About the Author

Virginia Gilbert is a BAFTA-nominated, award-winning writer and director in film, television, radio and fiction. Her screenwriting work has been placed on the BritList and she was named as a 'Star of Tomorrow' by Screen International. Her debut feature film as writer-director, *A Long Way From Home*, based on her short story and starring Brenda Fricker and James Fox, premiered in competition at the Edinburgh International Film Festival 2013 and will be released in Ireland and the UK in late 2013. Her short fiction has been published internationally, broadcast on BBC Radio 4 and RTÉ Radio 1, and her debut collection of stories was shortlisted for the Scott Prize. *The Travelling Companion* is her first novel.

First published in 2013 by
Liberties Press
140 Terenure Road North | Terenure | Dublin 6W
Tel: +353 (1) 405 5701
www.libertiespress.com | info@libertiespress.com

Trade enquiries to Gill & Macmillan Distribution
Hume Avenue | Park West | Dublin 12
T: +353 (1) 500 9534 | F: +353 (1) 500 9595 | E: sales@gillmacmillan.ie

Distributed in the UK by
Turnaround Publisher Services
Unit 3 | Olympia Trading Estate | Coburg Road | London N22 6TZ
T: +44 (0) 20 8829 3000 | E: orders@turnaround-uk.com

Distributed in the United States by
Dufour Editions | PO Box 7 | Chester Springs | Pennsylvania 19425

ISBN: 978-1-909718-13-5
2 4 6 8 10 9 7 5 3 1

A CIP record for this title is available from the British Library.

Cover design by Anna Morrison
Internal design by Liberties Press

The publishers gratefully acknowledge
financial assistance from the Arts Council.

*All characters in this book are fictitious, and any resemblance to
actual persons, living or dead, is purely coincidental.*

Travelling Companion

Virginia Gilbert

For my parents, B.G. & S.G., to whom I owe everything,
and for the love of my life, K.F.

Miranda: *I pitied thee,*
Took pains to make thee speak, taught thee each hour
One thing or other. When thou didst not, savage,
Know thine own meaning, but wouldst gabble like
A thing most brutish, I endow'd thy purposes
With words that made them known. But thy vile race,
Though thou didst learn, had that in't which good natures
Could not abide to be with. . . .

William Shakespeare, *The Tempest,* I.2, 353-60

The scuffle was easily broken up, over almost before it had begun. Neither man seemed to have the strength to fight properly. It was a half-hearted attempt. And after they had been pulled apart – nothing. Nothing but the faint, distant hum of the cicadas, the slow, heavy breathing of the onlookers, the jagged, shallow rasping of the combatants. All else was empty. And the emptiness had a different sound, something all its own: a hiss, vaguely ominous, unsettling. That was all there was. Emptiness. Emptiness, breath and the hiss of silence.

It was a very early start: the flight left at five o'clock. So they had to be at the airport by three in the morning, which meant, for Michael, leaving the house at a quarter past one. Almost not worth bothering going to bed at all, with such an early flight. But he did go to bed – not ridiculously early, but early enough and then found, to his irritation, that he could not sleep.

Irritation quickly became despair. He had only fourteen days ahead of him to enjoy, two of which would be disrupted by travel, and if he was exhausted, there was no telling how many precious hours would be ruined. He was unused to sleeplessness. Normally routine-bound, he was usually out by eleven and he always woke seven minutes before his alarm was due to sound. But now his head would not shut down. It whirred with all sorts of silliness. Had he packed the right things? Did he need to bring shampoo, just in case? Would there be any posh evenings? Did he need to bring something smarter? What about women, if they met any women . . . ?

In the end, Michael nodded off at around midnight. The alarm sounded forty minutes later, dragging him unwillingly back to consciousness. Heavy with sleep, he felt only resentment suddenly that he had agreed to this holiday at all. Too many hassles, too much to organise. And Patrick, the bugger, had got away lightly. Yes, he might have booked it and sorted all those details, but Michael had taken responsibility for getting them both up and to the airport in time, even though to do so took him right out of his way.

Patrick lived south of the city and had no car, so Michael had gamely proposed that he collect him. At least that way they could be sure that both were there, and avoid any last-minute panic if one or the other was late. Even though at this hour of the morning the drive was quick, Michael could not help but feel a surge of anger with his friend that he should put him out in this way.

Was Patrick his friend? The notion sounded strange to his ears, but yes, he supposed he was. They were colleagues first and foremost, the only two unmarried men who worked the warehouse floor. By virtue of that status, they had been thrown together in the beginning. The other lads all teased them that they could go out on the pull together, ribbing them that they envied them their freedom. Michael knew that they were lying. They were so pathetically grateful to be married, all of them; grateful to be able to indulge themselves in pure comfort, never having to make an effort, having someone to take care of them. There had been no real pleasure when they had been single, no matter what they said.

At first, Michael had looked on Patrick with cool curiosity. Patrick was small, lean and energetic; he strode across the floor as if he always had somewhere important to get to. For all that the other men teased them, they barely exchanged greetings those first couple of weeks; the odd nod, the occasional 'how are ya?' So it was with some surprise that Michael found himself accepting Patrick's offer of a drink one Friday evening after work.

The local pub had been packed and rowdy, the clientele emphatically declaring that the weekend started here. But they had managed to find themselves a small corner table, squeezed in beside the snug and the ladies' loos, and there, armed with their pints, they began to talk. Patrick was twenty-seven – older than Michael by four years – though he didn't look it. Born in the city, he had been living farther afield, with relatives, until very recently. His father had died when Patrick was young and his mother hadn't been able to cope on her own; hence his being brought up, on and off, by his grandparents. But he had moved back to the city a year ago, and planned to settle there. He liked it, he claimed; he felt he'd finally come home.

Patrick was a man who liked *doing*; a man of action, he needed to feel in charge. He was ambitious, and saw the job they were both in as a stepping-stone to better things. He planned to set up his own business one day. He had it all worked out: he just needed to get a bit more experience and put by a little bit of cash and 'the banks'll do the rest,' he airily declared.

Michael hadn't known what to say. He had no expertise in business and no experience of men like Patrick: young, hungry, ambitious. As they talked, or rather, as Patrick talked, Michael felt the heat of embarrassment spreading through him. Michael was a big man, prone to sweating, and he could feel the back of his shirt sticking to him. But Patrick didn't seem to notice, and nor did he want to turn the conversation onto Michael, which was a relief. By the end of the evening – for it had turned into a full evening – Michael had relaxed a little, and was even able to laugh and attempt to banter (with Patrick taking the lead) with some of the drunker women on their way in and out of the toilets.

For the first time in his life Michael had taken a taxi home, being too drunk to walk, and as he lolled in the back seat, savouring the luxuriousness of it, he had felt a surge of pleasure. Now he understood what the other lads went on and on about, the Friday and Saturday night 'sessions' they so looked forward to. It was simple. All you had to do was sit there and drink and natter, or listen to other people natter. There was no secret, no real mystery. Just people getting drunk together. But for Michael it was a revelation.

So he and Patrick became buddies, proper friends, sharing private jokes and tall tales. The men on the warehouse floor teased them, calling them a couple of old fishwives or cronies. They ate their lunches together and went out every Friday night. And now, nearly a year into their friendship, they were going on holiday.

Michael had barely ever left the city, let alone the country. Up until the moment Patrick had proposed their trip, he had never really thought about travelling abroad. His holidays were spent at home in front of the telly. He enjoyed them, but was always ready to go back to work after a week. He had never before taken off two weeks straight, and had never thought to actually go away anywhere. Patrick had laughed at his surprise when he suggested taking a little package trip. He had had to explain that package meant 'package holiday', and had tormented him for weeks on end about the misunderstanding.

'C'mere – Mikey thinks I've asked him to drug-smuggle for me!'

Everybody roared. But eventually Michael's little slip was forgotten in the excitement of planning, organising and fantasising about the trip. They had booked through one of the local travel agents, who, Patrick assured him, would get them the cheapest deal. Together, they chose their destination country, but as part of the terms of their package, their actual accommodation would be told to them only on arrival. All they knew is that they would be self-catering. This small, unknown aspect added to the sense of adventure, although Patrick would occasionally sigh, shaking his head with a weary sense of doubt. 'You can get landed with a terrible kip, you know.' Patrick had been on packages before – well, once before, with a girlfriend, to Ibiza. And he'd been to Greece before, too, when he was a teenager; three times to the very island they were going to.

Patrick's mother had had a Greek boyfriend for a while, though it hadn't lasted – none of her relationships had. But during the year or so she had been with him, she, Patrick and the boyfriend had all holidayed in the boyfriend's place on the island. Unfortunately for Patrick, the house had been away from the main towns, and he hadn't been impressed with the scabby little village and half-dug quarry that was on offer for his entertainment. Driving from the airport to the boyfriend's place, the teenage Patrick had glimpsed riotous scenes: endless strips of nightclubs and bars, the wild hedonism of young holidaymakers. He had been obsessed with the place ever since, determined to go back and sample its delights as an adult. And though Patrick was full of worries about the possibility of landing in a dump of a hotel, Michael didn't care. He was nervous, but not because of the accommodation. He had never in his life spent two full weeks in the constant company of someone else.

Patrick was bleary-eyed and snappy when Michael picked him up. They drove quietly to the airport and Michael parked in the long-term car park, shocked to discover how expensive it was going to be to leave the vehicle there for the fortnight. It would have been far cheaper for them to have taken taxis in and out. But Patrick was too irritable to share Michael's concern, striding off towards the terminal without a backward glance. Michael supposed they would sort it out when they returned, but he wasn't happy that the trip had started so unpleasantly.

Inside the airport, Michael was staggered by the crowds there at that early hour. People were everywhere, already dressed for scorching heat, stumbling over their enormous suitcases. White flesh was goose-bumped, fake tan streaked, older children were over-excited and hyperactive, younger ones tired and complaining. The fluorescent terminal lights were unforgiving, and Michael suddenly noticed a smear of egg on the front of his shirt, which he had not seen in the gloom of the car. He'd only worn the shirt once, the day before, and had been careful not to dirty it. Ashamed, he put on his sweater.

After the security checks, they made their way to the gate. There was a little café open and a bar, which was packed. At the sight of it, Patrick perked up.

'Come on, Mikey boy. A little oil to grease the wheels!'

Michael did not want to drink – his stomach was acidic from lack of sleep, but there was no way to deter Patrick. So he sipped his pint slowly, taking everything in, as Patrick knocked back his beer and ordered another, alert now, bright-eyed, wired.

'We're gonna have the best fucking trip of our lives, man!' Patrick told him. 'I'm telling you, this is gonna be something else.'

Patrick made a great show of flirting with a couple of girls at the bar who were off on their own holiday, and the girls, excited, already a little drunk, flirted back. Patrick nudged Michael. 'Isn't this great?' Michael wasn't sure. The girls were loud and mouthy, too much for him. He disliked the way a certain type of girl seemed to think she was too good for everything and everyone, bolshie and aggressive in manner, almost rude. What did they have to be so proud of? They were fat and ugly, nothing to write home about. So why shout about themselves so much? Michael couldn't get into the spirit of it, not at that early hour. He hoped he'd be able to relax a little more once they were properly on holiday.

Within minutes of settling down on the plane, before they even took off, Patrick was asleep. He'd flown before, many times; there was nothing for him to be excited about. Michael had not, and he watched with awe out of the window as the fields next to the runway rushed by, faster and faster, before suddenly they were lifting off. The roar of the engines was so loud, he was amazed that Patrick could sleep through the noise, but there he was, out like a light.

An hour into the trip and Michael had accustomed himself to the view of the clouds outside. It had been truly staggering, watching the sunrise from way up high, but now there was little outside to hold his attention. The plane was full and he looked at the other holidaymakers who were going to Greece. Lots of young families. A few groups of lads. Some girls, mainly travelling in twos and threes. The girls all wore heavy make-up, and chatted as they put on even more make-up, while reading silly magazines with pictures of famous people in bikinis on the front. They passed around the magazines, pointing out bits of gossip about people they had never met and were never likely to meet. Michael couldn't see the point of it.

Many passengers were asleep. But across the aisle from him, a young couple about his own age, maybe a little older, sat reading quietly. The woman whispered something to her companion and he chuckled. Smiling, she turned back to her book. There was something very calming about her, Michael felt as he watched. She wore a plain loose dress and a cardigan; her hair pulled back, simple, neat. She had on a little make-up, but not the slap that plastered the other young women. She just sat there quietly, reading a book – no stupid magazines for her – as if she hadn't a care in the world. She looked like the sort of person who went on holiday all the time.

Michael was surprised and a little disappointed to discover that he had nodded off and missed the landing. Patrick was wide-awake and nudged him brusquely: 'Get up off your arse!' Groggy, Michael grabbed his hand luggage and they disembarked. The mood had changed. The placidity of the journey had become impatience, and people jostled one another to get a move on.

They had to wait an age for their luggage. Patrick was pissed off because the little shop in the baggage hall wasn't yet open and he couldn't get anything to drink. Nor could he smoke, and he was itching for a fag. 'Fucking shite that you can't have a smoke any more. Fucking European bollocks.' But eventually, the bags came; Patrick's battered and worn, the mark of a well-travelled man; Michael's shiny and brand new. They made their way to the arrivals hall, where, according to Patrick, they would be met by a holiday rep from their travel agency and taken to their hotel. They pushed their way through the other tourists and found their lady: a plump, middle-aged Englishwoman, tired and harassed. She took their names, checking them off her list. And suddenly looked up.

'Patrick? Patrick Connor?'

'Yeah?'

'Oh dear . . . oh . . . look. You'll have to come with me.'

It all happened so fast. Michael was left standing with the bags as Patrick was taken to one side. The lady seemed very upset, and she was quickly joined by a colleague, a younger woman, who seemed more in control of herself. Then a policeman came up. Patrick did not once glance over, and Michael felt his heart pounding faster and faster. All that joking about a package holiday, Michael's foolish mistake about drug-smuggling. Had he been right? Patrick couldn't have been so *stupid*, could he?

Then suddenly, Patrick was gone, whisked off behind a desk and through a door. Michael looked around him, uncertain. Other holidaymakers, who were waiting for the same rep, were becoming impatient.

'Where did she bloody disappear to? We've not been crossed off the list!'

Flushed and red-eyed, the rep came back to her spot, only to be surrounded by the rest of her charges. 'It's Smith . . . *Smith*. Four of us – we're definitely on there.' As politely as she could, she held them off, and approached Michael, who was rooted to the spot, bewildered.

'Are you Michael?'

'Yes.'

'My dear – would you come with me?'

'What's happened? Has something happened?'

The others looked at him curiously. They supposed he was some sort of troublemaker. He could feel the sweat dripping down his back as he obediently followed her, like a naughty schoolboy on his way to the headmaster.

He was taken into a little office behind one of the sales desks. Patrick was sitting in the corner, his head in his hands, and didn't look up when Michael came in.

'What's going on?'

The holiday rep put her hand on his arm to quieten him. He looked at it with surprise.

'Michael, your friend Patrick here has had some very bad news, I'm afraid. His mother passed away this morning.'

Michael took this in. A policeman came into the room, with a couple more official-looking people. They were going to put Patrick on the next flight home. They were kindly and solici- tous, the officials, taking care of things smoothly, sensitive to the situation. Michael didn't know what to say, to them or to Patrick, who seemed in a state of shock. He hovered, uncertain, scared. The holiday rep took control and with that gentle gesture that had startled him, put her hand on his arm again.

'I know it's a terrible situation, dear, but we really can only accommodate poor Patrick's return trip for the moment. It's the height of the season you know – everything's absolutely jammed solid. But never you mind, we'll keep an eye out and if there's anything in a couple of days . . .'

And so it was that Michael was alone for his first ever holiday abroad.

~

As usual, they had been extremely early arriving at the airport. Georgie was a stickler for punctuality, and invariably made them leave far too soon for their destination. The thought of being late panicked her, and Rob had learned to give in to this necessary assuagement of her anxiety. It was minor in the greater scheme of things, he reasoned, and certainly better than having a row; winding her up and having her sulk for hours after the panic had subsided. He preferred to give in and make her happy. Far easier that way. So after checking in – and they were pretty much the first – they had spent a relaxed hour or so pottering around the airport bookshop, having a coffee and generally amusing themselves. They liked to travel and, far from merely tolerating airports, they genuinely enjoyed them, giving themselves over to the experience of the journey, refusing to fight it as an inconvenience that held them up in getting from one place to another.

Both of them needed this holiday. They had been working flat out for most of the year: Rob on a major project for the pharmaceutical company that employed him as a consultant engineer, Georgie on a deadline for a children's book she was illustrating. Though their work was very different, there had been, of late, a certain competitiveness between them as to who was busier, the more in demand. They vied for status, good-naturedly enough for the most part, but when they were really stressed, there was an undercurrent of resentment. Though Georgie could not claim that her work saved lives, as Rob just about could (if the vaccine he was developing was successful), she certainly had the high ground when it came to hours spent labouring. For the last six weeks she had toiled late into the night on top of her normal day's work, crawling into bed and invariably disturbing Rob from sleep. He didn't mind, though. He slept better when she was with him.

They hadn't been to Greece before, though this was not their first holiday together. The previous year they had snatched a week in Spain, too brief for total relaxation, and almost instantly forgotten about once they had returned home. But the year before that, they'd had two blissful weeks in Sardinia, lounging by the pool and doing nothing but eating, sleeping, swimming and making love. That Sardinian trip had been their first proper time away as a couple. They hadn't been together very long when they went, but it was that trip they hoped now to recreate: idleness, peace and quiet, and some good, old-fashioned fun together. They could do with it. They'd hardly spent any proper time together for weeks.

But for all that, for all the minor stresses and strains of their day-to-day lives and work, it was with no little sense of pride that Rob reflected that they did pretty well as a couple. They were still in love, still enjoyed one another's company, liked their shared routine, for the most part. And if their ardour had cooled somewhat, it was far more to do with the demands of their lives than with any sense of disillusionment or boredom with one another. There was not a great deal they did not know about each other any more – very little mystery left to discover – certainly when it came to matters of taste and preference. In most ways, their individual rhythms and routines had merged so well it was impossible to tell who had compromised where. So yes, granted, the heat of passion was less than it had been at the start, but after nearly three years that was only to be expected, and it wasn't something that worried Rob unduly. They had to make that bit of extra effort, that was all. Hence the importance of the holiday, of carving out some time together.

Rob had not yet asked Georgie to marry him, though friends and family were gently prompting him to with more regularity now. His hesitation was not to do with the strength of his feelings, or with any private reluctance to commit. The truth was (and it was a truth he had not shared with anyone; indeed, he refused to examine it in too much detail himself): the truth was that Rob was not entirely certain that Georgie wanted to marry him. There was nothing she had said or done that had given him this sense, but it was there: a nagging, underlying feeling that he might somehow be misjudging things by pressing for marriage; that she was happy for the moment, but would make no promises. He reasoned that it was more than likely his own resistance prompting such feelings, but he couldn't be sure. Not sure enough, anyway. So he hadn't asked her. Not yet.

Such thoughts, however, were far from his mind as they settled into the flight. They were both armed with holiday reading, and plunged into their respective novels as soon as their seatbelts were fastened. Rob had chosen a thriller, trashy but fun, and was hooked by the end of the first page. Georgie was reading what he could only describe as a 'woman's book – chick lit', even though she chided him for the phrase. It was something about a lost child, not his bag at all – no escapism there. They sat companionably side by side, Georgie reaching for his hand on take-off, an old routine. She was occasionally a nervous flyer, and had become superstitious about holding his hand for take-offs and landings, as if their shared grasp had some sort of power to prevent engine failure or fire or God knew what. Still, they had never (touch wood) been in a plane accident, so perhaps there was some merit to it. And Rob liked it – he liked indulging her – but more than that, he enjoyed the feeling that they had their private ways of doing things. Though both were tired, they were too tired to sleep, so they chatted to one another a little during the flight, spending the rest of the time reading. And, of course, they were excited about their holiday and wanted to save their energy for their arrival. They didn't want to waste a day.

The only hitch in the journey was an unexpected delay once they arrived. They had got their baggage without too much fuss, and were searching around in the arrivals hall for their holiday rep, but no sooner had they spotted her than she left with one of their fellow passengers, returning only to fetch a second man. There were irritated murmurings from some of the other travellers. Nobody seemed to know what was going on, and as the delay increased, the speculations got wilder. Georgie, normally placid in the face of unexpected hold-ups, was feeling the strain of the early start, and was itching to get to their hotel. She looked around angrily, her exasperation visible. 'Unbelievably annoying,' she muttered, to no one in particular.

Finally, after what felt like an age, the holiday rep came back with the second man in tow, who looked shaken and pale. She apologised for the delay but made no attempt to explain it, and began ticking their names off her list, then herding them onto the coach outside. Georgie and Rob, opening their welcome package and listening to the rep blather on at the front of the coach, discovered that they were going to be among the last to be dropped off at the Hotel Bougainvillea. Upon hearing the name, Georgie's irritation faded and she laughed, singing softly in Rob's ear: '*Welcome to the Hotel Bougainvillea! Such a lovely place, such a lovely face . . . !*'

The journey took almost an hour in the coach, through some of the most unprepossessing countryside the island had to offer, but they didn't mind. The sun shone brightly, and, to them, everything looked beautiful. Rob squeezed Georgie's hand as they caught their first glimpse of the sea, and raised his eyebrows at her as it promptly disappeared from view, blocked by highrises. There were several drop-offs along the way – Rob was quietly relieved to note that the very loud Glaswegian family with five young children was not staying in their residence – and eventually, there were only five of them left for Bougainvillea: Rob and Georgie, an older couple, and the solitary man who had been led away and then brought back at the airport.

'Strange to be travelling alone,' Georgie whispered, as they pulled up outside the hotel.

Rob shrugged. 'Maybe he's joining someone?'

'No, his friend – I think it was his friend – was with him on the flight. He's the guy they took away.'

Rob glanced at the man with vague interest. There was nothing special about him, as far as he could tell: nothing to mark him out as an obvious troublemaker. Heavy-set, mid-twenties, maybe, or even younger, bad skin, but he didn't look like your average lager lout, or at least didn't give off that vibe.

'I feel sorry for him,' Georgie whispered.

'Yeah, it's a bit strange' was Rob's only pronouncement as they made their way to reception.

~

The hotel was small but pretty, the building laid out as three sides of a rectangle, overlooking a swimming pool in front. True to its name, rich, pink bougainvillea plants cascaded down one side of the whitewashed façade. In fact, it was more of a self-catering affair than a fully functioning hotel, with small self-sufficient apartments rather than rooms. There seemed to be few staff about to help or provide service and there was no restaurant on-site for lunch or dinner. Guests would have to eat out or cook; all the apartments were equipped with a little kitchen unit. Clearly, the residence was used to hosting holidaymakers on a budget. For Michael, it was beyond anything he could have imagined.

There were two single beds in his bedroom. Next door, a small living area with a sofa and table, and a basic galley kitchen. A separate bathroom with a shower he'd never seen the like of before: the plughole was just in the floor, right next to the toilet. No bath. But off the living room-cum-kitchen, a balcony overlooked the swimming pool. Directly opposite was the facing wing of the hotel, and Michael could see into other people's balconies, strewn with flapping towels and beach gear. Beyond, in the distance, was the sea. It was unlike any view he'd ever seen before, and he stood out there for a long time that first morning, taking it all in.

He had barely had a chance to speak to Patrick before they'd whisked him away. Patrick had been as white as a sheet, and had half-muttered that, if he could, he'd try and get back out, but Michael knew there was no chance of that. Patrick liked to play the hard man, but he had been close to his mother, particularly in recent years, when he'd got to know her as an adult. His devastation was palpable. Michael, stunned by the rapid turn of events, hadn't known what to say. A mumbled 'mind yourself', and a quick pat on the shoulder was all he'd been able to muster.

He supposed he should unpack. He hadn't expected it to be quite so hot. It was a dry, scorching heat, not like good weather back home, what little of it there was. When he had first stepped off the plane, he'd felt it slam in his face with an unexpected force.

He took off his jeans and put on his shorts. The only shoes he had with him were trainers, which would do, he reckoned, though most of the men down by the pool seemed to be in sandals or flip-flops. Luckily, he'd thought ahead and changed some money at the airport, so he knew he'd be all right for the first day or so, and if he needed to buy some sandals, he could, as long as they weren't too expensive. There had to be some place to buy shoes on the island.

After hanging up his clothes, Michael thought he'd better get to know the neighbourhood a little, and pick up a few supplies, since there was nothing available at the hotel. The thought of eating alone every night, in restaurants packed with happy families, friends and couples, unnerved him. Inwardly, he cursed Patrick's mother for having picked such an inconvenient moment to pass on, then immediately felt guilty and apologised to her in his head.

Tucked just behind the little hotel complex was a well-stocked supermarket. Unfortunately, all the labelling was in Greek, and Michael had to select his purchases based on sight alone. For the most part, he could manage, but milk was a problem. He was hesitating over a carton, uncertain as to whether it was normal milk or something strange, when he heard a voice behind him.

'Hello there!'

He turned, startled, and the carton slipped from his hands, sweaty from the heat. Milk spilled everywhere. Shame-faced, he bent down, at a loss as to how to clean up the mess. The young woman crouched down too; it was she who had spoken to him. He recognised her from the plane: she'd been the one across from him, sitting next to her husband or whomever, reading. The calm one. The one with the loose dress.

'I shouldn't worry about it. Someone'll mop it up.' She picked up the broken carton briskly and put it to one side. 'You were on the same flight as us. I think we're in the same hotel.'

She smiled at him. Up close, he could see that she was a little older than he had thought – late twenties, maybe even thirty. She had circles under her eyes, and there were little lines at their corners, but the eyes themselves were a lovely hazel colour, rich and warm. She thrust out her hand.

'I'm Georgie.'

Hesitating slightly, still thrown by the unexpected nature of the encounter, Michael finally shook her hand, conscious that his palm was hot and sticky with milk.

'Michael.'

'Nice to meet you, Michael. Was it milk you were after? Here, why don't I give you a hand?'

They picked up the last few bits and pieces they needed and made their way to the checkout. Georgie explained that her boyfriend Rob had fallen asleep back in their room, leaving her to do all the sorting out, the unpacking and the shopping, though she said she didn't mind, because she liked to get settled quickly. She let Michael go ahead of her at the till, and he waited for her as she paid, confessing that this was his first time abroad.

'Really? Really and truly? You've never been abroad before?'

Michael flushed crimson. She took him by the elbow, steering him gently away from the checkout, where other customers were impatiently jostling for space to pack their bags.

'And am I right in thinking that your friend – you were travelling with a friend . . . ?'

'Patrick. His mother died. They told him when we landed and put him straight on the next plane back. There wasn't room for me.'

'My God! The poor thing. And poor you – stranded here all alone. Your first time away, too. I can't imagine how awful that must be.'

Michael shrugged. She still had her hand on his arm, and he was conscious of its pressure, its warmth. It felt comfortable, her hand on him, easy, casual. Not like the lady at the airport, the holiday rep, whose touch had made him jump.

'Michael, listen.' She was looking at him seriously. 'If there's anything you need – any help, any questions – please don't hesitate. I've been to Greece before. I mean, I'm no expert, but if you need anything. And if you want a bit of company, don't be shy. We'll be down at the pool most days anyway. Not planning to go very far.' She smiled at him, sincere. Michael didn't know what to say. She squeezed his arm, friendly.

He looked at her. 'Thank you. You're very kind.'

~

Though mid-afternoon, the sun was still extremely hot. Michael had avoided the midday heat, sitting in the cool of his apart-ment, eating some bread and cheese. He'd picked up a pair of cheap sunglasses at the supermarket, and when he finished his meal he put them on, wandering out onto his balcony, gazing down at the people below. Most had retreated out of the glare to eat in their apartments. Some were sitting on their balconies, but there were a brave or reckless few who remained by the pool, sunbathing, dozing. A vigorous older gentleman swam laps, taking advantage of the relative peace.

Georgie was down there. Clearly, she didn't want any lunch. Her skin was milk-white against the black of her bikini, and she lay stretched out, offering her body to the sun. She wore a large straw sunhat, and between that and her sunglasses, Michael could barely make out her face. She was reading, her book held up high so as not to cast a shadow. She seemed oblivious to those around her. Every twenty minutes or so, she would lean forward and check her legs, belly and chest to make sure she wasn't getting burned, and would reapply a dab or two of sun cream. Her boyfriend was obviously still sleeping. Michael wondered if it wouldn't be a good idea to go and sit with her, seeing she was on her own, but he didn't know what on earth he'd talk to her about, and he hadn't brought a book to hide behind. So he remained on the balcony, watching from behind his sunglasses.

It was nearly four o'clock by the time Georgie's boyfriend joined her. Rob, that was what she'd said his name was. She looked as though she'd fallen asleep. She had left the poolside only once all afternoon – to her room, Michael presumed – and had come back down alone, clutching a bag of crisps and a drink. But other than that, she had barely stirred, and Michael had had ample opportunity to study her. She lay so still when she was reading, it was as if she were a statue. He noticed that her legs were getting a little red and blotchy, but she seemed unaware of it. She was entirely her own self in her own world, unconcerned (though not unfriendly), utterly self-possessed. Michael had never known anything like it, certainly not from a woman. The girls he knew were what the lads on the floor affectionately termed 'slappers': loud, brash and well aware of their charms. He couldn't imagine any of them stopping to offer a stranger help in a supermarket.

Georgie's boyfriend was yawning loudly as he approached her, and rather than giving her a kiss or a smile or any other form of greeting, he merely pointed at her legs. Hurriedly, Georgie pulled them up for inspection and seemed annoyed, whether with herself or with him, Michael couldn't tell. She was about to cover them with a towel when Rob took her by the hand and pulled her to her feet. Michael could hear the half-laugh, half-cry that she let out in protest as she struggled to take off her hat and glasses. But Rob had already tugged her to the edge of the pool and jumped in with barely a backward glance, yanking her behind him, so that she stumbled awkwardly and fell in, ungainly. Michael drew back with distaste. That was not the way to treat a lady.

But then he heard her laughing, and peered back down over the balcony to see her swimming towards Rob, who was lounging nonchalantly against the edge at the deep end. Free of her hat and glasses, Michael could see her face more clearly, and it surprised him a little, being slightly different from the way he had remembered it. She had been so close to him in the supermarket; so close that her features had almost become distorted in his mind as separate entities: her eyes, her skin, her mouth. Seeing them from this distance though, as a whole, he was not disappointed. He studied her closely, even when she reached her partner, and pressed her mouth to his for a kiss.

~

Rob had slept exceptionally well: the deep and dreamless sleep of the exhausted. It had taken him a moment or two to remember where he was, but even in his slightly disoriented state, he loved the room he was in. Plain, simple, almost entirely white, with a little wooden table and a small wardrobe. Shutters on the windows, with the sun streaming through them. It was pretty, almost picture perfect. It had been a long time since Rob had felt so peaceful, and when he remembered it was the day of their arrival – that they had the whole holiday stretching out before them – he almost laughed out loud with happiness.

He stood naked for a moment, getting used to his new home, enjoying the luxury of having slept in the middle of the afternoon. Their suitcases were neatly stacked in the corner, the wardrobe full with their clothes. Georgie had unpacked already. Wandering into the little living area, he noted that she had shopped as well. That was Georgie through and through: she could not settle anywhere unless things were secure and organised to her liking. In periods of high stress, her agitation irritated and angered Rob, spilling, as it did, into unnecessary corners of their lives. She could become obsessively insistent about all sorts of trivial things – where they were going, what they were doing, their schedules – and easily threatened by any comment or observation, no matter how innocuous, leading Rob, on a couple of occasions, to call her shrill and shrewish. But now, witness to the small and useful results of her neurosis, Rob simply smiled, savouring the intimacy that enabled him to know her little ways so well.

Outside, the heat was spectacular, but he thrilled to it, feeling every muscle in his body uncoil that first little bit. He knew it would take a good few days before he really began to relax, but he was damned if he wasn't going to try. Georgie was spread out on a sun lounger and was clearly getting burned. *Silly girl*, he thought. He'd warned her about it before they'd left. The first four days of their idyllic trip to Sardinia two years ago had been marred by her sunburn: she'd fallen asleep without protection, and her entire left side had been red-raw.

'Your legs are bad,' he told her, when he came down.

'Shit.' She leaned forward to look, her bikini top slipping slightly. 'I've put loads of cream on. I don't understand it.' Her tone was plaintive, piqued.

The paving stones were hot under his feet, and Rob had a sudden impulse to pick up Georgie and hurl her into the pool, book and hat and all. Instead he grabbed her hand.

'Come on, you.'

'Rob—' she protested, but he didn't give in, pulling her swiftly to the water's edge. 'Hang on. My hat!'

The water was shockingly cold, but delicious. Rob surfaced and swam fast and hard to the other end, feeling his blood start to pump, his body beginning to respond to the exercise. Georgie took a moment to get the hair out of her eyes, but then swam gently over to him. He reached out and pulled her close as she approached. She laughed.

'Isn't this lovely,' she said.

He looked around. The pool was quiet. The hotel pretty. The sky bright blue. The water clear.

'Rob?' He smiled at her. Good God, apart from her face, the rest of her was very red. He closed his eyes and kissed her.

~

Michael ventured downstairs when the little poolside bar reopened for evening drinks. He had eaten another sandwich in his room, having no desire to eat out in a restaurant alone. He had tried to doze, but to no avail; the strangeness of his surroundings and the loneliness of his predicament had prevented sleep. At least he wouldn't feel so strange and out of place sitting at the bar. People did that – went alone for drinks – either waiting for someone to arrive, or stopping off en route before going somewhere else to meet friends. Solitary drinkers were solitary only for a certain amount of time, it seemed to Michael, except for the sad old men who sat in the pub during the daytime, near where he worked. They really were on their own. No matter, though – he figured he could get away with one or two without appearing too much of a misfit.

After showering, Michael put on a fresh shirt. He had always thought of it as his summer shirt back home, but the cotton seemed too heavy in this heat, even at sunset, and it clung to his skin, almost as if to trap him. He felt silly in his socks and trainers, but what else could he do? He would have to venture out in the morning and see if he could find better footwear. Better summer clothes, for that matter.

A sprightly Greek called Les, according to his name badge, ran the poolside bar. He must have been in his mid-forties, but he was trim and fit in his tight trousers and white shirt. His dark hair glistened – he seemed to use a lot of gel, and the colour was so black it could not possibly be natural. Les was vain about his hair. Michael had noticed him that afternoon on numerous occasions, checking his reflection in a small mirror hung behind the bar. But he was a hard worker; he'd been there all day, serving drinks and snacks, closing only for an hour in the late afternoon, presumably so he could have some dinner, and now he was back, chatting to a couple who, judging by their suntans, had already been on holiday for some time. They were clearly on their way out to dinner; the woman was very dressed up. Les had turned on the fairy lights that were gaily hung around the front of the little building, and the radio blared jaunty Greek pop music from a local station. All in all, there was a certain tatty charm to the place.

'Aha! You must be one of the new arrivals.' Les's English was excellent, although his accent was an odd hybrid of Greek, inner-city London and possibly American. 'Come, sit – have a drink, my friend.'

Michael pulled up a barstool, nodding politely to the couple at the table, who smiled at him.

'What's your poison?' Les grinned, showing off his fluent vernacular.

'Oh . . . just a pint of something, please.'

'No pints, only bottles. Why you don't try something local? We have some excellent beers.'

Les handed him an ice-cold bottle before Michael could refuse. 'Is very good – try. You don't like it, no problem, I give you another.'

Michael shrugged and took a sip. He wasn't a discerning drinker and it tasted much like every other beer he had ever had.

'It's good, no?'

'Yes. It's good.'

Les nodded. The couple stood up to go. 'We're heading off now, Les.'

'Have a good night. Remember to try the calamari salad! Tell Nico not to put too much sauce on it.'

'We will. Thanks for the tip.'

They nodded their goodbyes, and Michael watched as they made their way around the pool towards the exit, the man's arm slung causally over his partner's shoulder.

'They make a good couple, no?' Les was leaning over the bar, watching as well.

'I s'pose.'

'She has good ass, he has good assets!' Les burst out laughing at his witty turn of phrase. Michael blushed, a little uncertain. Les reached over and clapped him on the back. 'Is the only way to get the good ones, no?' He rubbed his thumb and forefinger together in the universal sign of money. Michael shrugged. Les continued, unperturbed.

'Is why I work like a donkey – all day, all night. You know, even on my day off, I have another job, in my cousin's pizzeria. I work like a crazy – mainly it's for me, but also, I must confess, the women like it. They really like it, you know? A man who works hard, has money – they get hot for that.'

Michael sought refuge in his beer, taking a long sip. Patrick would have known how to banter with the man properly, how to handle his sudden shifts and turns and jokes: the light, the serious, the little dance of male conversation that left Michael at such a loss.

'You – you look like a man who likes to earn his money. Look at you: young, on holidays. The girls will go crazy for a man like you! You going out tonight?' Without asking, Les handed him another bottle of beer.

'I dunno. Maybe. I'm still pretty tired—'

'You on your own?'

Michael sighed. He supposed he couldn't avoid having to explain. 'It wasn't the plan. I was travelling with a mate, but his mum died while we were flying and he had to go home.'

'Holy Jesus – goddamn bad luck. But still, at least you're here. And is a good resort here, lots of clubs and young people. You'll have fun, plenty of fun, my man!' He winked, lewd, grinning. 'Lots of English girls here. They like to have fun. Oh yes, the English girls, they're the ones to go for, my friend. But I guess you know that already, no?'

Michael coughed and stood up. Clearly hanging out at the bar was not going to be an option for him. 'Maybe I'll go and check it out. The town, I mean."

Les opened his mouth to protest, to tell him to stay longer, drink his second beer – what was the rush? But Georgie was walking towards them, smiling.

'Hello, Michael. How are you?'

Les immediately busied himself with cleaning some glasses. A charming smile was fixed on his face, all salaciousness banished.

'Another new arrival!' he called. 'And a very beautiful one at that.'

Georgie smiled but raised her eyebrows sardonically. 'I'll have a gin and tonic, please,' she told Les briskly. Slightly taken aback with her refusal to mess about, Les complied, without further comment. She pulled up a stool and sat next to Michael.

'How's the local brew?' she asked, nodding at his beer.

'Oh . . . pretty good.'

'Maybe I should try one.' She smiled at him. A small flicker of confidence surged within him. He leaned in a little closer, lowering his voice.

'Actually, I can't really tell the difference between this one and any of the others we have back home.'

She too leaned forward. 'Bet it's cheaper though!'

'I don't know. I haven't paid for them yet – he's just been handing them to me.'

Les plonked down the gin and tonic on the bar. Georgie took it with a nod of thanks and raised her glass to Michael.

'Cheers.'

'Cheers.'

Now that the sun was setting and the light less glaring, Michael could see how burned Georgie was. Her chest and shoulders were a dark crimson. She didn't seem to mind, though, and hadn't covered up anything, wearing a short sundress that skimmed her thighs. It had thin straps and was quite low-cut: it was clear she wasn't wearing a bra. But she didn't look sluttish to Michael – far from it. She looked cool and elegant. She wasn't dressing to show off, Michael thought, though on someone else the dress might have looked tarty.

They drank for a moment in companionable silence. Les broke it. He'd been eyeing Georgie, trying to get the measure of her.

'I was telling your friend here – this town is great for the nightlife.'

'I'm sure.' She was polite, but there was no warmth in her tone.

'You like drinking and dancing? I can tell you very good places to go—'

'I'm not much of a clubber really.'

'You don't like?' Les was completely taken aback.

'No.'

'So what you like to do?'

'Oh, you know – long meals, walks, cafés. That sort of thing.'

'Yeah? I know very good places—'

'Maybe some other time. My boyfriend's been here before. I think he knows a couple of nice spots.'

Michael was amazed. The ease with which she'd rid herself of the barman dumbfounded him. Les himself, unused to such brisk dismissal, snorted loudly, making his displeasure clear. He checked his hair, self-conscious in humiliation, and disappeared out the back. Georgie glanced around to make sure he was gone.

'That's a bit of a fib,' she told Michael, smiling, conspiratorial. 'Rob's never been here in his life. But that man's non-stop!

Every time I came up for a drink today, he wouldn't leave off. Real sleazebag.'

'He's all right, I reckon. Just . . . likes the ladies, that's all.' Something about her presence emboldened him.

Georgie nodded. 'What a bore.' She sipped her drink and grimaced slightly. 'And he makes a rotten gin and tonic!'

'Shall I get you another?'

'God no, not from here! Thanks, though. Anyway, Rob'll be down any second. I wish he'd hurry up. I'm starving.'

Michael shifted a little in his seat. Georgie glanced over at him. 'What about you?'

'Me what?'

'Where are you going to eat this evening?'

'Oh, I dunno . . .' He could feel the heat rising in his cheeks.

'Must be pretty awful being stuck on your own, particularly on your first night. And it doesn't seem very lively in this place, which is good for us – me and Rob, I mean – but maybe not for you.'

Michael shrugged. He'd rather avoid this topic of conversation: his solitary status, the odd-man-out. It made him feel worthless, sad. Pathetic.

She studied him for a moment, thoughtful. 'Though, if you don't mind my saying, you don't strike me as the clubbing sort, either. Correct me if I'm wrong.'

'I don't mind 'em. Bars – clubs, I mean. Long as they're not too loud. Although . . .' He hesitated, unsure as to whether or not he should confess. But he had started now; he had to finish. 'I've not been to many really. Just a couple of discos round my way. I prefer the local. The pub. That's where I normally go.'

She was listening to him attentively and he could feel her eyes on him. He was unused to such thoughtful care when it came to conversation. Most girls turned away from him, or sought to bring other people into their chats. He presumed he bored them.

'That's nice,' she told him. 'It's nice to have your one cosy spot. Your local.'

'Don't you have one?'

Georgie sighed, fiddling with the napkin underneath her glass. 'I suppose we do. I mean, there's a pub around the corner that would be our local, if we ever went. I used to have one when I was a student. There was a bar we'd all go to – dirt cheap – grotty little place really, but we'd all hang out there, nearly every night. It was great. Even if we started the evening some-where else – just for a change of scene – we'd always end up back there for some reason. I knew every inch of that bar by the end of college. Sometimes I'd go in there in between lectures, not to booze or anything, just for a coffee, do a bit of reading. It was popular with our gang. We were the only youngsters who hung out there. Other than that, there'd just be a handful of old men, if anyone at all. Bit sad, I suppose. I guess we thought we were being cool, a bit retro, going to the old man's pub.'

'Sounds good.'

'Yeah. It was. I think it's closed now. We were probably the only ones keeping it alive.' She smiled at him and, almost with-out thinking, he found himself returning her smile. But her eyes suddenly flickered, distracted by something, and he lost her.

'Rob!'

'Sorry I took so long.'

She stood to kiss him. Rob put his arm around her. Michael sat up a little straighter, not sure if he too should get up.

'Darling, this is Michael – you remember – we met in the supermarket. I told you . . .' Clearly Rob knew all about Patrick and his mother, had been told of Michael's sad predicament.

'Oh yes – hi there. Good to meet you.' He thrust out his hand. Michael shook it. Rob's grip was firm. 'What a shitty start to your holiday.'

'It's okay.'

'And he's never been abroad before. It's dreadful.' Georgie was looking at her boyfriend earnestly, eyes wide with the drama and the unfairness of the whole situation.

'God, really? Never been out of the country?'

Michael grunted a reply and knocked back the last of his beer. He had no desire to go through it all again, particularly not with *him*. Georgie tugged at Rob's sleeve.

'Darling, he's all alone here. Maybe . . . .'

Michael looked up just in time to see Rob shoot a warning glance at his girlfriend, but, instead of being cowed by it, she simply smiled more broadly. Rob closed his eyes and half-laughed, then leaned in and kissed her lightly on the lips.

'Michael.' She turned to him, mock serious, unable to hide her enthusiasm entirely. 'You must come out for dinner with us. You can't be abandoned on your first night.'

Michael shook his head. He didn't want to. What on earth would they talk about? And he sensed that the guy, the boyfriend, wasn't keen on the idea. 'No, I'm fine, honestly—'

'We absolutely insist!'

'No, please. I've already eaten anyway—'

'I won't take no for an answer!' She pretended to stamp her foot, playing out a little tantrum. Rob squeezed her shoulder, a gentle warning. 'Darling—'

'Ow! Not too hard. Sunburn.' She grinned up at Rob, then unexpectedly leaned forward and put her hand on Michael's arm. 'Come on. We won't be late or anything. It's holidays. You're supposed to meet new people. Please, Michael. For me!'

Michael gazed at her hand for a moment and felt a sudden lurch in his stomach, as if he had been given a piece of devastating news. He took a deep breath.

'Okay.'

~

Rob was surprised at his lack of irritation. This was so bloody typical of Georgie, picking up a stray, adopting the bloody man. Now of course, they'd be fobbing him off for the rest of the holiday, for Georgie had a way of making people feel more wanted than they actually were. Yet even knowing all this, Rob found himself in a happy state of nonchalance. He couldn't have cared less that the man – Michael, was it? – was coming to dinner with them, even though it was their first night and everything. There were plenty of other nights and, besides, it was only a meal.

Strolling down the little hill that set the hotel slightly apart from the rest of the town, Rob basked in the sheer pleasure of being away from home, in a beautiful location, enjoying the novelty of the break in routine. If they'd been at home now – but Rob still wouldn't be home, most likely; stuck in the office, grabbing some crappy pizza or something, texting Georgie when he could. He became aware of her laughter; she and Michael had been chatting almost continuously since they'd left the hotel bar. Rob hadn't been paying the slightest bit of attention.

'What's so funny?' Rob asked.

'Oh, nothing, really. Michael was just telling me about some of the initiation rites they put the new boys through at the warehouse where he works.'

'Oh?'

Michael shrugged. 'Just messing about.'

Georgie giggled. 'Apparently, the oldest guy on the floor takes the newcomer aside, before he's even had his tea or been shown round the place properly, and sends him out on a mission – a very serious mission. He has to go out and purchase a pair of sky hooks. Sky hooks!'

'I'm not sure I . . . Oh.'

Georgie turned to him, eyes wide, and lightly punched him, playful. 'You'd be useless, Robbie-me-lad. You'd actually go out and try to buy the things.'

'I did,' Michael told them.

'No!'

'I did. I went round to all our suppliers. They shook their heads very seriously and sent me packing. I was all over the place by the end of the morning. It was my first day; I thought the boss would be furious. I didn't know what to do.'

'What happened? What did you say when you went back?'

'I didn't go back. I spent the whole day trawling round the town, desperately looking for sky hooks. But I was lucky in the end. The final shop I went into knew my boss, like, and rang him. Put me on the phone to him and he told me it was all a joke.'

'God! I think I'd've burst into tears.'

'Or punched someone,' Rob said. Georgie glanced at him, smiling. He was only teasing.

'No. Didn't do either of those. But I did piss in his coffee next time I made him one.'

Michael's tone was serious. Georgie glanced at Rob, mouth slightly agape, nonplussed.

'Well. Remind me never to play a joke on you.'

They had reached the bottom of the hill, and the main drag of the town was bustling. Full of tourists. And English bars: 'British Bulldog' pubs and large, tacky nightclubs and fast food restaurants. They stopped for a moment, surveying the scene. A large group of lads in football jerseys wandered by, shouting, laughing, already pissed out of their skulls, though it was barely eight o'clock.

'It's a bit like home from home, isn't it?' Rob whispered to Georgie, sensing her dismay. She took his hand and gave it a squeeze. 'We'll find somewhere lovely,' she told him. 'Let's just get off this main bit.'

'Michael?' Rob glanced over at him. He was standing transfixed, gazing at the simmering madness in front of him. 'We think we might try and head down one of the side streets or something.'

Michael nodded but he couldn't tear his eyes away. There were so many people – so many young men and women – all in one place. He'd never seen anything like it. He was shocked. It was so unexpected, so busy and loud. Watching the groups of people passing by, he suddenly felt again the weight and burden of his loneliness.

After a good half-hour of wandering they found a quiet little taverna, tucked away in a cobbled street in the older part of the town, a couple of blocks from the beach. It seemed ideal. The clientele appeared to be mainly locals, bar one or two rather elderly Germanic-looking couples sitting in silence, eating methodically. They settled down at a table outside and immediately fresh warm bread and olives were placed before them.

'This is perfect,' Georgie beamed, munching happily. 'I think we might have found our favourite place.'

'It's only the first night, sweetheart. There are other places to try.'

'Yes, but everybody needs a local, don't they, Michael?'

She smiled at him conspiratorially. Michael half-nodded, but he was too preoccupied with the menu to pay close attention. He hadn't heard of most of the things on it and wondered what on earth he was going to eat. Rob watched him. There was something stolid and lumpen about the man which was beginning to grate on him. He was being unfair, he knew, but the size of Michael, his heft and weight, his ungainly proportions, made Rob irrationally irritable: an irritability he was beginning to have to work to fight. After all, the guy was perfectly pleasant company, genial, not too pushy, mild-mannered enough. There was no sense of the competitiveness that Rob was used to in his dealings with other men in his life: clients, colleagues, even friends. It surprised Rob, now that he was thinking about it, how an undercurrent of rivalry was so present in his everyday life. Rivalry over nothing in particular – status a little bit, he supposed – but it was more abstract, more amorphous than that. The men he knew were ever on alert, always ready to leap or pounce, to make sure they were top dog, even if it were only in conversation.

Georgie had summoned the waiter for some drinks. 'I feel like some red – how about you, darling?'

Rob nodded his assent, but also asked for a beer. 'Red wine do you, Michael?' he asked him.

'Oh . . . yes. Yes, fine.'

He was hesitant, Rob noticed. If he wanted to, he could press him on it, make him squirm a little – the man clearly hadn't a clue – but he resisted the impulse and instead opened the menu.

'What are you thinking?' he asked Georgie, who was in an agony of indecision. She'd already read the menu through at least twice.

'Salad for me to start, then maybe some mussels . . . Or the lamb looks good . . .'

Rob knew Georgie would take a while to decide and probably change her mind at the last minute, depending on what he ordered. They would have to get different things so that she could try some of his. She had a good appetite, and always cleared her plate before him, happy to 'help' him finish. Rob looked at her as she studied the menu. He hadn't really looked at her all evening, not properly. Her hair had come loose a little at the back, and had curled in the heat. Though she was burned, the gentle light spilling out of the restaurant softened the colour to a darkish red, almost bronze, if you didn't look too closely. Her mascara had smudged a little under her eyes, thanks to the heat, but the effect was charming and louche, rather than messy. Altogether she looked fuss-free and lovely. Just lovely. Rob reached out and put his hand over hers, suddenly longing to be alone with her.

'All right, darling?'

She barely glanced up. She was hungry. But she smiled that little half-smile that told Rob she was simply, purely happy.

~

They woke early, both still in work mode, and decided to take their breakfast down to the pool. They had slept exceptionally well, being full after their meal of the night before; the portions at the little taverna had been enormous. Dinner and the wine had made them drowsy, even though Rob had already slept most of the day away. But they had a lot of missed sleep to catch up on.

The evening had gone well enough. They had managed to sustain polite chitchat throughout dinner, and Michael had raised no objections when they suggested heading straight back to the hotel without a nightcap somewhere else. And once back, having said their polite goodbyes, Rob and Georgie had thrown themselves into bed, discovering that they were not quite as tired as they had thought. Rob smiled at the memory as he stretched out on his sun lounger, basking in the heat.

'I want to do absolutely nothing today.'

'Fine by me. I wasn't planning on anything anyway.' Georgie was lying rather uncomfortably on her front, determined to even up her skin tone.

'You sure you've put enough cream on?' he asked, concerned about the tender backs of her thighs.

'I'm covered in the bloody stuff. No chance of burning – promise.'

He reached out and stroked her arm gently, utterly relaxed. It was so simple, lying under a hot sun. That was all it took. Why didn't they do this more often?

'Maybe we'll go up for a nap later,' he whispered to her suggestively. She smiled, coy, encouraging. Back home, their lovemaking had been a bit fraught of late, done more out of a sense of duty than of pleasure. They were both too tired, too stressed out, their heads not really in it. But here, it was different. Here, they really wanted to. He did, anyway. In fact, he'd surprised himself with the heat of his desire the night before; he'd been ready for her again almost as soon as they had finished. Georgie had laughed with delight. It had been a long time since they'd been in that situation, and she welcomed him a second time, with almost as much passion as the first. She'd been the one to call a halt to things in the end, laughing that she was worn out, getting sore. Afterwards, they'd sprawled out together on the bed, tired and spent, but reluctant to fall asleep just yet. That marvellous sense of holiday freedom was growing on them, that sense that they could do whatever they wanted whenever they wanted. So they'd stayed up talking, giggling, like two naughty schoolchildren breaking the rules.

'He's a funny one, isn't he?' Rob had said to her of Michael. 'Bit of an odd-bod.'

'I think he's sweet. Shy. He means well. God, I don't know what I'd do if I were stuck here alone.'

'You'd be all right. You'd pick yourself up a toy-boy within minutes. Have a whale of a time!'

'What – one of the lager louts? Hmmm, now I come to think about it . . . .' He'd goosed her and she'd squealed, laughing. 'I don't know, though. I don't know if they could compete with you. Twice in one night! Who'd credit it?' Now it was her turn to goose him. They'd rolled around, laughing, both wondering in the back of their minds if they could manage a third round, both pulling apart, too tired to muster the energy.

'You've got to feel sorry for him though, Rob. He's a bit hopeless. Doesn't know which way is up.'

'As long as he doesn't bother us. We didn't come on holiday to make a new best friend.'

'Come off it. He's not going to. He's scared of his own shadow. And anyway, since when are you so anti making friends? You should be more open to things.'

'I'll follow your lead there, shall I, my love?'

She'd laughed. She liked it sometimes when he was dirty, not too often, but in the right mood. 'Don't be so bloody cheeky, Robert!'

Georgie had fallen asleep quite quickly after that, but Rob had taken a bit longer to settle. He had been thinking of the last few months, which suddenly, quite miraculously, seemed very far away. The pressures that had so consumed him felt like nothing now, although certain bits and pieces that he'd had to leave unfinished before departing nagged at him. He knew he was liable to get the odd phone call from some of his colleagues in the first couple of days, knew that at any moment he could be dragged back into the grim realities of the daily grind. The thought of having to make the effort, having to switch back into work mode, even temporarily, made him exhausted. He liked his work, for the most part, but lately it had all been a bit too much.

Georgie was sleeping now, by the pool. Sun cream notwithstanding, the backs of her legs were turning red, and Rob covered them gently with her sarong, trying not to disturb her. It was still early enough that the pool was quiet. The older couple who had been on the coach with them were sitting reading in the shade. A young family paddled in the shallow end, both toddlers in armbands. Rob picked up his book. He had been enjoying it on the plane, but now, as he opened it, he couldn't seem to focus, couldn't seem to get a handle on the words, the sentences. He wasn't quite ready to concentrate. Idly, he watched as

Les, or whatever his name was (was Les even his real name? It didn't sound very Greek), opened up the little poolside bar, sticking on the radio. It wasn't loud, but it was irritating to have bland pop music disturb the silence of the morning. Rob was tempted to go over and say something, but no one else appeared to be bothered, so he held off.

Another young family came out on to one of the balconies. These kids were older than the toddlers in the pool; a boy of around ten and a girl of eight or so, and Rob could just about discern from their quiet chatter that they were English, middle-class, polite. The parents kept them in check, hushing them if they got over-excited, making sure they finished their breakfasts. Rob smiled to himself, remembering being on holidays just like this one when he was the kids' age, remembering the almost overwhelming excitement of wanting to get down to the pool in the mornings, a need so strong that it almost became anxiety. Hard, as an adult, to recapture the power of that feeling. So easy to forget! Looking up at the children sitting there, squirming with impatience, Rob could see their throbbing anticipation, barely masked by their demure obedience to their parents. Let them enjoy it, he silently urged, let them hurry up and come down. They'll never feel such unmitigated excitement again.

The children got up from the table, duty done, breakfast eaten. They'd be down any minute. Rob's eye wandered and, two balconies above the family, he spotted Michael, standing as still as stone, leaning against his balcony rail. But almost the minute Rob laid eyes on him, Michael moved, turning abruptly back into his apartment, as though he'd been caught out at something. As if he had been watching them, him and Georgie. Rob sat up, suddenly on the alert, though a part of him knew he was being ridiculous. It was fair enough that the guy should stand on his balcony of a morning. But how long had he been there? Rob gazed at the empty space intently, willing Michael to come back out, wanting to let him know that he'd got his number, that he'd noticed. A ripple of irritation ran through him. Was this how their kindness of the previous evening was going to be repaid? Was the guy a bit of a creep?

His eyes were still fixed on the balcony, his thoughts mounting in self-righteous anger, when a voice behind him startled him.

'Rob?'

He moved too quickly, knocking the sun cream and the bottle of water on the little table onto the ground. Michael, sheepish, stooped to pick them up. Georgie stirred a little in her sleep.

'Sorry, Rob. I didn't mean to startle you. I wasn't sure if you were awake or not.'

Rob stood up, flustered, motioning for Michael to step aside, away from Georgie, so as not to disturb her. Michael was dressed in long shorts and a rather garish summer shirt, both still creased from their packaging, evidently new purchases. As was his baseball cap with the word 'Celebrate!' printed on it. The price tag hung down on one side. In only his swimming trunks, Rob felt an odd mixture of exposure and pride as he stood in front of Michael; his lean athleticism fully on display, in contrast with Michael's lumbering, ungainly heft.

'Sorry!' Michael whispered, theatrically. 'I don't want to disturb you.'

'What's up?' Rob tried to keep his tone light. No point alienating the guy, not so soon. Not unless it was really called for.

'Here—' Michael thrust a small package at him. 'I wanted to thank you for last night. You were very good to invite me.'

Rob hesitated, feeling a twinge of guilt. But he still couldn't shake off his irritation. He took the package, unwrapping it quickly. Michael, clearly uncomfortable, spoke rapidly, wanting to explain. 'It's nothing much, only Georgie mentioned she didn't know the area, so I just thought this might be of interest . . .'

It was a guidebook to the region. Rob looked up at Michael. He knew he was supposed to feel touched by the thoughtfulness of the gesture, but he wasn't. Something felt contrived, whether by accident or design he wasn't sure, and he couldn't help but feel a little resentful towards the man. Michael really looked the part – played the part – the harmless, helpless introvert: gauche, unused to social etiquette, making such an effort. Rob knew he ought to feel sympathy, but all he felt was a renewed irritation that he had to struggle to conceal.

'That's very thoughtful of you, Michael, but you shouldn't have.' When the bill had come the previous evening, Rob had not offered to pay Michael's share. It wasn't as if Michael really owed them anything.

Michael shrugged. 'It's nothing much, but I didn't know what else to get.'

Rob nodded. How could he know? How could he possibly have any idea of their tastes or preferences? He supposed he should be grateful that the guy hadn't presented them with something garish or inappropriate that might be embarrassing. 'Georgie'll be pleased. She loves reading up on stuff.'

Michael seemed to brighten. 'I hope so. She did say she wanted to know about the area.' He glanced over at her, and Rob followed his gaze to his sleeping girlfriend. 'She's out cold.' Michael almost laughed. 'Keep her up, did you?'

It was intended as a joke, an attempt at affectionate banter, but something about his tone made Rob resist. He put the book down on the little table.

'Thanks a million, Michael. I'll tell her you dropped it over.'

With a self-consciousness that he cursed himself for, Rob settled back down on his sun lounger, picking up his novel, leaving Michael hovering uncertainly to one side. Rob knew he couldn't leave things like that, and with an effort that seemed entirely at odds with the offhandedness of the remark, he asked Michael what his plans were for the day. Michael shrugged, suddenly vague and distant. He still had some unpacking to do, he said, he might come down to the pool later. And almost as quickly as he'd appeared, he left, loping off to the little stairway entrance, disappearing into the gloom.

Rob watched Michael's balcony for a moment but he didn't come out. He knew he was being ridiculous; more than that, very unfair. Had Georgie been awake, she'd never have allowed him to be so terse, so unfriendly to the man. And he knew she would be touched by Michael's gesture. She'd probably want to do something to reciprocate. What was the big deal? Unable to settle, to shake off the irritation, the bubbling resentment, Rob stood, and without a second thought, dove into the pool, hoping against hope that the short, sharp shock of the water would jolt him out of his pettiness.

~

The day had started so well. Although he'd woken very abruptly, a little frightened momentarily by the unfamiliarity of his surroundings, Michael had quickly recognised where he was and was surprised to discover a surge of pleasure that he was here, in his little room in Greece and not at home. He hadn't expected to feel that way. Indeed, he had gone to bed the previous evening depressed and angry at the turn of events that had left him stranded, marked him as a sad-case, reliant on strangers for any bit of company.

The enjoyment he'd had, eating out with Georgie and Rob, had quickly dissipated when he'd arrived back in his room. They had seemed so eager to be rid of him by the end, walking slowly back up the hill entwined in one another, barely able to sustain polite conversation. He knew what they were so keen to get back for; he wasn't a fool. The wine had made him heavy-headed and morose. He had never drunk so much wine before, glass after glass, and his nerves had made him greedy for it. That, in combination with the unfamiliar food, which had sat uncomfortably in his stomach, and Rob's barely concealed tolerance for his presence, had made for an unpleasant walk home. He had come back up to the apartment seized with a determination that he would not stay another night, that the situation was unbearable. He had another nine days ahead of him! How did they think he could manage, stuck here, alone?!

Michael had sat on his balcony for what must have been hours. He'd heard the distant throb of the nightclubs in town starting up at around midnight, and heard them quieten down and tail off, much, much later, when the sky was starting to lighten. He'd watched a couple of people come back into the apartment complex, noticed the light going on in the apartment below him, listened to the hushed tones of their conversation, though he couldn't make out the words. He didn't think they were speaking English. The whole world appeared to be paired off, in groups: families, couples, friends. It was a new and strange awareness. He had been alone most of his adult life and it had never really bothered him before. But since Patrick – since their friendship and the shaking up of his old routine, since discovering the horizons that friendship offered, Michael had easily and happily embraced them, and the lack of those horizons now was a bitter pill to swallow. Lonely. He was feeling lonely, and the ache of it almost made him sick.

Eventually he had dragged himself off to bed, in a state of such misery he was convinced he would not sleep. But he had slept; almost instantly it seemed, for he couldn't recall any tossing and turning or prolonged wakefulness. And though he awoke only three hours later, with the sun streaming in through the window, he felt refreshed and happy. The brief plunge into oblivion had flipped the coin of feelings for him. The pool was empty – it was barely seven in the morning – and Michael sat on his balcony, sipping his tea, aware that everyone around him in the building was asleep. He was still getting used to the strange taste of the tea, the weakness of the brew and the slightly different flavour of the milk. The day before, he'd thought it pretty disgusting, but now he savoured it, enjoying it, feeling more at home.

Gazing out onto the stillness of the morning, he felt as though he were the only man alive. But rather than tormenting him, this sense of isolation now energised him, pleased him. How different everything appeared in daylight. How much simpler, and how full of possibilities. The world was his oyster, there for the taking. He had only to embrace it. So he was stuck on his own – so what? No one could make him feel bad, not for anything. Yet as his thoughts progressed, a sudden pang of guilt gave him pause. Georgie. She'd been so kind to him, and he had spent hours late last night resenting her; her and that boyfriend of hers, after they'd taken him out, kept him company for a while. They had been tired, that was all: tired after a long travel day. Michael had no right to think ill of them because they had wanted to go to bed.

He was resolved. Although he had nothing concrete to reproach himself for, the mere fact that he'd indulged unpleasant thoughts regarding Georgie upset him. Looking back over the evening, it hadn't been her at all, it had been him, Rob, who'd marched them back off home, him who'd slung his arm around her, pulling her close, determined that she should do as he chose. If anything, she might have wanted to stay out a bit, keep going. She had been laughing a lot at dinner. Michael had made her laugh! The memory of it made him smile. And hadn't she even suggested going for one more drink? Michael strained to remember. He could hear her speak the words but he didn't know if he was imagining them or not. No matter. He had been wrong last night, wrong to condemn her. He'd make it up. He'd make it up to her immediately.

It was a great stroke of luck that the supermarket opened so early. It was quite busy when Michael went down, full of locals who were evidently getting their shopping done before starting their day's work. He felt sorry for these workers, surrounded by happy holidaymakers with nothing but their own pleasure to worry about. He hoped one or two of the soberly dressed men and women, hot in their heavy suits, silently queuing with their purchases, checking their watches, would get a holiday of their own soon.

Michael felt much more confidant going round the shop that second time, now he knew the ropes. He browsed their clothing section fully. It was amazing, really, how much stuff they had for people who were purely on holiday. You didn't see that at home, but then, he supposed, people didn't really come for holidays to his part of the world. Certainly not beach holidays, anyway. They'd be hard pressed! But here, you could buy anything: inflatable pool toys, all manner of games, shorts, T-shirts, hats, swimming costumes, even flippers and snorkels if you wanted. He needn't have troubled bringing any clothes over with him – he could get everything he needed here. In a burst of reckless-ness, he selected a pair of shorts and a shirt for himself, then a hat and a T-shirt. He still needed sandals or flip-flops at least, but he couldn't see any for adults and he didn't want to ask. He was riding high on a wave of self-sufficiency, and didn't want to risk any possibility of it crashing down.

Then he'd spotted the guidebook. It was the perfect gift for Georgie. He knew she didn't have one already – hadn't she said they'd come a bit last minute, made the booking quickly? That they'd been completely unprepared? And even though Rob had been to Greece before, he'd never been to this particular island before. Michael smiled at the memory of Georgie's fib to Les, sitting at the poolside bar, fobbing him off so easily, so elegantly, but letting him, Michael, in on her lie. A little conspiracy between them. Though it was expensive for such a small book, he didn't care. She deserved it.

Back in the apartment he changed into his new clothes, delighted that they fitted him so well, since he hadn't been entirely sure of the sizing in the supermarket. Fully decked out, he waited on his balcony in a fervour of excitement. With any luck, Georgie's boyfriend would sleep in – hadn't she said he liked to sleep late? Michael could go down and meet her, hand her the gift, all casual like, maybe offer to buy her a coffee. The older couple who had been on the coach came to the poolside first, carefully pulling their sun-beds into the shade, settling down companionably side by side with their books. Then the young family with the toddlers. They took their time to settle, faffing about with a big umbrella, covering the kids in sun cream. Michael was getting impatient. It was nearly nine o'clock. Where on earth was she?

It felt as though he'd been punched in the stomach when he saw her. It was because she was with *him*, with Rob. He was up and active, dragging their loungers to get the best spot in the sun, setting up a little table in between. Michael watched them, paralysed. He heard Georgie chuckle at something Rob had said: a low, throaty sound that carried on the breeze tantalisingly, reminding Michael of the way she'd laughed with him the night before. He hadn't anticipated having to deal with Rob, not remotely. The thought of strolling down, of handing over his prized gift in front of them both – he couldn't do it. And anyway, it wasn't for Rob, not really, it was for her – it was something *she'd* like. Rob would probably laugh at him for it. He watched as Georgie stretched out on her front, her face hidden from him; watched as Rob smeared sun cream sloppily onto her exposed back, watched as he sat upright, glancing around the pool, smug, self-satisfied, for all the world as if he owned the place.

It was a shock when Rob locked eyes with him from down below. Michael had almost forgotten he was visible, so intently had he been staring at them. When Rob saw him, his heart beat faster, so fast, in fact, that he thought he might get faint and he rushed back into the living room, clutching the edge of the table to steady himself. He'd have to go down now. Rob would think him weird if he didn't make an appearance. Gathering himself as best he could, he'd grabbed the book and left, gone quickly down the stairs, taking the long way through the complex so as to get to the side of the pool closest to Rob. He didn't want the man staring at him as he walked all the way around.

Georgie was fast asleep, Michael could tell instantly as he approached. She looked so young suddenly – younger than she'd seemed the previous night – lying there so still, her hat perched precariously on the very top of her head, her hair slightly damp with sweat and sun cream. She looked beautifully peaceful, and the mere sight of her up close gave Michael the little surge of confidence he needed.

He didn't know what he'd been expecting from Rob, if anything at all, but it pained him to hand over his carefully selected gift to someone so unfriendly, so clearly uninterested. He hadn't been wrong about *him* the night before: the guy was totally up himself, superior. He reminded Michael of one of the bosses back at work, a man Patrick took the piss out of mercilessly, mocking him for his airs and graces. *He thinks he's above us all, that one, but I can tell you, his shit stinks just like the rest of us!*

Rob hadn't even bothered to flick through the book, hadn't shown the faintest interest. He'd tossed it down on the table as if he'd always owned it, and Michael had a strong suspicion he would forget to tell Georgie where it had come from – might even claim it as a gift he'd bought himself. What had he done to make the man dislike him so? Who did he think he was, to look at him so dismissively? He was only trying to be friendly, for God's sake – only trying to do the decent thing. Michael made his excuses as quickly as possible and left, desperate suddenly to be alone.

He couldn't go back out onto the balcony. Rob's beady eyes would seek him out, find him, glare him into submission. And, besides, he'd pretended he had unpacking to do. He couldn't reappear so suddenly. He would have to wait. An overwhelming rush of fatigue overtook Michael and he sat down on his bed, at a loss. She didn't deserve it. She didn't deserve to be with a man like that who was so rude, so arrogant. She must see it – she was so clever, so sharp – of course she saw it! If she could see through Les, she could see through Rob. So it must be something else. Perhaps she was stuck with him for other reasons. Perhaps she had no choice in the matter. Michael had seen it before: young women stuck with men who didn't deserve them, stuck because they were frightened and unsure and couldn't see a way out. Or because they'd been bullied into it, physically bullied. Men like that were the worst, using their strength to keep other people down. If that were the case, poor Georgie! She shouldn't be stuck in a situation like that.

His thoughts tumbled over one another, battling for attention, but to no avail. As he lay back on his pillow, Michael fell deeply asleep.

~

'I'm going to the room.'

Georgie sat up, drowsy, surprised by the annoyance in her boyfriend's tone. 'What's the matter, sweetheart? Is everything okay?'

'Work. They've been texting me nonstop for the past half-hour. I'd better give them a call. I don't want this to go on all day.'

She couldn't help herself. She pouted. Which was guaranteed to irritate Rob further. He shot her a glance – a 'please don't start with me' glance – and she rearranged her expression as quickly as she could. She knew he had been expecting the intrusion of work on their first couple of days, and she knew she had no right to be cross with him about it. After all, it was his income that had mostly provided for their holiday. Her work as a freelancer came in fits and starts, and, though she was well paid for the most part, cash flow was frequently an issue. Rob, the regular earner, often took care of their day-to-day expenditure, and on this occasion had been happy to pay the money towards the holiday upfront. Georgie would repay him when the final instalment for her children's book was due, this fact the stern condition of her acceptance of his outlay.

Until recently, she hadn't minded the disparity in their financial arrangements, particularly because she'd been on a roll during their first two years together, going from job to job, earning handsomely. But the last year had been more difficult for her. Work had been scarce and the fees much lower. Thus far, she'd just about managed to hold her own, but Rob had been shouldering more of the financial responsibilities of late and it unnerved her somewhat. She had never relied on anyone before in that way: had always, as a single woman, managed to make ends meet, no matter the circumstances. This had been a source of great pride to her: a badge of independence more thrilling than seeing her name in print (however small) on the front covers of books.

But life together brought increased financial demands, particularly now they were an established couple, getting older, with a desire – more on Rob's part than her own – to live like proper modern adults, with fixtures and fittings. Though she had no wish to live as a student, she couldn't help but feel a little panicked sometimes at the extent of Rob's rebranding of them: the espresso machine, the matching dishes, new cushions for the sofas, framed prints on the walls. She struggled to keep up, and resented Rob's easy attitude regarding the luxury of his regular salary. The imbalance was beginning to grate, and she had initially been reluctant in the face of his insistence that they take this holiday, because she didn't have the funds for it at the time. 'You'll pay me back – stop fussing! If we don't go now, we won't get a break this year.' That was true. Rob's project would need his undivided attention for the late summer and autumn months, and she had work lined up for winter – nothing exciting, just some bread and butter work she did each year for a greetings card company – but she knew she wouldn't be able to afford to turn it down. So it had been a question of now or never for their holiday, no matter that she felt she hadn't truly earned her place on it.

She smiled up at him, willing him to forget her momentary fit of pique. Rob, armed with his phone, went upstairs. She knew she shouldn't take it so personally, the intrusion of his work on their first morning, but it bothered her: not because of him, but because of her. No one was ringing *her*, needing *her* urgent advice. No one sought *her* out long-distance. The thoughts were petty and childish, and she chastised herself even as she thought them, but they were symptoms of a deeper concern. Georgie was talented, she knew that, but she was getting to the stage in her career where she recognised that her talent was nothing particularly remarkable; at least, nothing especially above the talents of others in her field. She was solid, diligent and imaginative, she was a reliable employee, never missed a deadline, was good at dealing with capricious clients. Publishers liked her and so did authors, who appreciated the care she took when talking to them, discovering what it was they'd visualised as they were writing, before gently offering her own suggestions. So there was a great deal to recommend her. But whatever it was she lacked – whether something temperamental or intrinsically to do with her creativity – it was becoming clear to her that she would never actually do anything extraordinary. Good – really good – was about all she could aim for.

The thought depressed her, and had been depressing her for some months, though she hid it well. She was grateful that it hadn't turned her against her work – quite the opposite, in fact. If anything, she clung to her projects all the more tenaciously, working harder, actively opposing the voices in her head that whispered of her mediocrity. She knew better than to indulge the dark side, to give too much weight to the inner insecurities. But her new awareness of the limitations of her talent was still something she was having difficulty facing up to. She was turning thirty in three months, and, though the thought of it, in and of itself, meant very little to her, she couldn't shake a nagging feeling that she had not made the most of her twenties – not pushed hard enough, been bold enough – had spent too much time and energy worrying about what others thought of her. She worried that she'd not even made sure she'd had enough fun.

Of course, Rob hadn't minded in the slightest when *he* had crossed the thirty mark a year before. A fresh new decade was a cause for joy in his book: his career going from strength to strength, happily settled in his relationship. What need for mourning? He wasn't losing anything by leaving his twenties, only gaining. In fact, turning thirty stamped the seal of true adulthood upon him, giving him a greater sense of status. He'd thrown himself an enormous party, with all his friends and colleagues, turning one night's celebration into a weekend of drunken antics. Georgie had been delighted for him at the time, and privately amazed that he had so many people he could call on to come and join him. She had few friends; or, rather, she had a small, tight circle of close friends, but few acquaintances. Rob was the one who knew everyone.

Georgie could hear Rob speaking on the phone from their apartment above. Cool and efficient, he sounded in complete control. Maturity – Rob's version of it – suited him. In his eyes, his numerical age had finally caught up with his level of professional competence and success. His voice carried on the breeze, the acoustics of the courtyard being somewhat deceptive, channelling sounds from the apartments down to the poolside. Georgie smiled, suddenly thinking that she'd have to remember to shut the balcony door if they spent an afternoon making love.

She hauled herself up into a sitting position, her back a little stiff and sore. She had never found it comfortable sleeping on sun loungers, even as a kid, when she'd been able to curl up properly, and she registered with a grim sort of amusement how prone her body had become to feeling all sorts of minor aches and irritations. Or perhaps it was just that she was more alert to them; ready to pay attention to any sudden shift in the blithe robustness of the body she had so taken for granted in her youth. Her youth! For God's sake, she thought, if she were like this at barely thirty, how on earth would she cope at sixty? She was being far too self-indulgent, harping on about her impending birthday, allowing herself to think that her youth was over. Pathetic – she was being totally pathetic! How her mother would laugh at her if she could hear her thoughts, her athletic, energetic mother, who the year before, at sixty-two, had taken a cycling holiday in France; her mother, utterly indifferent since the age of forty to not only the numeral but to the conventional assumptions assigned to her stage in life. Georgie still thought of her mother as young. So why couldn't she think of herself in the same way?

Having a swim would loosen her up, get her a bit of exercise. Another sign of the dreaded new decade: she'd started worrying about her weight recently, something that had never bothered her before. She had always been amazed at her capacity to withstand the pressures of the culture and even of her friends, most of whom obsessed about their size. Georgie had been lucky as a youngster (there was that word again), and had never really fluctuated much beyond what she was now. If she'd found her clothes getting tight, a small modification of her appetite seemed to do the trick. Only recently she had been dismayed to discover that weight was sticking to her more readily, that her metabolism had slowed somewhat, and that the amount of food she wanted and felt comfortable with was no longer the amount of food her body could comfortably process. Rather than restrict her diet, she'd determined to take more exercise as a means of offsetting the imbalance, but the habit didn't come easily. She preferred long walks to runs and loathed the thought of gyms. A stationary bike at home had had a certain novelty value for a while, with the additional benefit of being instantly accessible, right there in front of her, but after a month or two, she'd tired of it. She didn't enjoy pedalling frantically to nowhere in front of the television and, rather than energising her, it left her depressed. She enjoyed swimming, but there was no local pool; it would mean traipsing into town, taking up half the morning. Here, however, she had no excuses, and could easily get in a workout each day.

Whenever she confided her body worries to Rob, he laughed at her. He was probably right to, she thought, since she'd never actually gained or lost more than a few pounds, but his inability to sympathise with her doubts, his amazement that she should worry about a tiny pinch of extra skin or find cause for celebration should that pinch reduce a little, upset her unduly. She should be grateful, she knew, that he took no notice of the tiny fluctuations of her body. She should be delighted that he revelled in her, no matter her size; that he encouraged her hearty appetite, took pleasure in cooking for her or taking her out for a meal, loved to see her indulge her sweet tooth and couldn't give a hoot if she'd earned it through exercise or not. Yet his wholehearted, blithe support seemed to Georgie to

conceal within it a certain indifference – a certain lack of attention that had recently been gnawing away at her, creating a level
of preoccupation with her own belly that she'd never known
before. *Why* didn't he notice when she was bloated or heavier?
Why did only she find herself that much more alluring when
her jeans hung a little looser on her waist? Was it that he simply
didn't see? And if not, why not?

She stood up, stretching, feeling a satisfying click in her neck
as something unclenched. The English kids – the brother and
sister – were splashing about in the shallow end but they were
pretty well behaved. They wouldn't get in her way if she swam
a few laps. She took off her hat and sunglasses and, laying them
on the table, she noticed a guidebook to the island sitting there.
She picked it up, surprised. Where had that sprung from? Rob
hadn't been out that morning and they hadn't brought it with
them: Georgie had left their guidebook on the living room table
back home.

She flicked through it, pleased. She hadn't done much
research on their particular island, and though she planned to
do very little during their vacation, she wanted the option of
sightseeing, just in case. It would make their trip seem longer if
they took a couple of days out and about, rather than just lounging by the pool. She wanted to sit back down and have a proper
read, but the little voice of authority in her head, whose intrusions had become more regular and upbraiding of late, told her
she should continue with her plan, have her swim. Plenty of
time for reading later. With a sigh, she put the book aside and
edged to the poolside ladder, gingerly testing the water with

her toe. It was cold – far colder than she'd expected – and she hovered, unwilling to take the plunge. Unlike Rob, who preferred to dive in instantly – a quick, sharp shock, and get it over with – she liked to inch herself in, letting her body get used to the water before finally succumbing to total immersion. Strangely though, she was the sort of person who ripped off plasters in one bold motion, so why she should be so gingerly hesitant about a cold swimming pool, she couldn't fathom.

She was almost halfway in when she saw Michael. He was carrying a towel and a bottle of sun cream, making his way slowly around the other side of the pool. He had his head down, but Georgie knew he must have seen her as he came out of the building. Her impulse was to call out a greeting to him, say hello, but something made her hesitate. Perhaps Rob's teasing of the previous evening, his semi-serious warnings about not turning Michael into a pesky hanger-on. Or perhaps that pernicious inner voice of authority, cautioning her against distraction; urging her to swim her laps or face a monstrous fate of obesity.

She watched as Michael selected a sun-bed, some distance from hers and Rob's, laid out his towel and carefully removed his trainers and socks. He seemed preoccupied and she wondered how he was feeling. How awkward it must be, coming down alone, knowing that there will be no one to join you, no one to go back upstairs to, no one to eat with later, or chat to on the balcony. She almost shuddered at the thought of it. Travelling alone was something she had never done, nor ever wanted to do. Even on the odd work trip she'd had to take, she had never been brave enough to sit at dinner alone in a restaurant, resorting to takeaways in the privacy of her hotel room, finding company in the television. A couple of her girlfriends had trekked the world on their own, relishing the independence and the freedom, but the mere thought of it had frightened Georgie. She was alone so much in her working life that having to relax on her own was a contradiction in terms for her.

She watched as Michael lay down on the lounger, hesitant, as if it might give way beneath him. He was so young – had he said he was twenty-three? And though he looked robust physically, though he definitely looked like a man and not an overgrown boy, the way some young men in their twenties did, he had the manner of an adolescent in conversation: unsure of himself, eager to please. The way he'd listened to her the previous evening, as though she were the most fascinating person in the world! Clearly he doesn't get out much, she thought, wryly. Rob had noticed her playing up to it a little at dinner, had teased her about it later, and she'd blushed, acknowledging her vanity. But it was harmless, they both knew that. Just a way of making a casual connection that wasn't going to go very far. And, anyway, she'd teased in return – shouldn't Rob be flattered that another man found his beloved so mesmerizing? Screw him and his moralising. What was wrong with being friendly?

She was getting cold, half in the pool, half out of it, her hesitancy having become genuine delay. She'd better make up her mind. Steeling her resolve, she pushed off from the edge, feeling the icy shiver run up her spine as her body submerged itself in the water, and she paddled over to the side of the pool closest to Michael. No reason why she shouldn't say hello – it would be rude not to. Michael wasn't snubbing her; it was just that he was awkward. She was certain the reason he'd avoided coming to speak to her was that he wouldn't want to intrude, and wouldn't know how to conduct a light exchange of greetings properly. Aware that she was being slightly patronising in her thinking, she beamed a smile at him as she approached.

'How are you today?' she asked him, hoiking her elbows up onto the poolside, feeling that unpleasant twinge again in her lower back – she must really have twisted it or something. 'Sleep well?'

Michael seemed surprised that she should be talking to him; surprised and delighted, like an over-eager pup. 'Yeah. Good, thanks. How about you? How did you sleep?'

'Like a log – and more this morning, too. I think I'm finally starting to catch up.'

'Yeah? Haven't you been sleeping well before, then?' He sounded concerned. He really was very sweet, she thought.

'Not recently. Don't know why. Just very wakeful these past few weeks. Working too hard, maybe.' She smiled at him, noticing the newness of his clothes. 'I like your shirt. Very summery.'

'Thanks. I only got it this morning. I wasn't sure if it would fit.'

'Suits you. You look good.'

'Yeah?' He seemed to relax a little with the compliment and he edged closer on his sun-bed. 'Where's Rob?'

'Gone upstairs. Had to make a phone call.'

'Something the matter?' His tone was over-urgent and she shook her head, a little bemused, half-laughing.

'No, no, nothing. Just work, that's all. He's in the middle of a big project and there'll be teething problems these first few days without him. With any luck it'll quieten down in a day or two.'

Michael nodded, digesting the information. Georgie, feeling the cold again, was about to make her excuses and finally swim her laps when he blurted: 'Did you get it then?'

'Get what?'

'The book. The guidebook. I picked it up for you this morning. Rob said he'd tell you.'

She was taken aback. 'That was *you*? I wondered where it'd come from. God! Did you get that for *me*?'

Even in the glare of the sunshine and hidden under the shade of his baseball cap, she could see the sudden flush of colour in his cheeks. She smiled at him, touched that he should have made so thoughtful a gesture. 'Oh, Michael, that's ever so kind of you.'

He shrugged, clearly embarrassed. 'I just wanted to say thank you – for being so good to me yesterday. You were really nice.'

'It was lovely, wasn't it? Dinner.'

'Yeah. Lovely. And the drink before.'

She turned to glance at the poolside bar. Les was dealing with a couple of clients. She had studiously avoided him all morning, making Rob go and fetch their coffees. 'Yeah, it was. We'll do it again.' She turned back to Michael. He was grinning and she couldn't help but smile back. His obvious delight was infectious. 'Thanks so much for the book. You really shouldn't have.'

'You said you didn't have a guidebook.'

'You're right – well remembered. I shall have lots of fun reading up on the island. Might even plan a few sight-seeing days!'

'But Rob didn't tell you?' Michael's face was creased into a frown, the issue troubling him.

Georgie felt the need to apologise on Rob's behalf. 'I've been asleep all morning, then he got up to make a call. We've barely spoken at all today. I'm sure he'll tell me when he comes down.' She sounded too gushing, too over-eager. 'I'm sure he's as pleased as I am.'

Michael nodded, as if confirming something he'd suspected. She suddenly became worried that Rob might have been ungracious or offhand, thanks to his early morning grumpiness. 'He did thank you, didn't he?'

'Yeah.'

Michael would be too polite to tell her otherwise, she thought. Sod Rob and his arrogance! Why can't he get off his bloody high horse for once and act his age, not his shoe size. He manages to do it perfectly well when he's at *work*. Georgie kicked out her legs behind her, irritated. 'It's chilly in here.'

'Yeah. Looks it.' Her arms had goose bumps.

'You coming in?'

'Nah. I don't like swimming much.'

'It's very good for you – best form of exercise, they say.'

'I don't like getting water up my nose.'

'So don't put your head under!'

'Then what's the point?'

They smiled at one another. There was, perhaps, more

substance to the man than she had credited.

'Well, I'm going to do my laps, water up nose and all. See you in a bit.' Georgie pushed off before he could reply, and let her head sink below the water. She was thrown by the unexpected present, the unexpected kindness. They were pricey, those little guidebooks – a bottle of wine or something would have been far cheaper. And Rob had probably been rude to Michael, wanting to put him off. He could be so callous sometimes, particularly when it came to people he thought were stupid or a bit slow. His impatience got the better of him and Georgie had seen him be quite cutting on more than one occasion. He had been surprised when she'd confronted him with it – questioning his tone and attitude. He had never noticed how he slipped so easily into a manner that could only be described as imperious.

She swam her laps, fourteen in all, which she reckoned to be a pretty fair attempt at improving her fitness and burning off her breakfast calories. She would invite Michael for a coffee, she decided – do the decent thing – to thank him. Besides, it wasn't as if Rob was hectoring for her attention. When she looked up out of the water, breathless from her exertions, he still hadn't come down from the apartment.

Michael, sensitive to Georgie's dislike of Les, offered to fetch the coffees, but she insisted that she pay. She motioned that he should take a seat on Rob's sun lounger, so that they could converse comfortably, but Michael seemed reluctant, pulling up a chair instead. It was nearly lunchtime. The young families were slowly gathering their things to take the kids up to eat. The sun was searingly hot. Georgie had dried almost instantly as she got out of the pool.

'God, it's unbelievable, isn't it? The heat?'

Michael nodded, sweat beaded on his brow. 'The heat. Yeah. I've never known anything like it.'

'Yes – it's not like that round our way, is it? Amazing that the pool should be so bloody cold! Though it's lovely once you're in. Mind you cover yourself in sun cream – you mustn't get burned.'

They chatted companionably for a while, Georgie slowly dropping her fussy, maternal bluster, easing in to proper conversation. She was pleased to note that if she took a slightly gentle tone with him, respectful, encouraging, Michael would relax and respond. Actually, he could be quite funny when he felt comfortable enough – nothing remarkable though; his wasn't a searing wit – quite the opposite. His humour derived from a slightly childish literalism, playing up the dullard aspect of his character to good effect. They had been watching Les try to flirt unsuccessfully with the mother of the two toddlers, providing a hushed running commentary on his activities.

'"Are you sure you don't want to come clubbing with me? You can ditch the kids with your old man!"' Michael attempted to mimic Les's accent, not very successfully.

'I can't believe he thinks that all that leering and winking will get him anywhere!' Georgie sounded disgusted. Michael shrugged, his eyes still on Les as the young woman turned her back on him, leading her children away.

'Maybe it does. He had quite a fan before you came down last night – some middle-aged bird with too much slap on. He must get lucky sometimes; otherwise he'd give up.'

Georgie turned to him, interested. 'So what – this woman – was she flirting back?'

'Flirting? I dunno. She was with her husband – at least, I think it was her husband. But she seemed to enjoy the attention. Tell you the truth, she was a little bit . . . *tarty.*'

Michael spoke the word with a lowered voice, as if it were a shameful obscenity. Georgie smiled at his delicacy and shrugged, intending to convey worldliness.

'Some women like that,' she told him, happy to unite with him in judging the unknown middle-aged lady. 'Some women crave attention – doesn't matter who it's from.'

She threw a glance at Michael, who was nodding, clearly hanging on her every word. She felt a sudden stab of self-consciousness. Here she was condemning the innocent flirting of another woman, while she herself was so shamelessly courting Michael's favour. Her vanity really was remarkable! She smiled at her hypocrisy.

''Course, those kinds of women . . . women like that . . . well, they're not really worth bothering about.'

She looked up at him, surprised. It was the first time he had ventured so concrete an opinion.

'How d'you mean?'

He hesitated, and Georgie could almost see the cogs turning in his mind, as he tried to formulate a coherent response.

'They're all for show, you know. They want you to look at them. But what you see is what you get – only they don't know it. They dress up and parade themselves about and they want you to think how interesting they are, how mysterious, but really, that's it. That's all they've got. Tight dresses, too much make-up and lots of gold jewellery. Take that away, and they're nothing.'

Georgie watched him, with that slightly prickly sensation she sometimes got when a perfectly pleasant taxi driver revealed himself to be a virulent racist halfway through the journey. She chose her words carefully, praying that her amiable companion would not disappoint her.

'I think some women just choose to display themselves differently, that's all. Some women really enjoy all the dress and fuss. I've got no problem with it.'

Michael looked up at her, on the alert – or so it seemed to Georgie, who had thrown down the gauntlet and was waiting for him to pick it up or walk away.

'No, no, I've no problem with it either. It's their business, isn't it? I just think it's a bit sad, that's all. You'd think their husbands would do a better job of making them happy, wouldn't you?'

'Or that they'd be able to make themselves happy,' she replied staunchly.

He looked at her, a little puzzled. Georgie cursed herself inwardly for her heavy-handedness. It was guilt that had made her suddenly so serious, guilt at colluding in criticism, snidely craving Michael's approval and affirmation that she wasn't one of *those* women. Really, it was too much! Was she so insecure that she had to lower herself – even momentarily – to eke out backhanded compliments through nasty comparisons with others?

'Mind you,' she told him ruefully, 'we all need a bit of help sometimes, don't we? We can't always do it alone.'

'Yeah, that's true enough.'

He was looking at her and she smiled, suddenly distracted and impatient. She glanced up behind her at her balcony. It had been a good half-hour and Rob still hadn't returned. She could no longer hear his voice.

'He must have a lot of things to talk about,' Michael said, following the direction of her gaze.

Georgie shrugged. 'I suppose so.'

Something in her tone, in the little gesture she made with her hands, trying to give off an air of nonchalance and lightness, struck Michael as being not quite right. With a rapidly beating heart, he asked her: 'Is everything all right?'

She didn't respond and Michael felt a pang of fear that he might have overstepped the mark, that he might have lost her. Inwardly, he cursed himself for his clumsiness. If Patrick had been there, he'd have known how to handle things, though Patrick would hardly waste his time talking to a more or less married woman.

'Oh . . . yes. Of course.' She had taken too long to reply, she knew, and tried to cover quickly. 'I guess he's really having problems – with work, I mean. He must be as indispensable as he claims.'

Michael nodded. 'He must be quite important if they're ringing him on holiday.'

'Oh . . . not really. Well, in a way. There are a couple of other people in the plant at his level, but he's been the main one overseeing this batch of vaccines that they're working on. Sorry. It's a bit of a bore, and, to be honest, I'm not even sure what it is he does exactly. He has explained it to me, but it sort of goes in one ear and out the other. That's terrible, isn't it? I should know what he does in detail.'

She smiled, hoping Michael wouldn't press her any further. He seemed to take her cue for he shrugged self-deprecatingly.

'I don't think work would ever bother to ring me while I was away. Practically everyone on the floor could do my job.'

Michael wasn't looking for sympathy, or at least Georgie did-n't think he was. Nevertheless, something protective within her stirred a little – an impulse to defend him, make him feel valuable. She often had this instinct with the underdogs of life: a desperate desire to help, to make them feel good about themselves. It was a guilty, and, she knew, ultimately a profoundly patronising instinct.

'I'm sure that's not true. I'm sure you're very important to them.' It sounded lame, trite and she regretted it. 'I mean . . . .'

'Nah. My job's just a job. It's not a career, or anything like that. It's just something to pay the bills with.'

She didn't know what to say. She supposed there was no proper answer, though she felt a nagging need to apologise to Michael – not for anything she had done or said, but for his own lack of self-worth. A faint snatch of Rob's conversation floated down to them on the breeze. His voice was raised and his tone strident.

'—No—you're not *listening*! If you do that now, we'll have to alter it for every batch and that could set us back months . . . .'

Oh, he was busy and important all right. And though Rob might claim to be relatively indifferent to his work, Georgie knew he took great pleasure in the status it afforded him. It was something concrete – a career that had an instantly measurable progress, with updates and promotions that people could ask about. 'So what's next for you then, Rob? Heading up your own research team? Fielding offers from the States?' Whereas *her* work, her career, wasn't like that at all. Some of their friends had stopped asking her about it, unable to track the minute little victories that working for this or that author really meant. Who followed children's literature with any interest anyway? Until her drawings accompanied someone else's prose onto the bestseller lists, no one could place Georgie in the pecking order. All they knew was that she managed to earn a living at it.

'Does it bother you that he works so much?'

Michael's question took her by surprise. Quickly, she tried to shake herself out of her thoughts.

'We both work hard. Me more than him actually. Only I work alone for the most part, so there's no one to pester me.'

She sounded a little affronted, though she hadn't intended to. She'd become so prickly of late, about their relative status when it came to their professional lives. The financial imbalance had destabilized her.

'Oh yeah – I'd pegged you for a hard worker soon as I saw you. Anyone watching you swim can see that!'

Georgie blushed, childishly pleased by the slightly lumbering compliment. Putting in the hours and being recognised for it had long been a source of pride for her, a small wellspring of

consolation when she felt at her least talented and least reward-
ed.

'Well. I enjoy working. For the most part.'

'He must be very proud of you.'

Michael felt a little foolish. He hadn't intended to show
his admiration so clearly. Perhaps she would think him soft or
stupid. Women had laughed at him for less, but Georgie
suddenly turned to look at him, and to his amazement, he saw
tears welling in her eyes.

'Oh, goodness . . . I'm being so silly, Michael. Sorry.'

He was flustered. 'I didn't mean to upset you —'

'Oh, it's not you – really – really, it's not! God, no! It's lovely
talking to you. I'm enjoying it.' She glanced back up to the balcony, almost involuntarily.

So it was Rob, then. It was Rob who was making her cry.
Michael bit down on his lip.

Georgie shook her head, sighing. 'It's only a work call. And I
know he has to sort things out. It's just . . . .'

She was struggling to keep her tone even, Michael could tell.
He felt a strong impulse to reach out and touch her, reassure
her, but he thought that might be too much. Instead, he edged
forward almost imperceptibly and kept quiet, letting her do the
talking. He wasn't sure what he should say, anyway. Georgie
half-laughed.

'I'm overtired, that's all. I'm being childish. It's only that Rob
and I haven't really seen each other for a while – spent enough
time together. Sometimes I feel that we're just . . . going through
the motions, you know?'

Michael nodded, though Georgie wasn't looking at him. He was out of his depth. He didn't understand what she was getting at, but he knew that, in a strange sort of way, it didn't matter. All that mattered was that he was here with her, listening. She shook her head as if trying to get rid of her thoughts.

'I don't know . . . . I'm turning thirty soon, and sometimes I feel as if I'm still twelve. I don't know what I'm doing half the time. It's ridiculous!'

She did look up at him then, and Michael counted his blessings. This, he could understand. Feeling lost, feeling unsure. He nodded seriously.

'You don't have to tell me. I know all about it.'

They looked at one another for a moment and, to his immense surprise, Michael found that he was able to hold her gaze without difficulty. Something in her seemed to soften and she smiled, telling him she was happy to talk to him. He was a good listener. He felt as though he would burst with pride. He was about to offer her another coffee – on him this time – when a voice from above shattered their privacy.

'Oi! Georgie!'

Both she and Michael turned to look. Rob was on their balcony. Georgie scrambled to her feet almost immediately, walking briskly over to the edge of the pool enclosure so as not to have to shout too loudly.

'You all done?' she asked.

Rob glanced at Michael, who was still sitting on the chair next to Georgie's sun lounger. 'Everything all right?' he called, his eyes on Michael, not meeting hers.

'Lovely, thanks. We were just having coffee. To thank Michael for his present.'

'Oh, yeah.'

Michael looked away. Rob noticed, or thought he noticed, the hint of a smirk playing across the man's features.

'You coming down?' Georgie asked.

'Why don't you come up? I'll fix us some lunch.'

Rob saw Georgie hesitate, and he fought the impulse to snap at her. There was no need for it: she'd done nothing wrong. If anything, he was the one who owed her for having disappeared, letting work interrupt their first proper morning. He forced a smile. He had noticed that her resistance to him had been growing recently – not over anything major, just in small things, but it bothered him. And his reaction to it bothered him as well – he was too prone to irritability with her.

'Come on, gorgeous – come on up. It'll be worth your while!'

Georgie grinned at him suddenly, nodding, turning to gather her bag. Michael was still sitting on the chair.

'I'd invite you up but I can guarantee you he'll just be sounding off about work. It'll be an awful bore,' she told him apologetically.

But Michael could see she was covering up for the rudeness of her boyfriend. And he knew that a guy like Rob wouldn't summon her up just for a chat – not in front of him anyway. He was doing it on purpose. Rob wanted him, Michael, to know who was in charge, to know what was what. He'd seen it all before with his boss at work, the way he made people jump to it, do petty little jobs that didn't really need doing, just to prove he could make them. If Patrick had been there, he'd have had a quip all ready to win the round. But he wasn't Patrick, didn't have his nous, so he nodded silently at Georgie.

'See you later?' she asked him, smiling.

She wanted to be friends, that was clear enough. And she wasn't responsible for the bad manners of her boyfriend. If anything, she suffered more than anybody from them. Michael returned her smile with real warmth.

'Yeah, sure. See you later.'

~

Rob stroked her naked back, marvelling at the smoothness of her skin. He played a little game – one he hadn't played for a long time, probably not since the earliest days of their union: counting the moles and freckles on her back, using them as a sort of abstract join-the-dots, working out the shapes and pictures they might form. She chuckled: the deep, throaty sound that was so at odds with her small stature, reassuring him of her pleasure at his touch. 'S'nice,' she murmured. 'Keep going.'

It was work that stressed him out. Though Rob had known this intellectually for some time, he had only really felt it that afternoon, when Georgie had come up to him after the phone call. How his heart raced after dealing with work, how quickly and easily he focused his irritation and sense that he wasn't quite good enough on to her. No wonder she was resistant to him. It was damaging her – his stress level, his way of handling things – damaging them both, and though, in a way, it was a relatively minor sin, it wasn't a habit he wanted to get into. It wasn't how he wanted to be with her.

Rob had been mockingly sarcastic when Georgie first came up, teasing her mercilessly about Michael. 'Scintillating conversation – looked like, anyway. Could hardly drag yourself away!'

Georgie had worked very hard not to rise to it. He could see her swallowing her impatience, her own, legitimate annoyance with him. Rob knew he had taken far longer than necessary on the phone, going through everything with a fine-toothed comb. There was an insecurity in him when it came to his work – one that he masked well – indeed, one that he would never admit to, even if pressed. It drove him to action above and beyond the call of duty. It wasn't that he doubted his abilities, or doubted that others recognised them; it was more to do with a sense of uncertainty about his career potential. He didn't quite know where he wanted to go with his work. The actual nuts and bolts of chemical engineering and problem solving interested him, in and of itself; but in terms of sacrificing so much of his personal time to an occupation that didn't afford him huge creative autonomy or individuality, he hadn't made up his mind about how far he was prepared to go. He was earning well, even at his level, and though the material rewards of a higher-level career as a consultant engineer – working internationally, advising pharmaceutical companies about how they might implement the technical aspects of the creation and testing of new drugs – were incredibly attractive, Rob was apprehensive about the disruption that taking such a leap might cause. Paradoxically, though he knew he was being groomed for bigger things, his inner reticence about it made him nervous, as though everyone knew what he was thinking, knew his uncertainty. So he worked doubly hard to prove himself, even as he didn't want to face the rewards of it.

They had eaten lunch more or less in silence, Georgie being unwilling to provoke him inadvertently (or to be provoked herself), Rob with the dawning realisation of his behaviour towards her. Neither ate much, and eventually, as Georgie stood to clean the plates, he reached out and stayed her arm.

'I'm sorry,' he told her. 'I know I'm an awful shit with this stuff. I have been for some time. I hate it. I hate being like this with you. I've got to learn how to deal with it better.'

Georgie had cried then, and it hadn't troubled him, the way her tears often had in the past. He felt it as a sort of relief – a letting go for both of them of all the tension that had built up so stealthily in the midst of their busy lives. On impulse, they opened a bottle of wine, feeling as though they were breaking the rules, drinking in the middle of the day, but both united in wanting to free themselves of their oppressive feelings. They had proceeded to get very quickly and very happily drunk – laughing, joking, looking at one another anew – rediscovering what it was that had made them so delighted with each other's company in the first place. And then, with Georgie remembering at the last minute to close the balcony door, they had tumbled onto the sofa, grasping at one another, overwhelmed by their mutual desire. Rob had banged his knee quite hard, Georgie had hurt her head and her back had still been twingeing – they hadn't cared. Rob carried her into the bedroom and they continued, the alcohol heightening their sensations: each touch, each movement an exquisite pleasure.

The shadows had grown longer on the walls and the shrieks of the kids from the pool below got louder as the afternoon drew on. Rather than tiring, the children's energy seemed only to increase the longer they played; a state of being both Rob and Georgie wistfully remarked upon. How amazing summers had been as children, seeming to stretch on and on. After they had finished for the second time, Georgie had suggested going back down to the pool, but Rob shook his head, enjoying the isolation of their little world. She hadn't minded, and had snuggled up against him, smiling, happy, falling fast asleep.

Rob found it strange, looking at her, peaceful in repose, how little he really knew about her inner life. Georgie spent her days at her big artist's drawing board, working for hours on the painstakingly detailed illustrations that had become her trademark. It amazed him to think that she must spend so much of her mental and emotional energy immersed in a child's eye view of things: making the pictures that would bring to life their fantasies, helping them understand the text better, making real the imaginary world that each child would have their own vision of. Make it somehow truthful, appealing, universal. It was a monumental task in its own way, having to crystallize a response that was entirely your own: taking the author's words and then translating them visually in a way that would resonate with thousands of different readers. How difficult it must be for Georgie to unlock her responses if the words were bland and unimaginative!

Rob remembered those agonising jobs when she had felt drained and uninspired – hopeless, even, when nothing came. Nothing that she was pleased with, anyway, for Georgie's approach to creative work was disciplined. No sitting around waiting for the muse to strike. She was active, putting things on paper almost immediately, working through her uncertainty and fear. When projects left her cold, the amount of discarded drawings tripled – it took her so much longer to find her way with them. But her diligence and stamina were impressive. Rob would often be the one dragging her away, forcing her to take off at least one full day of the weekend. It must be lonely, he suddenly realised. No one to report to, no one to tell you you're doing a good job until the very end. No one with whom to share the quiet triumphs and disasters of the journey, for the details were too personal to explain. No one would ever know the battles that had to be fought in order to get there in the end. Nor should they. The trick was making it look effortless.

He would not be able for work like that. Rob thrived on attention, on teamwork – well, leading a team, if he were honest. He liked to be in charge, liked to be busy; loved nothing more than having a list of tasks he could cross off at the end of every day, with a sense of solid accomplishment. A part of him was proud that his colleagues should have called him on holiday, reassuring him that he was vital and necessary; for without his knowledge and insight, up to twenty people would be sitting around with nothing to do. But the part of him that took such pride was the part he had to watch. Indulging it too much brought out the worst in him. Demanding that he be valued for his accomplishments at work devalued what was increasingly becoming most important to him. Too much pride in the externals distorted what he craved from Georgie, which was an inner appreciation – a love for him, without bells and whistles – purely for him alone.

Rob would be lost in Georgie's world, hopeless in the face of the uncertainty that was part and parcel of her work. He didn't have the self-reliance that would be necessary to sustain him through long periods when no attention was being given. He'd go crazy. How did she not go crazy? It was miraculous to him, suddenly, gazing at her as she slept. She was a miracle. And that someone so extraordinary should love someone like him . . . He felt an almost overwhelming urge to clasp her to him, to hold her close and tell her what he felt – tell her he would always love her, always take care of her. Nothing would ever harm her, if he could prevent it. But he didn't want to wake her, so instead, he gently stroked her, feeling the heat of her under his hand; willing her to feel, through his touch, his strength of feeling.

His caresses woke her anyway, easing her out of sleep. She turned to him, smiling, her face creased from the pillow.

'I love it when you do that,' she told him.

'I know. I know you do. Turn round. I'll keep going.'

~

They didn't come down all afternoon. The only glimpse Michael had had of her, since she'd left him by the pool, was a couple of hours into the afternoon. He saw Georgie, still in her bikini, stumble, giggling, to her balcony door, closing it firmly, drawing the curtains. It was such a shocking sight that it almost made him doubt the truth of their earlier conversation. How could she go so quickly from tears and upset to laughter? For one awful moment, he thought he'd got things wrong. That it was all for show, that she was just as bad as that boyfriend of hers – actually, she was more responsible, because she was the one who pretended to be decent, to be good. It made Michael angry – with her and with himself – that he should have been so taken in. But then he remembered how she'd tried to hide it, tried to hide her pain from him, and how delicately she had left him. It had been clear as day that she didn't want to go upstairs, that she wanted to see him later. It was Rob she was playing up to, he decided: Rob she had to placate and soothe. Rob was the one she was dishonest with. The relief of this recognition was immense. Michael felt his muscles unclench and relax again, even though the truth of the revelation posed some unsettling questions for Georgie's safety in the apartment with her partner.

Sitting on the balcony, Michael was lulled by the heat of the afternoon. He'd eaten the last of his bread and cheese and would have to go down to the supermarket later, to pick up some more supplies. But he was too hot to move, so he stayed watching as the families returned to the pool after lunch, the parents sleepy, the children as energetic as ever. The older couple hadn't left: they still sat side by side in the shade, reading, occasionally looking up to exchange a few words. Les was there, manning the bar. When he didn't have people to serve or clearing up to do, he spent his time on the telephone, talking at full pelt in

Greek. Michael couldn't work out from Les's tone any sense as to the nature of the conversations – for all he knew they could have been arguments, business transactions or illicit exchanges. He must have dozed off for a while because when he looked again, the pool was half in shadow and Les had closed the bar, taking that precious break of his before he had to open again that evening.

Georgie hadn't returned. Her balcony curtains were still closed, and the bedroom shutters firmly shut. Perhaps they had gone out, and Michael had missed them? She had said she would see him later. She must have thought he would stay down by the pool. But he hadn't wanted to – he hadn't wanted to sit there alone where he couldn't see anything, and where he himself would be on show. Suddenly panicked, Michael craned his neck to look. Georgie's towel was still on her sun lounger, as was Rob's, just as she'd left them. So was the guidebook, sitting there on the table, untouched. She can't have come back down after all. What the hell was keeping her so long?

A movement from the corner of his balcony caught his eye. A tiny lizard, no longer than his little finger, was writhing its way up the wall. Michael watched it, mesmerised. The fluidity of its movements, its perfect form – he'd never seen something so small and yet so intricate. He got up to look, scraping his chair clumsily. Almost instantly, the lizard froze, locked in place, feet splayed against the wall. How did they do it? he wondered – how did they manage to stick there and not fall off? Michael brought his face up close, studying the patterned back, the tiny scales; noticing the funny way the lizard's tongue darted in and out, following some internal rhythm of its own. He reached out to touch it, certain it would feel dry and scaly. The lizard didn't move. Perhaps it was frightened. Perhaps it could feel his breath on it and thought Michael was a predator.

'Don't worry, I'm not going to hurt you,' he whispered, and almost laughed at the silliness of it. As if the lizard could understand!

Its skin was surprisingly soft and pliant to the touch, not leathery at all. Michael took his finger away. Still the lizard didn't move. If he were careful, he could cover it with his whole hand and hold it for a while, see how it felt. Slowly, so as not to panic the creature, he did just that, cupping his hand a little so as not to crush it against the wall, gently edging his fingers down to knock the feet from their perch. He felt a flutter of movement: the creature wriggled wildly in his closed hand, lashing its tail, scrabbling for a foothold.

Michael suddenly panicked. What was he doing? Did lizards bite? Were they poisonous? The movements grew wilder and he became frightened. Something rose in him, matching the frantic struggle of the creature in his hand, urging him to clench his fist, press down, end the battle. But, as if sensing an impending doom, the thrashing suddenly ceased and, slowly, Michael's panic began to abate. Uncertain as to what he might find, he gently unclenched his hand. The lizard lay motionless, and for a moment Michael thought he'd killed it, had crushed or suffocated it. But feeling the air on its back, the reptile suddenly lurched into life and shot off his palm on to the edge of the balcony. Before Michael could react, the lizard had raced down the side of the wall into a little crevice and was gone.

A laugh from downstairs broke Michael's reverie. He leaned over to see if it was Georgie, but it wasn't – it was the mother of the two English kids, laughing at something her husband was telling her. Over the way, Georgie's shutters were still closed. Michael sighed, trying not to worry. She'd surely be down soon. He stepped inside to the cool of the kitchen and washed his hands carefully at the sink, removing every last trace of the lizard. He shook his head. If nothing else that afternoon, at least he'd had the opportunity to see a lizard up close! That's something he wouldn't have been able to do back home. He wondered what Patrick would say if he were there now. He'd probably laugh at him for being such a geek. Smiling, he took a beer from the fridge and went back out to the balcony.

~

It was dark by the time they dragged themselves out of the room, worn out, muscles aching as if they'd run a marathon. They were hungry, and dazed with the pleasures of the afternoon. They didn't stop for a drink at Les's bar, even though they could hear the radio going and some chatter and laughter from the poolside. Slowly, arms around one another for support, Georgie and Rob wound their way down the hill to the main drag, heading straight to the taverna of the previous evening, too tired to bother looking elsewhere. They drank more wine, enjoying the

way it increased their weariness, making them heavy-headed.
Only as they were leaving the restaurant did Georgie remember
that she had left their towels by the pool all day.

'I hope they'll still be there. They're the only ones we have.'

Back in the room again, both fell quickly into a deep sleep,
legs and arms entwined. Rob had told Georgie over dinner that,
in spite of his earlier determination to make sure everything was
okay with work, he was turning off his phone for the rest of the
holiday. He was going to break his routine and really take advantage. He'd given work plenty of forewarning about his holiday –
they could bloody well sort themselves out! If he woke early the
following morning, he would go back to sleep, would ignore the
body clock that was still set to the demands of his daily life.
Georgie had smiled at him, pleased. She wanted him to relax,
wanted him to be there with her, only with her. After all, wasn't
that the point of going away? And, for her part, she promised to
enjoy herself as well. She might not stay in bed all morning (she
was bad at lying in) but she would certainly indulge Rob any
time he liked in the afternoons! She pledged to bask in the sun,
improve her swimming and hang out. No sketching, no indulgence of any little pangs over her current project back home. It
was a deal.

Rob stuck to his pledge the next morning. He rolled round
in bed quite early to find Georgie gone, but, rather than following suit, he smiled to himself and settled in for more sleep.
Georgie, happy to be up, was by the pool, determined to make
headway with her novel. It had become a bit of a luxury for
her to read books intended for adults. When work was all-

consuming, she had time for little else, reading and re-reading the simple prose and fantasy journeys of the children's books she was illustrating. She never managed to get past the first page of anything more substantial when she tumbled into bed at night. So now she was going to take full advantage of the free time ahead.

When she got too hot for comfort, she plunged into the pool and diligently swam her laps, pushing herself to twenty. She felt a little burst of pride and satisfaction that she should be so disciplined, so virtuous while on holiday, even though she knew she was being ridiculous, and going against the spirit of everything she had promised the night before. She must not allow the nagging voice that bullied her over her physical appearance to become too dominant. Georgie already had a nagging voice that bullied her when it came to her work. One was enough. She had to fight against it – and she would, she resolved – she'd fight it properly as soon as they got back home.

She hadn't noticed Michael's presence, so engrossed was she in her book again, after her swim. It was only when he cleared his throat awkwardly that she looked up, surprised. He was carrying two coffees.

'Am I bothering you?' he asked. Georgie had been alone long enough that he was a welcome distraction and she smiled up at him, accepting the coffee gratefully.

'That's very sweet of you. You shouldn't have.'

Without waiting to be asked, he pulled up a chair and sat close to her, as he had done the previous morning. His face looked pale, his eyes slightly red-rimmed and, unfortunately, he had caught the sun on one side of his body: an arm and leg were burned red-raw.

'What happened?' she asked him. 'Did you fall asleep on your side?'

Michael nodded.

'Poor you. That's exactly how it happens to me – every time! D'you have some after-sun?'

Michael shook his head, confused. He'd never heard of it.

'I'll bring some down for you in a bit. It's good for sunburn – helps the skin to heal.'

Michael drained his coffee almost in one go. Georgie watched him, half-laughing. 'You needed that!'

'Didn't get much sleep.'

'Was it the burn?'

'Nah, that wasn't so bad. Just couldn't drop off.'

'Did you go out last night?'

'For a bit – just into town. It's crazy down there.'

'Yeah, I can imagine. They're always a bit full-on, these kinds of resorts. We've got lucky with our hotel, where we are – off the beaten track a bit, not right in the middle of it all. Even though it's a pain to get to the beach, I prefer that to being on the main drag. I think I'd go mad with all the noise, especially at night.'

Michael nodded, but he was clearly preoccupied with his own thoughts. Georgie watched him, curious as to what was troubling him.

'Everyone's drunk down there,' he eventually offered. 'They're all . . .' He broke off, unable to articulate his dismay.

'It must make it hard to talk to people,' she offered, sensing that his loneliness and inability to reach out might be at the heart of his distress.

'They only want one thing. That's all. They don't bother with you if they think you can't . . . you won't . . . .'

Women – it was women he was talking about, but in a different gear to their conversation of the day before. Georgie sighed to herself. This was potentially a thorny issue. Michael wasn't a particularly attractive man at first glance, and his way of dressing and carrying himself didn't display him to best advantage. He was someone who needed careful attention: he needed to warm to someone first before he was able to relax. When he smiled, his face lit up – there was something spontaneous within, but he seemed unable to access it easily. Georgie wasn't sure what to say, and she had a fear she could all too easily bruise him, overstep the mark without meaning to. She couldn't help feeling that a man like Michael would be hypersensitive to criticism.

But he surprised her. She had been going to offer a tentative thought, that perhaps he could go out earlier, even during the day, and meet people in more relaxed circumstances at the beach or in a café, before they got too drunk. But he had started to speak again, revealing himself to be less vulnerable than she had imagined.

'I know I'm no great catch. I know I'm not a looker. And I can't chat to people right off the bat. My mate Patrick, he's great at that – he's the one that always starts things. Me, I'm no good. I never know what to say. I don't know how to act. And, to be honest, most of them girls down there – they don't interest me

at all. They look at you like you're a piece of meat. They're . . .
horrible.'

This last was spoken with a hint of bitterness, but Georgie
had to acknowledge the truth of it. She disliked generalisations,
and was particularly sensitive to generalisations about women;
which was why her collusion in mocking the middle-aged lady
by the bar the previous morning had unsettled her briefly. Pangs
of long-instilled feminism stirred within her, and yet she knew
that what they were talking about was more to do with class than
sex. That made it even more complicated, required even more
delicacy. For Michael was firmly of a certain class. Georgie
couldn't bring herself to name it, even in thought – it sounded
so judgmental: working-class, proletariat. Michael belonged to
the class of blue-collar workers who lived for the weekend; those
whose greatest pleasure in life was a night out with the gang,
drinking themselves into oblivion, grabbing sensation quickly,
greedily: fast food, sugared drinks, shags. How unfortunate it was
that he should recognise the limitations of his social world, and
feel so at odds with them. Georgie hoped she might jolly him
out of it, without having to tackle the issue head on.

'It's never easy, getting to know people,' she said. 'Girls.
Especially when they're in groups. God knows, half the men I
went to college with were too scared to talk to us when we were
out on the town, but what they didn't realise was that we were
only sticking together because we were scared, too. I think most
people find it difficult, you know? It's not just you.'

Michael was watching her, a hopeful expression on his face.
Georgie wished she could tell him the trick of it: the way to walk

with confidence, not caring what others thought. Tell him that if he looked, if he looked hard, he'd find plenty of girls like him: quiet girls, who also recoiled from the brashness of their peers, who longed for something different. But she knew it was useless – knew she would be unable to articulate such things without an embarrassing and potentially patronising display of middle-class over-sensitivity that would confuse matters completely.

'I did all right with you though, didn't I?' he asked her. 'I mean – we're getting on all right.'

She smiled. 'Yes, but it's not quite the same, is it?'

Michael shrugged. He didn't see why not, and Georgie had a sudden sense that they might be getting into tricky territory. She wanted to change the subject.

'You know, Rob and I mightn't have met if he hadn't been brave enough to come up and talk to me.'

This wasn't entirely true, but it was a start. Michael glanced at her, frowning slightly. She pressed on, regardless.

'We were at a party. Friends of mine from college had just got engaged and Rob had sort of gate-crashed. He didn't know the hosts, but he was good friends with one of their brothers. We hadn't been introduced, but he came up to me towards the end of the evening and started chatting. It all went from there.'

Michael nodded. Georgie wondered if he were picturing it in his head, wondered what images he was seeing. She knew Rob hadn't made a very good impression on him so far.

'So – what, you just . . . fell in love?'

He was looking at her, his expression unreadable. She let out a short laugh. He really was a bit of a baby. His tone reminded her of the children's books she illustrated. *Martha and Billy fell deeply in love and lived happily ever after.*

'I suppose so. Not instantly – not me, anyway. It took a little while. But we started spending more and more time together and just . . . it just happened.'

'It just happened? But not like love at first sight or whatever?'

She shrugged, not sure where this was leading. 'Not quite. If that even exists anyway, though plenty of people say it's happened to them. It hasn't happened to me yet – I mean, not in that way. It didn't happen that way for me.'

She corrected herself quickly, regretting the 'yet'. Where had that come from? Michael was about to ask another question, but she wanted to pre-empt him, get him talking about himself.

'What about you?' she asked teasingly. 'Has it happened to you?'

He blushed a deep crimson, the colour flooding his pale cheeks. 'To me? Nah, I don't think so. Not like that.'

Georgie looked away, sensitive to his embarrassment. She shouldn't have been so careless, asking him outright. But she was finding it a bit of an effort to think of Michael as a fully grown adult, the way he was responding to the subject matter. She had to stop and remind herself that he wasn't a gawky teenage cousin, someone she could tease with impunity.

'How long you two together then?' he asked.

'Almost three years. No, wait – just *over* three years. Something like that. I lose track.'

'You live together?'

'Just over a year. We bought a flat.'

'Yeah?'

'We needed more space. Both of us had one-bedrooms before. I work from home, you see. I need space and peace and quiet.'

'And what – Rob goes out to work?'

'He's on-site at the plant, yes. Up early and out late. He's got a proper job!'

'You don't get lonely? Being on your own all day?'

The question was innocent enough, but, to Georgie's surprise, it touched a sudden nerve.

'Yeah, I do, actually. It's okay for the most part, but . . . Rob's hours are long. He's usually so knackered by the time he gets home, he just wants to go to bed – which is fine, 'course it is. Don't get me wrong – I mean, I love my work, and I need to be on my own to do it, but . . . yeah, it can get lonely. Lonely and boring and frustrating.'

She bit her lip a little, concentrating on the articulation of her feelings. 'The worst part is when I'm between jobs, when I've nothing in particular to do. That's hard. I feel like I should be inventing something new, something of my own, but often I can't be bothered. So I just . . . drift about, worrying about where the next gig's going to come from. All my friends work regular nine-to-fives, so there's no one around during the day. And in the evenings, usually I just wait for Rob to come home. I mean, I do go out, occasionally, but maybe not enough. You know, I sometimes think . . . well, not really, but sometimes I wonder if I might be better off doing something more . . . normal.'

'You don't like what you do?'

'Yes, I do. It just gets a little . . . wearying sometimes.'

'I bet you're good at it.'

'You haven't seen any of my work! I could tell you anything and you'd believe me.'

'But you must be good to make a living like that – earning money from drawing pictures. It's amazing.'

Michael was so earnest that Georgie was touched and pleased; glad of the impressive reflection he was holding up to her, even though he knew nothing about it. It *was* pretty amazing, now that she thought about it. That she had managed to build her life around sketches on paper. She shrugged modestly.

'I'm a hard worker. People say I've got a good eye, but I'm no genius. You're not looking at the new Picasso or anything.'

Michael frowned, missing the reference. She sat up, not wanting to make him uncomfortable. 'What about you? Do you like drawing?'

'I've always wanted to do something with my hands. Something creative like.'

'Why don't you?' Her confidence had been restored by his evident admiration. She wanted to bestow some on him.

'I was always rubbish at art.'

'What about something more practical – woodwork or carpentry?'

'Not good at any of those. I used to think I might be handy at a bit of engineering – machines and stuff. I was going to do an apprenticeship when I was younger. I was always messing about with bits and pieces as a kid, taking things apart, putting them back together.'

'You're very young – you could still go for it. Plenty of cours-es available, and we're crying out for skilled technicians, aren't we? It can be a very well-paid career.'

He shook his head. 'It's all the studying, like. There's exams to pass and stuff. I didn't realise. But if I want a qualification, I have to do exams, write essays and stuff. I was crap at all that at school. I'd still be crap now.'

She was about to interject with a mild yet encouraging, 'I'm sure that's not true,' but he hadn't finished.

'There was this whole module on health and safety – you couldn't pass the course unless you did it and I couldn't make head or tail of it. Neither could the instructor, if you ask me.'

Michael shot Georgie a grin and she returned it, sympatheti-cally. He sighed, straightening up.

'Nah, it's not for me, all that. I don't like it – writing about everything you're doing instead of doing it. Can't hack it.' He wasn't plaintive, just straightforward.

Georgie felt a pang of pity for him, but she didn't press the point. She recognised that she was out of her depth, fearing once again that she might inadvertently offend him with well-meaning suggestions that were utterly beyond his reach. It made her angry suddenly; angry that quiet, shy young men like Michael should be so excluded from even the most basic of occupations, thanks to red-tape bureaucracy and short-sighted government edicts that punished those unsuited to mainstream education. What happened to people like him? They failed in the exam-ridden school system, then came out blinking cautiously into the sunshine, only to be thrust back in to yet another system of exams and reports that they couldn't fathom, thus ruining any enthusiasm they might have for a trade requiring manual dexterity and practical learning. It was completely wasteful – not to mention cruel. So here was Michael, and probably thousands like him, stuck in a dead-end job that would never take him anywhere, while his talents were left to rot.

Yet even as her self-righteousness swelled, Georgie recognised the flaws in her argument. Everyone needed a bit of basic literacy; and a mandatory course in health and safety wasn't such a bad idea. No point hiring an engineer who would blow up your car as soon as look at you. She pushed away such thoughts, determined only to nurture Michael's fledgling ambitions, to be the one to offer that little bit of moral support he'd clearly been lacking. There was no harm in it, and, after all, it was as easy to be dismissive as to be kind, so why not be kind? She smiled, hearing her mother's voice ringing in her ears with that early childhood mantra.

Georgie was about to speak, about to say something light and neutral to move things forward, find safe ground again, when Michael got up suddenly.

'I've disturbed you long enough,' he said. 'You're very good to listen to me rattle on.'

She stayed his arm, surprised at his sudden desire to leave. 'You don't have to go. It's nice talking to you.'

She wondered if perhaps she had offended him, if she'd missed some subtle cue that had upset him. But he smiled at her, his face lighting up in that boyish way she'd noticed.

'Thanks, Georgie. It's really nice talking to you too. But I'm going to go up now. Might see if I can get some kip.'

She nodded and let him go, watching as he loped around the poolside, his head lowered, the stance of someone apprehensive, hoping to avoid confrontation or trouble. Poor guy, she thought. It was an insight, talking to him. All that confusion and yearning underneath the surface – you'd never think it to look at him. You'd just write him off as an oaf.

She settled back down on her sun lounger, and was about to pick up her book again when two hands covered her eyes from behind, making her jump.

'All right, gorgeous?' Rob had roughed up his accent for amusement. 'What's cooking?'

~

The days passed. Everyone in the hotel complex had settled into their own private routine. Holidays demanded as much structure as everyday life, even though the circumstances were so much more enjoyable. The elderly couple, for example, could be relied upon to be first up and out by the pool, spending the day in the shade, reading, taking their lunch of sandwiches and chips from Les, nodding off for a while in the late afternoon. They were usually the last to leave the poolside, when long shadows covered most of the courtyard and the English kids had finally been dragged upstairs. The couple would have one drink at around seven-thirty at the bar, then go out to dinner. They'd be back without fail by ten o'clock, lights out in their room by eleven.

Everyone followed a routine and it was comfortable, reassuring. Nothing got in the way of it for any of the guests, unless by their own design: heading out for the day to sightsee, going on one of those tourist excursions that were advertised so prominently in the downstairs lobby. But even when they had spent the day doing something different, their evening routines would be more or less the same. People's little ways were respected, were known or sensed now by the others, who would nod greetings, exchange the odd 'hello', trying not to interfere with the structure of anyone else's day. Everyone was tolerant, easy-going – as long as they weren't disturbed.

Michael, too, had developed a routine, and it suited him. It had taken three days for things to settle in to place – not a long time, in the greater scheme of things – but on holiday, where every day was precious, it had seemed like a lifetime. Mornings were the best. Those were his times, their times, because in the mornings, from about nine to eleven, Georgie was alone by the pool.

Rob had stayed true to his word and slept in late. Georgie, too restless to ignore the early morning sun, would be up and about. She napped in the afternoons, either by the pool or in the apartment. Michael slept then as well – soundly, heavily – right through until evening, because he was up all night. He had flipped his routine right round: it was as if he was on night shift at work, starting his day when everyone else was ending theirs, going to bed when the rest of the world had just got up.

Mornings were his joy: the sole and primary reason for his changed routine. He would stroll down casually at around nine-thirty, buying coffees for him and Georgie. They would have a good hour, and sometimes more, before Rob appeared. An hour in which Michael experienced the sheer happiness of simply being with her. He was amazed at how effortlessly things had all fallen into place, how easily they had slipped into a friendship, a routine. Georgie accepted their morning chats without hesitation or resistance – indeed, she welcomed him, beaming as he approached each morning, carrying their coffees. It seemed the most natural thing in the world, and Michael was delighted. He was a part of her daily life now, and she a part of his. It was perfect.

And in that precious hour or so each morning? Revelation. Michael had never dreamed that conversation was possible with a woman. Nothing in his experience had prepared him for the pleasures of talking with a woman like Georgie. The girls he had chased (or rather, the girls he'd had to distract while Patrick was chasing their friends) had been hard, almost impossible, to talk to. When they realised (pretty quickly, for the most part) what was going on – that their more attractive friend was being chatted up by the more attractive Patrick – a sort of defeated sneer would play across their lips and they would look Michael up and down, dismissing him with a contemptuous glance, before they had even bothered to get to know him, though both were rejects, as it were, in the hierarchy of the mating game, the women wouldn't lower their dignity to concede to a mere chat. They felt affronted – not by Michael, but by Patrick and their prettier, sexier friend – and they were damned if they were going to make the best of it. It was one of the ironies of less-attractive girls: far from being easier to get, they surrounded themselves with a wall of superiority and bitchiness.

Michael had spent long evenings tongue-tied, sitting next to someone from whom only hostility and bitterness emanated. On one occasion, when he'd had way too much to drink and was fed up with it all – fed up with Patrick wearing the face off some particularly tarty number – he'd earned himself a slap, having turned to his reluctant companion to tell her that she may as well put out since even dogs have their day. Michael had been rather proud of that line. He didn't know where it had come from; it had just popped into his head, like a nursery rhyme long forgotten. And even though the slap had stung (the girl was wearing heavy, ridiculous rings and had caught his skin with one of them), he hadn't cared. The stupid bitch deserved it anyway.

Georgie wasn't like any of them. It was as if she was from another world: a world where people looked at one another differently, took time to find out about each other, were gentle and polite with their remarks. There was almost an art to it, if you paid attention: the way she spoke, the way she conducted herself in conversation. Delicate, kind. And if some of the things she chose to talk about were a bit barmy, well, what did it matter?

She had been playful the previous morning. There had been something restless and energetic in her manner. She had finished reading her first novel – 'Wasn't great. Disappointing ending, not very emotionally satisfying' – and was preparing to start another one, a huge book that she was excited about.

'It's all set on a Greek island. Very famous – I've been meaning to read it for ages. I've read a couple of his others and really enjoyed them.'

Michael had glanced at the paperback: it was as big as a doorstep.

'You think you'll get through all that?'

She'd laughed. 'Oh yes – and then some! That's pretty much all I plan to do this holiday – read.'

There was a twinkle in her eye that Michael had picked up on, though he couldn't be sure what it was about.

'Well,' he'd said, rising slowly, pretending to be weary and preoccupied. 'I'd better not keep you from such important business.'

She'd giggled, pulling his arm so that he'd sit down again. 'You're important business too, you know. Plenty of time for me to start this later. All the time in the world, the way Rob sleeps.'

There was something almost cheeky in her tone, which made Michael blush a little. 'You'll be a right brain-box by the end of your holidays then' was all he'd managed.

She had been quiet for a minute, gazing at the enormous novel on her lap. Michael wasn't frightened by those moments any more – not the way he had been at first, when he thought he might have said something wrong, something to offend. But still, those little lulls in which she seemed to drift away, out of reach, made him a bit sad: sad that he'd lost her, even temporarily; sad that he didn't know what she was thinking, where she'd gone. He had managed to jolly her out of it that time, making a joke that the size of her book must have cost her in excess baggage.

'Oh, I had to sacrifice three pairs of shoes to bring this one along.'

'Three! I only bought one pair with me.'

'Yes, you men seem to get by with just the one. I think Rob only brought two pairs, which for him represents huge choice. But it's different for women. Shoes are important.'

'Only so you don't hurt your feet when you're out walking.'

'Oh, Michael, you're missing the point! Most women's shoes *do* hurt our feet but it doesn't matter if they're extremely pretty. Especially if they make our legs look longer. Beauty comes at a cost, you know.'

She had been smiling, teasing him probably, but he couldn't be sure. He hadn't known what to say to that, hadn't felt comfortable talking about her legs – even thinking about them – but luckily she'd changed the subject, asking him if he'd managed to find a pair of sandals yet, since he'd mentioned he was on the lookout. From there, they had moved on to the pleasures of shopping in a foreign country: how Georgie loved nothing more than spending time browsing in foreign supermarkets, looking at all the different foods she might take home with her, though she'd learned to buy carefully. One year, in Sardinia, she had packed a bottle of olive oil in Rob's suitcase (hers had been full of other goodies) and it had cracked, ruining most of his clothes. Not a great welcome home present. But, still, she wasn't going to be put off. She had already been eyeing a couple of things in the supermarket down the road that she'd like to take home with her: stuffed vine leaves and some really delicious-looking biscuits.

She'd laughed. 'You must think I'm a real saddo, getting so excited about biscuits. Ah, it's the simple things, Michael.' But after all, she said, as if defending herself from an unspoken attack, hadn't they first met in a supermarket? If she wasn't such a foodie, as she put it, they might never have met properly at all, and wouldn't that be a shame? 'You see? Some vices have their upsides, though people are reluctant to admit to it.'

It was as if Michael had unlocked something in her. He didn't know how he had done it, but it must have been because he was so careful, so polite, making sure he listened properly, not interrupting, even if he didn't understand what she was on about sometimes. It seemed that all Georgie wanted was for him to sit and listen, and occasionally offer a quiet suggestion, a thought, an observation on what she'd been saying. Make her laugh if he could. It came easy after the first couple of times. Now he didn't even have to try. He knew exactly what to do.

And she talked a lot, with only the most minor promptings on Michael's part. Once the preliminaries had been dispensed with – the 'how are you this morning?' and the 'sleep well?' – Michael let her set the pace and tone, just let her talk. Sometimes she wanted to joke around a bit, like the previous morning, almost as if she were buying herself time, gearing up to more important matters. But it didn't take much to lift the lid on the tumult of contradictions and emotions that appeared to dominate her. She seemed to be a bubbling well of thoughts and feelings, crowded under the surface, just waiting to be released. And now, with Michael, she'd found someone she trusted enough to talk about them with.

He had been a bit surprised at first by some of the things Georgie had said. He'd never heard anyone speak at such length about things that seemed to him perfectly obvious. Things like how one *had* to work, how strange it was that one should have to earn a living *doing* something, and how one became defined in so many ways by what one did.

'It's always like that, isn't it? One of the first questions people ask is "so what do you do, then?" as if it's the most important thing about you.'

Michael nodded, even though it seemed a funny way of looking at it. What was the harm in asking what someone did for a living? But she hadn't finished.

'I mean – it's not as if *what* you do is all that you are, is it? It's not as if it's all that matters. God, people get so full of themselves about their work, so full of pretension. My profession's the worst for it: people wafting about, calling themselves artists, as though it makes them somehow superior. Real artists, people with talent, don't bother telling everyone about it; they just get on with it. They're independent, original – they don't try and *prove* how original they are all the time just by giving themselves a label!'

If Michael were honest, there were times when he did zone out, unable to follow the intricate logic of her thoughts, but he had become more used to it – like those little lulls of her, when something shifted imperceptibly underneath; when her mood might switch suddenly from quiet to energetic, from positive to negative. All he had to do was listen: listen and watch, intently, try to find a pattern to her conversation, try to understand what she was really saying. Try to really hear her. Yet the more Michael heard, the sorrier – and angrier – he felt.

Take her relationship, for example. Georgie told him all about herself and Rob, their life together: their work, their routine back home, how they liked different things, even down to the sorts of books they read. How sociable Rob was, while she preferred quiet nights in. How he worked so hard, even though she knew he didn't love his work, hadn't yet discovered what it was he wanted to do with his career.

'I think a part of him hasn't really decided the person he wants to be, you know? Mr Career Man, running all over the place, busy and important, or Mr Regular, with a life, hanging out with friends, having more of a balance. And I can't tell him what to do – I wouldn't dream of it. I know how hard those choices are to make. He's got to do it himself.'

'Yeah.'

'The last thing I'd want is to box him into a corner, and then have him resent me for it for years. That wouldn't be fair to either of us. Oh, God, Michael – no offence, but you men stay boys for the longest time.'

Rob was apparently reluctant to talk seriously about some of the bigger things that were looming on the horizon for them, given their age: marriage, children. Rob wasn't sure he wanted children (or, at least, certainly not yet): an awful thing to say to a woman, though Georgie said she knew it came out of his own fears and a certain immaturity – a refusal to face up to where he was in life.

'It's all right for him – he can have kids at any time, doesn't have to think about it. Obviously, it's not the same for me.'

She wanted children, she said, she was pretty sure of it, but she didn't want to have them with someone who was uncertain or reluctant. Not that she was planning to have them immediately, but she had to think about those things, didn't she? Didn't everyone?

Then there was the more private stuff about her. Her work, her ambitions. How she loved what she did but how she'd always dreamed, as a kid, of being a truly great artist (once she'd given up her ballerina obsession which had taken her through to puberty). How stifled she felt by the niche work she'd found herself in, though she didn't want to dismiss it out of hand: it paid the bills, had given her a good reputation – she couldn't knock it – most people weren't so lucky in her profession. But she had a nagging sense that she was selling out in some way; turning her back on something important to her, not taking a risk she knew she ought to take, lacking the courage.

'It's a funny thing. When I was starting out, anything – any gig that paid money – seemed worth it. But now I realise they're just distractions, in their own way, stopping me from being brave and looking at what I really want to say as an artist, how I want to spend my time. Does that make any sense? Otherwise, I'm just a hack-for-hire. That's not what I want, I don't think. Although I'd be hard-pushed to tell you what grand projects I'm brewing over. Honestly – I want it both ways, don't I? Not content with what I've got but no idea what I want to replace it with.'

Strangely, Georgie smiled a lot as she talked – she laughed, too. Michael found it a bit odd at first, that she should pretend to be so happy in the face of the painful things she was talking about. Was he missing something? Then he realised: she was doing it for his benefit. She didn't want to upset him. It was so like Georgie to be so thoughtful, so concerned for his feelings! It made Michael want to smile and cry at the same time, which must have been how she felt. He wished he had the courage to tell her that she didn't have to pretend, didn't have to hide anything from him. If there was anyone she didn't have to hide from, it was him.

'It's the big irony in my line of work. You have to be out in the world to get all your ideas, but then you need to be alone – fully alone, shut away – to do it. It's hard to get the balance. There've been weeks on end where I haven't left the flat. I end up looking like I've crawled out from under a rock. I often think if I could live somewhere like Greece – in a hot country – I'd get a better balance, you know? I think I'd almost be forced to – the rhythm of life here is so much more relaxed. I'd get outdoors more, out into nature. Just the simple things: being in the sun for a bit each day, having a swim. I'd still work, but I could enjoy all this as well.' Georgie swept out her arm, taking in their surroundings. 'I don't need much more, you know. I'm easily pleased!'

'Sounds to me like you could do with a bit more of that, then. A bit more fun.'

'You're right.' She smiled, turning the beam of her eyes upon him like a set of headlights. 'I shall try and persuade

Rob. Pack up and ship out – part and parcel.'

She glanced up at her balcony, as if expecting to see Rob there, ready to acquiesce to her plans. But it was empty. Michael watched as she gave her head a little shake.

'You know, if there's anything I regret, it's that I didn't let my hair down more when I was your age.'

Michael looked away. He didn't like it when she pointed out the discrepancy in their ages. It made him feel distant from her and a little foolish.

'I wish I'd just . . . I don't know . . . *gone* for it more, you know? Got out into the world, travelled. I always wanted to go to more places, see more things. I had a girlfriend who was going off for a year to trek the world after we finished college. She asked me to go with her and I could have – I had enough money, I wasn't working at anything serious.'

'What stopped you then?'

Georgie pulled a face. 'A man, of course. I was desperately in love with my boyfriend at the time – a complete disaster, as it turned out, but . . . he had a steady job, we were living together. It all seemed so . . . settled. I wasn't prepared to risk it. I was a fool.'

'You're not a fool.'

'I was then. Believe me, I was then. And I sometimes wonder . . . .'

She'd stopped short then, her eyes distant and vague. Michael had been about to speak, about to try to bring her back to him, but she gave a little laugh before he could begin.

'Don't mind me. I'm being terribly sentimental this

morning. You shouldn't indulge me you know, you really shouldn't. God, d'you ever catch yourself just wittering on, sounding like the biggest . . . ? Anyway, I'm going to shut up now. It's too lovely a morning to spoil. And I've got absolutely *nothing* to complain about!'

She did ask Michael questions sometimes, bits and bobs about himself. But he didn't really like it when the conversation steered over to him. Georgie had a way of looking at him when she asked him something, as though she were expecting the most interesting reply in the world. Michael would get a bit tongue-tied, trying to think of what to say and how to say it in his head first, which meant he spent too long in silence, halting the flow of conversation. It was hard to suddenly switch back into his head, after paying such close attention to what she was saying. And half the time he hadn't thought about the kinds of things she was asking him. Or they were things he didn't like talking about.

But luckily, as the days went on, her questions were less to do with him directly than with her. What did he, Michael, think about what Georgie had just said? Did he agree with her feelings on such and such? Had he ever had a similar experience? He had become good at answering these sorts of questions, giving his opinion when he had one, offering, sometimes, a slightly different perspective. It didn't take all that much to keep her interested. He just had to parrot back a bit of what she'd said and turn it around a little.

As, for instance, when she had asked him if he thought about what he was going to do in life, if he'd thought about what he'd like to do if engineering wasn't an option for him. Michael had pretended to think about it for a bit, then told her that he was happy enough doing what he did, and that he didn't think his job was all there was to him. His job just paid the bills, and if he enjoyed it, all the better. What he became in life would have less to do with his work than it would with who he was. He was proud of that answer, remembering an earlier conversation where she had mentioned her despair at being thought of only in terms of her career. And he was prouder still when she nodded thoughtfully, and told him that she thought he was right.

'We shouldn't define ourselves by what we do. It makes a mockery of everything life's about.'

He didn't see what she was getting at exactly, but his answer had seemed to cheer her and he could have laughed with happiness.

'And your friends – your friends back home – what do they want out of life?' She was looking at him eagerly.

'How do you mean?'

'I don't know – do they want careers, houses, marriage, kids? Are they happy where they are?'

'My mate Patrick – you know, the one whose mum . . . . He wants to set up his own business. He probably will, as well. He's smart, Patrick. Much smarter than me.'

But Georgie wasn't really listening, Michael could tell, even though she nodded politely. She smiled, but it wasn't a warm smile. It looked more like a grimace.

'My friends . . . I think a lot of them are quite frightened of life. Oh, you wouldn't know it to look at them, but underneath

I think they're very unsure of themselves. I think they *want* to care about important things but they don't know how to do it properly. Like, you know, everybody has a girlfriend who's amazing in her life – got a great job, great career, but is just *hopeless* with men. Can't ever attract a decent guy, doesn't know what to say or do, ends up totally lost. But my friends, they're *all* like that! The men and women alike. They either find some *completely* dysfunctional partner and just stick it out, even though they're unhappy, because they're so relieved to have met someone, or . . . .'

Michael gently prompted her. 'Or what?'

Her eyes had got that distant look again. 'Or . . . they find someone they really like, really connect with, and then screw it up by following all sorts of stupid rules about how they think relationships should work. It's amazing to see. The lack of honesty. The fear. The game-playing. And it's not just to do with relationships. It's everything – their work, their sense of themselves, how they think about other people. It's as if they don't quite know how to live properly. Or that the rules they're following don't work. Like they're caught up in some vision of life, some image of themselves or the way things should be that doesn't really exist. But the image is the most important thing and has to be maintained at all costs. It's strange, isn't it?'

'Yeah.'

She'd gone quiet for a moment. Michael's mind was working furiously, trying to untangle everything he had just heard. Fear. Honesty. Unhappiness.

'I suppose we're a bit of a lost generation,' she went on. 'We're not political, but we have *issues*, causes. We're all liberals, whatever that means. But we're cynical, too. We don't *really* believe in much – nothing that has to trouble us, or make us do anything, in the day to day. Like, we consume like crazy, but we reassure ourselves that we're *ethical* consumers, because we pay more for certain labels and religiously recycle. We claim to hold culture in high esteem, yet we tolerate all sorts of rubbish on the telly, in our books and movies, and we don't really care about the effect it's having. We believe in freedom, in tolerance, in equality, but anyone who expresses an opinion that isn't widely accepted is condemned as a fascist. Sometimes I wonder if all we really care about is the *appearance* of goodness, and can't be bothered with the thing itself.'

Georgie was smiling, shaking her head, as if trying to unblock her thoughts. She didn't look at Michael.

'It all comes from our education, I think. Our upbringing. There's so much pressure, isn't there? To get everything sorted so fast. I mean – God help you if you're thirty and you still haven't found what you want to do with your life. Or, worse, you know what you want to do but you don't know how to go about doing it. You're screwed. And everyone runs around pretending everything's great, when most of them hate their jobs or can't hold down a relationship. There's no room to breathe. No wonder everyone's frightened. Dysfunctional. You go from school to university to a job and then – what? It's what we've been taught, this inbuilt anxiety that my generation all carry around with us. We buy into so much crap! Because, on the one hand, we were told that we could be anything, do anything, yet on the other, our parents, our teachers, were worried for us. Everything had to be an investment – "security" – it was all about the future. We were all supposed to be incredible high-flyers in remarkably satisfying and impressive careers. Status mattered, being recognised. Doing the right things to get you to the right places. Nothing mattered just for itself alone. Anything that was really valuable was just . . . dismissed.'

She picked at her coffee cup, breaking its plastic rim. Michael frowned a little. He wasn't entirely sure what she was getting at. Worries for the future in his household had come and gone on a week-by-week basis. Enough money for fags and booze. Teachers worried only if you were making trouble in class. That was about it. He glanced at Georgie, straining to make sense of what she was saying. It was hard to know just what she was making a big deal about. It was like having to decipher a code that changed every time. She was talking about the future, so she must be *worried* about the future – that was it. Worried that all her plans would come to nothing. Worried that she would never have security or success. Worried that she'd be stuck for ever with *him*, with Rob: stuck with his bullying, superior ways.

'I had this friend, Lydia – incredibly smart, incredibly beautiful. She did law at uni – she qualified and everything, started practising, was doing very well. Only thing was, she hated it – she'd always hated it. She only read law in the first place because she couldn't be bothered arguing with her parents. Lots of my friends were like that. But what Lydia *really* wanted to be was a writer. That was what mattered to her most, she told me. When we'd be at parties or something, she'd tell people she was a writer, moonlighting as a lawyer to pay the bills! It was a bit stupid, but I didn't think much of it at the time. In fact, I think I admired her for not buying in to any box-ticking definitions of yourself, and all that. Anyway, Lydia was working the corporate life, trying to write on the side, and just becoming more and more miserable. And one day, out of the blue, she quit. Just upped and left, no word of warning. Sold her flat, her car, all her designer clothes and moved to this arty village on the coast. It was amazing. I went down to stay with her a few times, and it was . . . I was a bit in awe actually. She'd made such a break with everything she'd had – everything so many people would have killed for: money, career, status. And now she was living in this cottage, simple and perfect, staying up all night to work, sleeping all morning, hanging out with other artists in the afternoons. It sounded wonderful. I was a bit jealous, to tell you the truth. She seemed like a proper bohemian, a free spirit. I used to feel really boring and pathetic. Lydia had all sorts of plans: she was going to write a novel, a play, short stories. She was bursting with ideas; almost manic, in a way. I didn't realise, at the time, but later, the more things went on, I began to understand. Lydia was more in love with her new lifestyle, her new image of herself as a writer, than she was in actually doing the work. It took me ages to work it out. She talked so well about everything! Talked everything up so . . . *fluently*. I kept expecting to get a phone call telling me she was about to be published, or a play was being staged. Nothing. It turned out, she couldn't hack it. Not the reality of it – being on her own so much, working in solitude, not getting any immediate praise or attention. And, more than that, when it came down to it, I think she probably discovered that she didn't actually have anything she wanted to say. Not really.'

Georgie leaned forward a little, stretching out her arms in front of her legs, as though she were warming up for a race. Michael could see small beads of sweat on the top of her chest.

'She's working as a journalist now, a critic, of all things! She's quite well known. Speaks on the radio a lot.'

'Wow.'

Georgie sighed. 'Yeah. The thing that bothers me about Lydia is I feel I got her so wrong. I misjudged her. I couldn't see through any of the self-presentation – I bought into it completely. And I don't know why, but it makes me wonder about myself a bit – if I'm not as much of a fraud as she is. After all, I've made this great show of following what I love and all that, but I've made it my business to get a reputation as a really solid illustrator who can turn her hand to any old thing. Plus, I've got the security of Rob and his regular pay cheque if things happen to get tight. I get all the benefits of the label "artist" without any of the risk. And you know what? I'm still dissatisfied. I still don't know what I want out of any of it. I still can't work out whether or not I'm just playing some sort of game with myself, pretending my ambitions are bigger than they really are. I think, in my own way, I've stayed as safe as Lydia has. I didn't realise that until now.'

Michael nodded, even though she wasn't looking at him. He wished he could see her face properly. He couldn't work out what she needed him to say. She smiled suddenly, crunching up her plastic cup in her hand.

'No one ever tells you, do they? They never tell you that everything matters. Every choice, everything we do, counts. Changes us. And there's no time. It all happens now! You know, I think that's the worst bit about getting older. You realise you have to stop living in your head so much and start getting real.'

She was flushed, bright-eyed. Michael wanted to laugh at her expression, but knew it wasn't the right thing to do. Still – to get so het up over what your friends were doing! It's not like any of it made any difference to her. Except that . . . . Maybe she wasn't really talking about her friends. In fact, the more Michael thought about it, the more obvious it became. She was talking about herself. Wondering what would become of her; wondering about her choices.

No one had ever explained to Michael before the way to think about life, about the future. No one had ever told him that there was more to it than just plodding along, day in, day out, never lifting your head above the parapet, never thinking beyond the weekend; or, as it had been in his parents' case, never thinking beyond the next drink. Never thinking about yourself, not properly – not beyond whether you were hungry or bored or tired. Not thinking about what you wanted for yourself, for your life. Oh, he had learned pretty quickly how to duck and weave, keep out of sight, not attract attention, but somewhere along the way that had translated into something bigger: not making any plans, not thinking too far ahead, keeping the world in check by limiting it, or his place in it.

But, Michael was beginning to understand, you had to have

some goals in mind, or what was the point? Take this holiday, even: it had needed Patrick to show him how important it was to plan things, to have something to look forward to. And what an amazing experience it was turning out to be, even if at first it had been terrifying. As the weeks had drawn closer to departure, Michael had started to think of himself differently; had begun to think of himself as a man with a friend, going on a holiday like anyone else. It had made him feel good, in spite of his nerves. Might doing other things, making other plans – bigger ones, more important ones – have the same effect? Was there a way to feel differently about yourself, simply by *doing*?

Listening to Georgie made Michael realise that things could go even further. You could think about your life in terms of years, decades even. You could project an image of yourself, where you'd like to be – *who* you'd like to be – and it was something to aim for, something important. You could make plans and do things based on what you wanted in the future.

'I'm sorry, Michael. I've been going on and on. You must be bored stiff.'

'No. I like listening to you.'

'I don't know how you can make head or tail of it, because I really can't. God, honestly – sometimes I catch myself in the middle of a sentence or something and I think, "is that really me? Is that what I sound like?" It's awful, the sound of my own voice! Bores me to death. Rob laughs at me when I'm off on one of my rants – "having a little meltdown, are we?" he says. Doesn't take me seriously at all, and he's quite right.'

Rob. Of course. Everything changed when Rob arrived each

morning. Georgie would change. Rob would become the sudden centre of her world. She'd get up to greet him, fuss over him, make sure he was settled on his sun lounger, offer to buy him a coffee. It was as if she had to make sure she wasn't going to upset him. It sickened Michael; sickened him to see the hold Rob had on her, the way she bowed down to him, made him feel like a king. Michael's mother had been the same way: fussing around his father like he was a baby, and fine thanks she'd had for *that*. It unnerved him to see Georgie, so different in every possible way from his mother, follow suit. It lessened her, not much, but a little: it made her seem more ordinary, somehow, even a bit pathetic. It should have been the other way around. Rob should be fussing over *her*, worshipping the ground she walked on. Instead, he flicked his eyes at her, grunted at her questions, taking her care for granted. Didn't he see what it cost her? Probably he did, and he didn't care. Sometimes it was all Michael could do not to cry out, challenge Rob, tell him like it was. But he didn't say anything. Instead, he was as pleasant as he could be when Rob came down, asking him how he was, if he'd slept well. Once or twice, Rob was reasonably friendly back, engaging him in a bit of chat, even offering him another coffee. But he never protested when Michael got up to go, never asked him to stay a bit longer. Michael guessed that Georgie had probably asked him to be nice, and he could imagine Rob laughing at her. Well, let him. One day he'd laugh on the other side of his face.

So Michael would make his excuses, and Georgie would flash him a smile full of warmth, of hope – a shared smile laden with meaning – a little validation of their time together. She would always tell him that she'd see him later, even though Michael would have no contact with her for the rest of the day. But it seemed to be important to her, seemed to reassure her, and he would always tell her that yeah, he would, he'd see her, would catch her later. Rob would grunt a goodbye and Michael would go back up to his apartment where he'd fix himself a snack, eating it from his hidden spot on the balcony, watching as Rob and Georgie sat together, sometimes talking, sometimes quiet. She would get on with her reading, for the most part, shutting him out. Michael could see the logic in her having brought such a big book with her: anything to keep Rob off. As noon approached and the sun became too powerful, Michael would retreat inside, closing all the shutters and crawling into bed, sinking into a deep and heavy sleep.

He would wake about six, or just after. He was surprised at how little sleep he seemed to need. Back home, if he didn't get his eight hours he was a useless lump at work, forgetful, scatty, heavy-headed. Here, six hours did him fine – more than fine: he awoke alert, alive. Michael had never had such energy before. He would shower and dress for the evening: a clean shirt or T-shirt and his jeans. And when the time was right, just after seven, he'd take a beer from the fridge, the first of the day, and settle, out of sight, on his balcony.

He would watch the elderly couple have a drink at the bar, the old fellow nattering to Les as he waited to be served. Then the young family would arrive back from dinner – they always ate early. The comings and goings of the people in the complex were as regular as clockwork. And at eight o'clock, give or take, Georgie and Rob would come down to the pool, sometimes stopping for a drink, but more often than not heading straight out into the night. When they had gone, Michael could relax a little bit, for he knew he had a two- or three-hour wait ahead of him. He'd wander back into the kitchen for another beer and make himself a snack; stand on the balcony a bit, unafraid, not worrying about prying eyes. A couple of times, he had even gone downstairs to have a drink at the bar, chatting to Les, less worried now about his intrusions, better able to handle him. But he wouldn't linger too long. He didn't want to be distracted, just in case he missed her.

By ten o'clock he would be back in position, sitting on his chair, the lights in his apartment off so as not to attract attention. Rob and Georgie had never come back later than eleven, and mostly they were earlier. Michael would hear them before he saw them most nights: her low laugh, Rob's louder, more strident tones. Invariably, Rob would have his arm round her, holding Georgie close whether she liked it or not. They'd go straight up to their apartment and Michael could sometimes see them in there, when they'd forgotten to close the curtains or the shutters, though Rob would always remember to do so before they finally went to bed.

Michael loved seeing into Georgie's apartment. Catching glimpses of her pottering about, even if *he* was around. On two occasions, she'd turned on her balcony light and had sat out there, on her own, reading. Michael had had to stand back in the shadows of his room in order to watch her. Georgie looked

different at night. Michael loved the way her face appeared
clearer, somehow, more of a piece, not broken up by sunglasses
or shaded by a hat, the way it was in the daytime. He loved to
see her hair hanging loose, carefully brushed, gleaming when it
caught the light. She wore it scraped back during the day, pulled
tight off her face. But more than anything, Michael loved the
way she dressed; the way she made simple, basic items like skirts
and T-shirts look so special, so unusual, as if the clothes had
been made for her alone. It was the way she moved in them, he
reckoned, the easy grace she had that wasn't for show, wasn't for
display. You had to pay attention to notice it. There weren't
many people who'd know how to value a woman like Georgie.

Michael would watch until their lights went out, never later
than one o'clock. And then, abruptly, he'd get up, close his balcony door and head out into the night. He had no interest in
staring at a black apartment. He didn't want to think about what
might be going on in there. Michael could well imagine what
sort of demands *he* would make upon her. Once he was certain
Georgie was back, was safe, and would be there the following
morning, the rest of his night's entertainment could begin.

~

Rob was feeling like a new man, a fact he happily proclaimed
often to Georgie throughout the days. The long sleeps, the sun
on his skin, the swimming, the strolls around the town, the food!

The good, fresh food! And the exercise she gave him – who knew working up a sweat could be so pleasurable! He was hungry for her, for Georgie was looking wonderful. Her sunburn had darkened into a ripe, deep tan; her hair had lightened in the sun and her daily swims were firming up her muscles – not that they had needed any firming, he would hasten to add: she'd always looked amazing. But just now, after nearly a week of pure relaxation, she was looking magnificent: carefree, happy, without strain. And, of course, Rob finally had the time and the inclination to see this change in her, to properly pay attention.

He hadn't realised it could be so easy – or if he had, he'd forgotten it. There was a reason they had both spoken so wistfully of their Sardinian trip, because they had learned the lesson then. But it had so quickly dissipated as they'd slipped back into normal life. How fast they had forgotten the simple pleasures that had so enraptured them: time together with nothing to do; carefree self-indulgence; reading, resting, letting go of the 'have to's and 'should's that so dominated their everyday lives. They had promised to try and maintain that holiday spirit as long as possible back home.

It had all vanished, of course, almost within a fortnight of their return. The sense of real freedom that the holiday in Sardinia had awakened two years before, had for a little while spilled out and over, beyond the confines of the trip. Rob remembered his sense of a broader perspective on life during that period, even upon their return home. He had awakened to the fact that they could have freedom of choice in everyday life, as well as on holiday. Both of them had recognised – albeit briefly – that so many of the concerns and demands of their day-to-day existence had been contrived by their own hand, and could be looked at afresh. They could, if they chose to, take back a little control: they didn't have to be passively bound in the prison of daily life – the prison of their preoccupations that was, to a large extent, their own creation. The holiday in Sardinia had made them question themselves and had given them hope: they had freedom, room, space and choice. They could become the old cliché of working to live, and not the other way around. They could be alive to the sheer joy of the simple pleasures in life – hold on to the simple pleasures!

'We could live here, Rob – we really could.'

Georgie had said this so often in Sardinia, gazing around at the landscape, blood heated by the sun, that it had almost become a mantra.

'Property's so cheap – just think of it. We could enjoy all this and still do our work. You could consult internationally and me, well, I can work anywhere. We could have all that and *this*!'

An expansive sweep of her arm, encompassing sun and sea and languorous hours spent over meals, relaxed schedules, a proper life balance. 'All this as well. It would be glorious, would-n't it? Get up early, a swim before breakfast, work all morning, then doze and read on the beach in the afternoon. Another swim, work until the evening, then a late dinner with fresh fish and salad, looking out over the sea. Wouldn't it be perfect, Rob? And we could do it – we really could.'

Rob had played along for a while, indulging the fantasy; quite seriously once or twice, because Georgie had, at the time, seemed deeply serious about it. Rob hadn't known her well enough at that point to understand what lay behind the urgency in her tone. It had been less to do with property or upping sticks to the Mediterranean than with a sudden, stricken sense (that the holiday itself had provoked) of being stagnant – away from life, not in it. Rob hadn't understood Georgie's profound fear of disconnection, of getting lost in the chaos of things. Back then, he had mistaken it all for mere impetuosity, a passing whim – 'let's move over here' – that she'd latched on to as a sort of perverse test of his faith in her, his commitment.

They had fought about it, towards the end of the Sardinian holiday, when Rob, bristling at her endless, wistful fantasising, told her quite sharply that he *liked* their life back home, and if she didn't, she only had to say. Georgie had clammed up, whether angry or upset, he hadn't known, and had dropped the subject of moving. But she hadn't been able to – or perhaps had chosen not to – mask her intense reluctance about returning home as the holiday drew to a close. She let rip every now and then with almost hysterical pleas that they try to extend their vacation, even if only by a couple of days. Because weren't they having the most wonderful time? Didn't they deserve just a bit longer? They worked so hard! Rob had greeted these pleas with easy laughs, carrying within them a hint of warning. But Georgie had really feared going back to what she called her 'prison'. And even if the fear had been mostly unwarranted (for she'd settled in again quite happily back at home), Rob felt he was beginning to understand at last what it had been about.

They had been together for three years now, living together

for two of those three. They weren't just starting out, as they had been back in Sardinia. Things were different. And Rob had a feeling that something of importance had occurred over the past couple of years which he had perhaps wilfully missed or evaded, through laziness, fear or blithe assumption. Some sort of boundary had grown up between them, he recognised; a boundary that neither had thought to name, let alone challenge.

It had been an unspoken term of agreement that Georgie would make her own choices for herself, and Rob would do the same, with no intrusion by the other, except offering advice when it was asked for. That was just that. No overstepping the mark, no imposing oneself on the other's personal territory too much. It had made sense at first, when they'd been a newish couple, with neither wanting to come across as too pushy or, worse, too needy: both wanting to preserve an image of independence. Everything had schooled them for such self-preservation: their friends, and the rules and regulations that accompanied their romantic relationships; the culture they had grown up in, screaming self-fulfilment above all else; the dissolution of the marriages of their parents' generation – the careful groupings and regroupings of almost everyone they knew. If things weren't working, if you weren't happy, you owed it to yourself to walk away – everyone knew that. But now, three years in, such strictures felt hollow and ridden with pretence; they were keeping one another at arm's length for no reason. It was a distortion of everything they really felt for one another, yet their holding back had become a habit. What were they so frightened of?

Rob knew all too well that there was quite a bit he hadn't

shared with Georgie over the years – nothing dangerous, nothing untoward – just petty stuff he thought she wouldn't understand or wouldn't know what to do with. Like how he felt about himself sometimes. How he sometimes looked in the mirror and didn't get it: didn't understand the bloke, the fully adult bloke with a job and a girlfriend and a flat, staring back at him. How he still felt like a kid inside, which was partly why the thought of having a child of his own scared the life out of him. How a part of him still believed he could do anything, be anything – that it was all ahead of him, even though he was into his thirties. How another part of him just wanted to run away and hide. Georgie must have sensed some of it, Rob thought, even though he hadn't bothered to articulate things to her. Just as he now was sensing all the hidden drives and fears behind her words and pleas of years earlier. Had they really thought themselves so fragile that they couldn't cope with the vulnerabilities of the other? He didn't think of them as fragile, not as individuals. Why then as a couple, a pair?

At dinner on their fourth night, back in the taverna Georgie insisted on returning to, Rob had started really talking to her. And the more he talked, the more he found he had to say. He discovered – rediscovered, for a central part of him had always known it – that Georgie was the person he wanted to say things to. And that he, in turn, wanted her to share things with him. He wanted to know her, really know her: now, as she was, at this moment in her life. He wanted it all: the good, the bad, the frightened, the indifferent. He wanted the permanence of her.

Georgie had found it a bit awkward at first, Rob could tell. It had been a long time since they had spoken to one another so openly; spoken of their inner selves, unfettered by work constraints or the worries of daily life. After their initial courtship, when they had talked late into the night, shared their pasts, their hopes, the shutters had come down. Both were able to acknowledge it, and recognise the unwritten rules each had carried with them – the unwritten rules they had been led to believe guided the way relationships were supposed to be conducted. Georgie had laughed. How she upbraided all their friends and acquaintances for doing what they themselves had done for so long.

For it was ridiculous, now they looked at it, how censored they had been. Each partner should firmly maintain their individuality; no one, not even the beloved, should be allowed to muddy the delicate waters of personality or freedom. What nonsense. They had both bought into the fact of youth as a precious commodity, not to be squandered or given up too easily; something to be fiercely guarded for oneself and oneself alone. And this in spite of their inner yearnings, their inclinations to the contrary. Rob felt dazed with relief that somehow the two of them had stuck it out, for all their immaturities and deficiencies. He couldn't fathom how they had managed it, with all the burdens they'd been carrying. Yet they were still together, still holding out for more. It was remarkable.

And as the days went on, with Rob showing no sign of retreating or withdrawing, Georgie gained in confidence and their conversations flowed. It amazed him how much she had thought about things, privately. How deeply she had considered her choices, and the implications of those choices. How she had chosen to stay with him, no matter what her worries or frustrations. Her loneliness, even. Her fear that perhaps she was taking an easy option – yes, she confessed to having thought about him in those terms! Though she explained that such fear stemmed from her own insecurities: deep-seated beliefs that she was a fraud, a sham, with nothing to say for herself and nothing to offer. Feelings she had been battling with, of late, almost daily.

But Georgie believed in him, in his character, his soul. She had such faith – had had it from the start. And she had seen so much, had understood so much (as Rob was beginning to understand now), though she hadn't dared articulate it. How tentative they had been together, how unambitious in their communication! Yet it was so simple to do otherwise. The ground of their relationship was rich and fertile; it had only to be tended to and all would blossom. He would blossom. So would she.

It was this thought, which had come late at night, as Georgie slept in his arms after making love, that made Rob realise the relationship was what he wanted, above all else. For it seemed to him it was the only thing that mattered: the only thing of proper value that would give his life the meaning he sought. He wanted to mind the relationship, to nurture it, for it had the capacity to nurture them both so well. He wanted to give himself over to her and he wanted Georgie to do the same. He wanted, he decided, to marry her.

Rob had never known such clarity. Nothing had held such certainty for him before. He wanted, more than anything, to make Georgie his wife. He recognised in her an attitude to life and living that he admired, and felt in his bones to be true for himself, too. Together, they could make a fortress, keep each other safe; protect their vulnerabilities, their inner selves. Shield one another against the cruel, unpredictable buffetings of the outside world.

Such feelings were new. Not a few short weeks before, if Rob had heard a friend expressing such things, he would have laughed out loud at the pretension, the abstractions. He would have been wrong. The words might have been clichés; the feelings weren't. Rob had thought he'd been in love – he *had* fallen in love with Georgie, and yet, it had not been like this: so powerful, so unshakeable. For the first time, he looked at himself and asked if he was truly worthy. Asked himself what it was that *he* might give *her*, how he could best serve her.

He felt a sudden, desperate urgency to be a proper man; a man who, through his quality of spirit and steadfast resolve, could help this woman – *his* woman – become the absolute best that she could be. And, to his profound joy, Rob discovered, under the glare of his own scrutiny, the certitude that he was right for Georgie. That when it came to it, when it came to weighing up the balance of their union, he would not be found wanting.

Rob's dilemma was how to go about asking her. It wasn't that he doubted her eventual acceptance. A proposal of marriage could not now be felt merely to be a move born of obligation or duty, done because that was just the next thing to do. Rob knew he understood Georgie better than he ever had, and he knew he'd offered himself to her in recent days in a way he had been unable to before. His only fear was prematurity – that she might think he was just carried away with the happiness of their holiday and was acting impulsively. Georgie was more of a sceptic than he, both in nature and from her experience of life, and would not look kindly on any dramatic outburst or theatrical gesture. She would doubt him, and Rob knew he would not be able to bear it. So he had to think carefully. Above all else, he did not want to screw things up. Not when he had recognised for the first time how important it all was.

He'd been watching Georgie closely for the past day or two, more closely than she knew. He was finding it difficult to take his eyes off her, now that he was seeing her as his life partner, his true match, and these new feelings created a strange sensation of seeing her as if for the first time, though so much was familiar. But Rob's overwhelming feeling was one of gratitude. However lumbering and blundering he had been all those years before when he'd first met her – however full of trivial concerns and pathetic hang-ups that had blinded him to so much that was important – thank God some instinct, some innate sense of quality, had led him to make the relationship happen, led him to pursue it, even though he hadn't realised at the time what it was he'd got.

So Rob stood on their balcony in the mornings, watching as Georgie chatted with the poor, hapless fool who had taken such a shine to her. She was so patient with him – she never brushed him off. Rather, she welcomed him with open arms, the way she had welcomed Rob when they'd first met: happy to share herself, happy to make a connection, to be in the world, rather than in her own head. If pressed, Rob would have admitted to one stab of jealousy – very brief and fleeting – as he watched her speaking with Michael one morning. Not jealousy towards the man himself, for there was nothing about him that could trouble Rob, but jealousy over what he was able, without any apparent effort, to unlock in Georgie. How could someone so trivial bring her such pleasure?

The thought chilled Rob momentarily, for it prompted a sudden and unwanted glimpse of Georgie in the world without him. If Rob were not there, she would survive perfectly well on her own, he felt. More than survive: she would build a rich and fulfilling life for herself. And in that moment, above all else, Rob wanted Georgie to be more discriminating in her happiness, even as a part of him delighted in her capacity for it. He wanted her to need him more. And though he knew it was childish of him, selfish and beyond silly, Rob needed to hear her tell him how lost she would be without him.

But he was trying very hard to grow into his newfound sense of things. He had been making much more of an effort when he came down in the mornings to be agreeable to Michael, though he couldn't feign interest for long. He wanted Georgie to see that he recognised and appreciated her kindness, and, following her lead, was able to be kind himself. He wanted Georgie to know how much he admired her, how much she impressed him; how she made him want to be worthy, though when he asked her, casually and half-joking, how she managed to put up with Michael every day, she seemed a little put-out, reminding Rob that he still had some way to go. She felt sorry for him – didn't

Rob? Stuck out here on his own, adrift. They just chatted in the mornings, that was all – Michael didn't have much to say for himself but seemed happy to hear her natter on. Georgie was at her most alert at that time of day and not averse to a bit of company. Of course, if Rob would only haul his arse out of bed a bit sooner, then he could be the lucky beneficiary! But since he preferred to sleep until noon rather than luxuriating in the presence of his beautiful girlfriend, he could have very little to say on the matter.

'But he comes down *every* morning!'

'Yeah, pretty much. Just for a bit.'

'And sits with you. Just you.'

'Brings me a coffee, usually.'

'Ah, so he bribes you!'

She rolled her eyes, laughing. 'Yes. I'm a cheap date. A coffee'll do me. You should know that better than anyone, darling.'

'What do you talk about?' Rob was genuinely interested, watching as she lay back on the pillow, blinking up at the ceiling. Everything about her fascinated him at the moment. Her every move, her every gesture seemed somehow revealing.

'We just natter, that's all. It's no big deal.'

'So he doesn't bother you? It's not . . . weird?'

'Not remotely. Why do you say that?'

'I dunno. He's taken a real shine to you, that's all.'

'Rob, he's a baby! He's twenty-three years old and he's stuck out here all alone. Of course he's taken a shine to me – and to anyone who'll give him the time of day.'

'So what do you say to him?'

'God, I don't know. Nothing much. Work, life. This and that. His job, my job. What we had for dinner last night. He doesn't have a vast amount to say for himself really. He's a bit naive.'

'And not the sharpest tool in the box.'

'Rob!' Georgie pouted, but couldn't hide the smile in her eyes. Rob raised his eyebrows, unwilling to back down, and she propped herself up on one elbow as she considered. 'Okay, he's no Einstein – but he's not stupid either. Just a bit . . . basic. And he's sweet.'

'In a creepy sort of way.'

She rolled her eyes, but smoothed over the interruption. 'I don't know – there's something so helpless about him, so . . . lost. Sheltered – no, that's not quite it either. It's as if he lives in a little bubble just comprised of the essential activities: eat, work, sleep, drinks on a weekend. He's got no ambition, no sense of the bigness of the world, of anything outside himself really.'

'Sad.'

'Yeah. But it's also quite touching.'

'Oh God, Georgie, you're getting sentimental. The nobility of the working classes! The purity of the put-upon. The revelations of an idiot savant!'

'Try and credit me with some intelligence, Robert.'

'On what basis?' He grinned at her, relishing their playfulness, delighting – almost with purity – in their private world, though he couldn't deny that a small aspect of his pleasure was at Michael's expense.

'It's all so simple – everything he wants for himself; or rather, what I imagine he wants for himself, because I don't think he'd know where to begin.'

'So what do you imagine?' Rob was teasing a little, but was still interested, watching as Georgie thought about it, enjoying the sensation of being the person who had provoked her into thought, who had drawn her into conversation. 'What do you think he wants for himself?'

She hesitated. 'I think he'd like to meet a nice girl – he's very big on that: he doesn't like the drunken slapper sorts. But he's got no confidence. He's vaguely interested in engineering, but he doesn't want to have to do any exams or proper training.'

'So he expects the world to hand things to him on a plate?'

'Not at all. Quite the opposite actually. He's quite . . . humble. Doesn't think much of himself, doesn't rate himself very highly. If he sees anything at all in his future, it's more of the same, only, with any luck, he'll have a meek little wife in attendance, some good, home-cooked dinners and eventually, perhaps, a rug-rat or two, whom he'll look upon with the same befuddled amazement with which he regards the rest of life.'

Rob laughed. 'I'm surprised you haven't drawn him yet. He'd be the perfect subject for a book. A more sober, realistic children's tale, perhaps, as a warning to middle-class kids. "The boy who didn't want much". Aim low and you too can attain the lofty heights of apprenticeship and domestic discord.'

'You're being very rude, Robert. And your title sucks.'

'So you spend your time encouraging him, do you? Is that it? Reaching out to a real-life member of the downtrodden?'

Georgie had laughed, but it was a laugh tinged with guilt, and when it had run its course, it left a small silence between them. Rob reached over and stroked her hair gently, watching as she retreated for a moment into the privacy of her own thoughts, any lingering jealousy over Michael dissipated. He hoped he hadn't gone too far in his teasing. He thought not, for it had mainly sprung from a cleaner source than his trifling, fleeting twinges of resentment. There was a latent idealism in Georgie that rarely found expression in the outside world: it all went inwards, into her work, her obsessions, her worries. With Michael, it seemed, she had found the perfect outlet, and Rob didn't want her to expend too much of that energy on him – didn't want Michael to stir up, however unwittingly, those guilty and unsubstantiated feelings that she was on holiday to get away from.

'Well,' he said, wanting to bring her back to the surface, 'as long as you don't prefer him to me.'

'At least he's not a lazy lay-abed,' she shot back instantly, daring him to press her further. Rob smiled, and moved a little closer.

'He doesn't like me much, does he? Always hotfoots it when I come down.'

'I think you probably intimidate him.'

'Am I that impressive?'

'No, but you're also not at your best when you've just woken up.'

'I think I'm glorious in the mornings.'

'You would.'

'So where does he go for the rest of the day? He never comes back down.'

'I think he sleeps. He goes out at night apparently. Down to some of the clubs and bars.'

'Yeah? And do you long to go with him? Recapture a bit of your lost youth? One final fling on the dance floor!'

Georgie goosed him, frowning, but not seriously put out, Rob could tell. He nestled close to her, happily. 'So he's trying to meet a nice girl. Good luck to him down there – it's a meat market.'

'Yeah. But what else is he going to do with himself?' She sounded almost concerned. Rob wanted to shake her out of it and spoke briskly.

'It's good for him to get out and about in the world a bit. At least you're not his only source of amusement.'

She bit her lip. 'It's sad though, isn't it, when you think about it? He knows that he wants something better for himself, but he hasn't got the first clue how to go about getting it. Must be a pretty horrible trap to find yourself in.'

Rob knew he had to end it, before he lost Georgie to her inner self, and lost his patience. He nudged her cheerfully, careful to keep things light. 'Are you done with the pop psychologising, Dr Freud? I'm getting hungry.'

To his immense relief, she indulged him. Perhaps she also recognised her displacement on to Michael of her ordinary, workaday concerns.

'Why don't you come a little closer, you cruel, contemptuous man. I'll work up an appetite for you . . . .'

Another afternoon, another evening. It could not have been better.

~

It was a different world down there on the main drag of town. It seemed implausible that within such a short distance – a mere stroll down the hill – a teeming mass of people should be engaged in such determined and wild pursuit of what they called pleasure. It was extreme, and unlike anything Michael had ever seen. The contrast with the ordered quiet of the hotel, where people 'pleased' and 'thank-you'd, where considerate conversation was as loud as it got, and where all lights were out by midnight more or less, could not have been more marked.

Initially, he had felt only revulsion. Everything seemed to conspire against him. The lack of inhibition, the manic drunkenness, the loss of control – sometimes the violence – but, most of all, the sex. It was everywhere. You couldn't pass a bar or a street corner, let alone head on to the beach, without seeing writhing bodies pulled tight in embrace, wandering hands, flashes of skin. No one bothered to stumble to the privacy of a room and no one else seemed to care. It was shameless and ugly. The grasping, leering nature of it; the way the girls responded just as eagerly as the boys, more so in some cases. They called out obscenities, lifted up their tops, flashing milk-white skin. They were night owls, crawling out of bed when the sun went down, stumbling back when it rose again in the morning. They would return home after a week with no hint of a tan. Michael wondered why they bothered to come all the way out to Greece, only to do what they did every Saturday night back home. And the size of so many of them, the fleshiness! Rolls of fat bulged out from tight straps and tops; rolls of flesh to be hung on to for dear life, clutched at desperately. Wantonly. There was no moderation: in dress, in appetites, in vulgarity. The whole place existed to serve greed on every level. It was a wonder most people managed to survive it.

The first time Michael had ventured out, he'd gone from bar to bar, club to club, never stopping long, looking to see if any place might be different; discovering, to his dismay, that they were all the same. He hadn't spoken a word to anyone that first time, and no one had approached him. But, somehow, he passed the whole night through and was amazed to discover it was getting light when he emerged from his final club of the evening. Slightly dazed with it all, he had bought himself a coffee and a bacon sandwich from a little greasy spoon stand, queuing up behind the lines of sozzled men and women eager to seal their night's activity with the familiarity of egg and chips. *'Here, Shaz, that bloke you were with the other night – that guy who fingered you on the dance floor – isn't that him over there? God, he's bit rough in daylight!'*

Michael had strolled down to the beach, stepping over prostrate bodies and busy, writhing couples, avoiding the bigger gangs of people who had clearly been partying there all night. Sitting on the sand, with his back to the mayhem of the town, the view was remarkable. Clear blue sea, glittering in the early morning sun, stretched to the horizon, its vast expanse interrupted only by the hazy outline of a small island, some distance from the shore. The bay itself was spectacular: the land to the left dramatic – a strong upward sweep of hillside, dotted with distant villages. To the right, the land curved gently, gracefully, hugging the water. Along the coast at regular intervals, other tourist resorts were visible as far as the eye could see, until all of it – land, sea, sky – seemed to merge into one.

Michael now made it a habit to end his nocturnal wanderings at the beach, having a bite of breakfast in the relative calm, gazing at the view. He loved it. No matter how long he looked, how many times he saw the same thing, it didn't lose its mystery, its beauty. The colours of the landscape – the rusty browns of the scrub, the dark greens of the trees, the rolling white mountains and the vast blue sea – were combinations he had never seen before. And the land itself was so old, primitive-looking, craggy and rocky. Michael imagined it was how the whole world must have looked when it was first made.

The expanse of it made him feel tiny in comparison, but, rather than unsettling him, he enjoyed feeling insignificant: feeling the world around him melt away to nothing, so that he was just a speck. Because if he was a speck, then everyone else was as well. And that being the case, nothing that he did, nothing that anyone did, mattered. Nothing could make a difference, good or bad, in the greater scheme of things. It was liberating, thinking of things in that way. It made Michael realise how narrowly he had thought of himself for so many years: how silly he'd been, being frightened of life, frightened of what other people thought, what they might say about him. Why, they were no more than a grain of sand, any of them! A random grain of sand on this beach which looked no different from any other grain, which wouldn't be noticed if it weren't there. The beach would still be a beach if a grain of sand went missing – even if a thousand or one hundred thousand grains went missing. It didn't matter a damn.

The little island in the centre of the bay pleased Michael most. On clear mornings, he could make out how deserted it was. There was nothing there except for a couple of small, abandoned huts. He couldn't imagine who might once have lived there. There was nothing on the island to support them, as far as he could see, no shops, nothing. It wouldn't appeal to your average person – it certainly wouldn't appeal to any of the people on the beach with him, who'd be lost without their beer on tap and their greasy takeaways on every corner. But it appealed to Michael. There was something deeply attractive to him about the idea of your very own island where you could do whatever you chose, where there was no one to answer to, no one to have to avoid or explain things to. Being away from it all, far enough out so that the great mass of land he was currently sitting on would be a hazy vista on the horizon, blurred, unreal.

Each morning, he spent some hours imagining what he would do to one of the little huts over there if he owned it. He imagined how he'd renovate it, turn it into a proper little cottage, make it hospitable and welcoming. He'd keep it simple enough – perhaps imitate the style of his hotel room: spare, stark wooden furniture, white walls, tiled floors. Everything clean and crisp. No fuss, no having to hide bits of damp and peeling wallpaper with posters, or covering old stains on carpets with threadbare rugs. As bare as possible, that's how he'd like it.

He would get a little boat, to sail back and forth to the mainland for supplies. He would have to learn to cook – learn all sorts of practical things, like how to run a small electricity generator and sort out a system for water supply. It would take a lot of hard work, but Michael didn't think it would be impossible. He liked the thought of such a challenge. It made him smile to think of himself, even in fantasy, doing such things.

And the other huts. He would make use of the other huts, too; maybe turn one into a workshop for himself, where he could potter about with machinery, try things out his own way. Stuff exams – if he had the time and space to do things himself, he'd become skilled in no time. Screw all their books and papers and the filling out of forms – he'd have his own bloody workshop, thank you very much; he'd be capable of running and maintaining his own bloody island! All that crap he had been given about how reading and writing were the most important, how if he didn't *apply* himself, he'd never get anywhere, how if he would insist on not paying attention, he'd end up just like his father, useless and full of shit.

Michael stopped himself short. He hadn't meant for his thoughts to go in that direction, and resented their sudden and unexpected intrusion into the pleasures of his fresh new world; his new, man-of-the-island self. His parents, his teachers – they had all called him a fool, but who were the real fools? Look at him, sitting on a beach miles from home, with money in his pocket, food in his belly, a roof over his head, friends! For he did have friends: two good ones, in Patrick and Georgie. Friends who wouldn't dream of telling him he'd never amount to anything; that he'd better take what he can get and be grateful for it; that he should count his lucky stars he hadn't been born any stupider than he was.

Michael usually sat undisturbed during his reveries, but on his fourth morning a drunken young woman had almost tripped over him, flailing in the sand, ungainly, laughing. Her friends had been standing behind him, laughing at her. 'Fuck's sake, you twat!'

She'd been one of those bulging girls, flesh spilling out over the waistband of her skirt, white and pasty, sweating in the early morning sunshine. She had grinned at Michael, and he'd smelled the booze on her breath, on her skin, seeping out through her pores.

'All right?' she'd asked him.

Michael, shocked at the intrusion, hadn't known what to say. Approaches like this weren't often made in daylight. He had stared at her silently, willing her to move on. But instead of going, instead of leaving him be, the girl had waited, interested suddenly, her friends behind him giggling, watching.

'Had a good night?' she'd pressed, her sharp accent slicing the morning air.

'Leave it, Amanda – let's get some food!' one of the others had said.

'Fuck off, Steph. I'm only chatting to the lad. Sitting here all on your own. What's that about then, eh? You lost your mates or something? Lost your missus?'

The girl had gazed at him, not quite focused because of the drink, yet strangely locked onto her mission; a mischievous mission, if he would allow it, if he would only play along and indulge her. Michael knew the girl was using him as a test of her will, her charms, her force of personality. And he also knew that she must triumph, be victorious, or else she'd turn. His heart had begun to beat in that familiar rhythm of panic and excitement. Clearing his throat awkwardly, he had garbled his words: 'My friend's gone back.'

'What did you say?' She tottered forward in the sand, getting closer, straining to listen.

'Oi, Mands! Greedy cow – you've already had one shag tonight.'

The girls behind were raucous, a perverse chorus, out to get him. Michael felt the heat of a blush rising in his cheeks.

'Do you want to talk alone?' he stammered, but the others had got in on top of him too fast.

'Leave him be, Mands, he's a weirdo.'

'Anyone can see he doesn't fancy you.'

'Steph, fuck *off*!'

Why do they do it? Michael thought. Why do they let themselves get that way, these leering women, reeking of fags, booze and grease, believing for all the world that they were catches, not to be missed? *Fat slags. Stupid fat slags.*

'What was that?'

He looked up, startled. Had he spoken out loud?

'We're going now, Amanda!' A singsong voice from behind, sensing danger perhaps, wanting to avoid it. Or maybe just plain greedy. It sounded like a fat voice. 'You coming or not?'

The girl had hesitated, her eyes narrowed into little squints, as if distorted vision would enable her to tell once and for all if she had heard something she ought to make an issue out of. Michael had coughed and looked away, knowing it was an admission of defeat and shame, but suddenly past caring, just wanting her to go, to leave him alone. He felt a stab of habitual fear, and he suddenly loathed her for it. Why did they always have to spoil everything, women like that? They seemed to exist only to spoil things. It sickened him to think that he was still such easy prey.

She had stared at him a little longer before deciding it – he – was not important enough to pursue. The energy it would take to mount an attack, fuel an out-and-out scene, was too much to summon after her long night. 'Fuck you then,' she'd told him, before stumbling on her way. 'Tosser.'

Michael heard the girls laughing as they left, laughing at him, taking the piss. A hot wave of anger had hit him, and he had longed suddenly to leap to his feet and go after them, to take that fat cow by the shoulders and shake her, tell her what he thought of her and her type. But almost as suddenly as it had arrived, the urge passed, leaving him flat and depressed. He had let the bitch get the better of him, had let her ruin his morning. Yet even as he recognised the truth of it, something in him clicked. No. She wouldn't do it – he wouldn't let her get away with it. Why should she be allowed to ruin things for him?

Gazing back out at his island, Michael willed his thoughts away to nothingness, letting himself slip into a state of blankness, not-thinking, not-feeling. And it worked. He had gradually become calm. He didn't know how long it had taken, but slowly he found himself coming round, reawakening to his surroundings, blinking back into real time as if he'd been asleep, only to discover himself still sitting there, on his own, on the beach. It had been the strangest sensation: a shutting out of everyone and everything, a complete retreat. But it had worked. He was happy again, positive. His sense of accomplishment was powerful, and he felt a sudden burst of pride that he had managed to restore himself so well. It was a tool he knew he would call on again, now that he had discovered it. If only he had known how to remove himself from the world – from himself – like that years ago.

There were no other disturbances in the mornings that followed. So Michael sat quietly each day, watching the sunrise, gazing at his island – for it was fully his now, in his imagination. Thoughts of what he would do with it cleansed away the grit and strangeness of the night in the frantic town. Apart from sitting with Georgie each morning, this time – just thinking, working it all out – was Michael's favourite part of the day.

Satisfied with his preliminary plans for his own accommodation and workshop on the island, he had turned his thoughts towards the final two huts. He couldn't just leave them like that – rotting old shacks on his doorstep; he'd have to make something of them, make them useful in some way. Perhaps he could turn one of them into a little guest cottage, if people wanted to come and stay. Maybe Patrick would come out, though Michael knew Patrick wouldn't be happy for long, stuck on a little island with no pubs or nightclubs. Still, there was always the mainland for that sort of stuff. It could work. One hut for Michael, one for his workshop, and the third for guests.

The last hut was on the far corner of the island, a bit removed from all the others, set closer to the shore. Michael was tempted to leave it alone, finding no immediate use for it. But it nagged at him. Perhaps it could be used for storage? Or as another workshop? No, he wouldn't need a second. He thought about it long and hard, unwilling to compromise. And then it occurred to him. He could do something special with it, a bit out of the ordinary. Make a different sort of working space. Other people needed places to work, not just engineers. People like artists. A studio – that's what they called it. Hadn't Georgie said she'd always dreamed of having a studio, rather than working in her spare room?

That fourth hut would be perfect for an artist: peaceful, remote – with a spectacular view. Of course, Michael would have to consult about what things artists needed in a studio. He hoped it wouldn't be too complicated. They could work all day: Michael in his workshop, and the artist in the studio. In the late afternoon, when work was done, the artist could swim in the sea, and stroll over to Michael's place for a drink and quiet conversation, watching the sunset and the lights coming out on the mainland, before sitting down to dinner – dinner that Michael would learn how to cook.

It was settled. Michael was pleased with his accomplishments, proud to have worked everything out so well. He was beginning to understand what it meant to make plans, think ahead properly about big things. He could see why other people did it. It was enjoyable, and it made him feel more solid, somehow, more sure of himself. If he could plan something like that – a whole island! But almost as soon as he had started to enjoy his success, a little voice in his head had begun whispering – quietly at first, but it became more insistent, more demanding. *Getting a bit too big for your boots, are you? Think you've got it all worked out, you great fool? There are one or two things you might have forgotten about.*

It was his mother's voice, sharp and unforgiving. It had been some time since Michael had actually heard it, but it had, nevertheless, frequently intruded over the years, needling him in private moments, tormenting him with its reproaches. And, more often than not, Michael had to acknowledge, the voice was right. It reminded him of things he had overlooked, hadn't done, or had done badly. It was right this time too. There were things he hadn't thought about. One big thing, in particular. Money. Not only money to purchase the properties, but earning it once he lived there. How had he been so stupid? How had he allowed himself to overlook such a vital thing? He felt the sting of shame cut through his plans, rendering them all a joke, a stupid impossibility. *That's right – you're finally getting it! Took your time about it though, didn't you?* He could hear the laugh that was coming, could feel the knot in his stomach start to tighten and clench. His foolishness would haunt him for days, he knew.

Yet even as the laughter started, to Michael's immense surprise, something within him reared up and resisted, much as it had done after the interruption of the drunken woman, days before. Rather than abandon everything, give up on it all, even in his imagination, Michael forced himself to stay calm. He could still hear his mother's voice, but he was able, with an immense effort, to bring himself into that state of nothingness where no thoughts, no feelings could reach him. It took less time than it had done before, and when he came round, calmer, he realised to his delight that the voice had gone. And instead of giving up, running away, he began to think more practically, pondering the situation, refusing to give in to any hint of despair.

All right – money. He'd have to get a job on the mainland. He wouldn't need much – it was cheap to live in Greece. Perhaps he could offer his services as a handyman? Or do security at one of the nightclubs? He could work at night, after the artist had gone to bed, and come back early in the morning, bringing hot food and coffee for her, to help her start her day. He could do a few things in his workshop and then go to bed for the afternoon. That was a good enough compromise. Problem solved.

But he wasn't strong enough. Though he had silenced the voice temporarily, after a while, it came back. Not quite so insistent this time, but nevertheless, it reminded him that he shouldn't be quite so sure of himself just yet. Money was one thing, but what about electricity? Running water? All very well to say he'd sort out a water system, but what did that really mean? How much work would it take to get even one hut up and functioning?

Though he had made a valiant effort, the stark reality of such a venture was all too much. When the voice became too strong, which, in spite of his efforts, it eventually did, Michael would haul himself up off the beach and make his way slowly back through the town, up the hill to the hotel. By then, the elderly couple would be by the pool, with Georgie not far behind. He would shake off his mood the moment he started talking to her. All the impossibilities of the situation seemed to melt away. Georgie deserved the best, and if other people could do impressive things – climb mountains, build empires – then he could, one day, manage to set up the island. Not that he told her about his plans, not yet. There were still too many practicalities to think about. The voice at least had some use. He wasn't going to be made a fool of because he hadn't thought things through. He wouldn't tell Georgie until everything was set.

Nor would he tell her too many details of his excursions into town after dark. When she pressed him a little, Michael told her that he went out a bit, chatted to some people, had a few drinks. That was that.

'And dancing? Do you like to dance? I haven't been dancing for so long!'

He could imagine Georgie dancing, though not in any of the clubs he went to. When he pictured her, it was always in a large, empty room – a ballroom – gliding around elegantly to gentle, lulling music.

'I'm not a very good dancer,' he'd confided.

'Nor am I,' she'd laughed, 'but I don't care. I just enjoy it. Maybe I should come out with you one night and we can strut our stuff.'

He knew she was joking, but a part of him wished she wasn't. Truth be told, it had been difficult for him at first, going out on his own at night. Michael had battled with himself to do it, forcing himself after the first time to go back again. But, somehow, the more he did it, the easier it became, and the nights out now seemed to exert a mysterious sort of pull on him, drawing him down into the town, demanding that he go. The compulsion to go was a force far stronger than whatever he might feel about it.

Because, after the first night, Michael had grown more used to the chaos, and had at last been able to hold a couple of conversations with other people standing at the bar. His forays into social life seemed to please Georgie. She had told him she was glad he was enjoying himself, getting out and about – that's what holidays were for. So, in a way, Michael felt he was doing her bidding, going out each evening: proving to her that he was just like anyone else, that he could make something of himself, do what she suggested. But there were some things about his nights in town that she should not know, that he wouldn't ever tell her. Things that even he found strange about himself, out of character, and implausible in the shock of sunlight and the routine order around the pool.

He wouldn't tell her, for example, that he drank steadily through the night. He wouldn't mention that he'd taken to getting to the beach a bit earlier each day, to watch some of the couples before the sun came up and he got lost in his island. Certainly, he wouldn't tell her that on his fifth night he'd found himself behind a club, with a girl whose name he didn't know. She'd been so drunk, she had fallen over when taking off her knickers, which she had done before they'd even kissed. Michael had been leaving the club and she had been outside. They had barely exchanged words before she'd grabbed him by the hand, dragging him round the back, beside the bins. He hadn't had time to say no – it had all happened so fast.

She had been a big girl. Michael remembered the heft of her, how difficult he'd found it to hold her in position up against the wall, how her eyes had rolled back in her head as she battled to remain conscious. He remembered his disgust, even as he went through with it. Remembered with a shock how the sensations had taken him over, his body acting independently of his mind. He remembered how he'd tried to move her afterwards, tried to help her up, get her back to the street with her friends, but how he couldn't manage it. He had left her there, slumped over some black bags. He had told the group of girls she'd been with where she was, and left them to it. They could sort her out. That's what they were there for, wasn't it?

He couldn't imagine having any difficulty lifting Georgie. Though she went on about her weight a bit, making sure she swam her laps each day, complaining about the amount she had eaten the night before, she was pretty tiny. He could manage her no problem, he reckoned – could carry her for miles if necessary. Not that it would ever be necessary. Georgie would never get herself into such a state. Not like the girls downtown. Michael knew pretty well what girls looked like and, of course, he saw Georgie wearing next to nothing each morning in her little bikini. But somehow, even in that – the tiny scraps of material that hugged her form – she retained a natural modesty that Michael honoured in his mind. He couldn't for the life of him imagine what she looked like naked, couldn't picture how she might feel or taste, get a glimpse of what her face would do when he . . . .

He was glad that she was so different. It wasn't the same thing when it came to proper women. Not women like Georgie, who liked just sitting with him, talking and laughing. Who liked books and painting. Who would thrill at the thought of a brand-new studio all her own, away from the madness, on a peaceful little island out in the middle of the bay.

~

They had quarrelled, unexpectedly. All had been harmonious between them since the minor conflict on their first proper morning, when Rob had been caught up in his work call. Subsequently, he and Georgie had been melded, enmeshed, attuned to one another. So when they fought, at the beginning of their second week, it was shocking to them both. It seemed out of all proportion, shattering the joy and sense of rediscovery they had been carefully tending.

The cause of Georgie's explosion had been ridiculously trivial. Something to do with Rob having taken too long in the shower and leaving it in a mess, but Rob knew that whatever it was that was really bothering her had started hours before. She had been nursing some grievance or other all day and he had misjudged her mood, taken it too lightly. He hadn't been paying close enough attention, putting her irritability down to hormones, though she had angrily denied it. Lack of sleep then, perhaps, or too much sun.

Georgie had been snappy with him from the first, when he came down to the pool in the late morning, nodding his hello to Michael, who had scampered away as usual, like a chastened puppy. She'd grunted when Rob asked her if everything was all right, if Michael had amused her well. Clearly she had not been in a joking mood. Rob hadn't taken her seriously, hoping it would pass, and had left her to it, escaping into his book, dozing in the sun, not rising to the sharpness of her tone whenever they exchanged a word or two. Whatever it was, he had reasoned, it must be minor, for there was nothing tangible that could have occurred to make her really angry. And sometimes with Georgie, it was better to let her stew – mull it over, work through it. When highly strung, she reacted badly to too much probing and prodding. She would tell him when she was good and ready, Rob figured. Until then, he was going to enjoy himself. He had been pleased with the maturity of his refusal to be petty over a bad mood, pleased with his refusal to allow it to anger him or ruin his afternoon.

But, unfortunately, the mood was not just Georgie's to nurture: it was designed for Rob too, and the whole thing had intensified up in their room with a startling rapidity. He found himself under attack, damp from the shower, towel around his waist. How was it possible that he, Rob, should be so blithely arrogant all the time, so unaware of other people, of her! The minor shower incident – taking too long when he had been chivvying her to get ready to go out for dinner – was, it appeared, merely the tip of an iceberg Rob had had no glimpse of. It was rare for Georgie to be outright angry. Sulky, yes, but not angry. So when she rounded on him, hurling accusations, he was so taken aback that he almost laughed.

'Where's all this come from?'

'All what?'

'Why are you so angry?'

'I'm not angry!'

'Jesus, Georgie, if this is you not angry, I'd hate to see you when you are.'

'Arsehole,' she'd muttered, knowing that he'd heard.

'What's the matter with you? Come on, sweetheart – what's happened?'

She had shaken her head, mute, her eyes glittering. Rob sensed that her rage, which had been triggered by some minor, external source – so minor that on another day, in another mood, it wouldn't have had the same effect – had drawn her thoughts down into the pit. He struggled to get the measure of it.

'Have I done something, said something to upset you? I thought we were having a lovely day.' He knew that wasn't true – she had been simmering all afternoon – but he needed something with which to defend himself.

'Of course, you would. You don't even notice, do you, Rob?' Georgie stood in front of him, feet apart, squarely placed, her stance that of a fighter's. 'You don't see it – you never bloody have!'

'See what? What did I do?' It had been hard to keep the exasperation from his tone. 'Is it because I hurried you? I was only conscious of the fact that you'd said you were starving!'

She barked out a laugh, cold and contemptuous. That he should even *think* her anger was in any way related to something so banal! That he could dare consider her to be in the midst of an immature reaction to his precious schedule for the evening! That laugh had irritated Rob, and he had struggled to keep his composure. As so often happened when they fought, he had a hard time maintaining his sense of things, his sense of her. When he was overtaken by anger (and it could happen quickly if he wasn't careful – he tried to be careful), Georgie took on a different form, became someone he didn't recognise: an enemy who had to be defeated at all costs, no matter that she was the woman he loved and cherished. They were unnerving, the distortions of his temper, giving an unwanted glimpse into a cruel and callous part of him that sought only to destroy, claim victory, no matter the opponent – almost in spite of the opponent – and all the tender feelings he held for her. Rob wished he were able to integrate those feelings better within himself; wished that he was able, when they argued, to see them both as three-dimensional people with a range of complex emotions, and not just as one-sided combatants, going at it to the death.

'Please, Georgie, I don't want to fight,' Rob had pleaded with her. 'If you won't talk about what's bothering you, can we at least agree to try and be civilised?'

He had gone too far, he realised, almost as soon as the words were out of his mouth. He'd patronised her, unwittingly, to be sure, and it had added fuel to the fire.

'I see – put up and shut up, is it? Keep the peace? So sorry, Rob – I completely forgot – mustn't intrude on your happy little world.'

He was scuppered. No amount of coaxing or trying to jolly her out of it would work. Whatever had been growing and why it had grown, would have to come out on her terms. Sitting wearily on the bed, he watched as she moved about the room, restless, gearing herself up for the onslaught of her anger.

'You always do that, Rob, you always turn everything back on to yourself! You're the poor victim, you're the innocent blameless one.'

'I still don't know what I've done —'

'No matter that you're rude or arrogant or just plain *ignorant.*'

Baffled, he glanced up at her. 'Was I rude? When?'

She rolled her eyes to heaven.

'I apologise for it if I was, though I really don't know what I said or did.'

'God, Rob – it's all so by the bloody book with you, isn't it? *I apologise for it!'* She mocked him, beyond caring that the childishness of the imitation was demeaning.

'Would you please tell me what this is all about?' Rob stood, his patience wearing thin. Georgie had stopped pacing and was staring at him. 'If I've said something or done something, I'd like to know about it because this is insane!'

'That's always your excuse, isn't it? It's me – I'm the crazy one, the one who gets it wrong. *You're* Mr Perfect, Mr Rational!

God, your *loftiness* is insufferable. Okay – you want to know what this is all about? Where this "came from", as you put it – because of course, you haven't noticed *anything* amiss *all day.*'

'Oh, I noticed, Georgie. Believe me, I noticed. You made it pretty impossible for me not to, snapping and grunting and glowering as if someone had insulted you —'

'"Someone?" Hmmm. Wonder who that could be.'

'All right then – me. I insulted you. I don't know how and I don't know when, but clearly it's been enough for you to act like a spoiled child all day.'

'That's right, be sarcastic – that's the way —'

'Then just spit it out! What's the fucking problem?'

She stepped towards him, apparently not in the least intimidated by his stance, his anger. The thought flashed through Rob's mind that she was able to let rip so openly because she knew he would never hit her; would never dream of hitting her. And though he was grateful for that fact – grateful for what it meant about their relationship, about him – it also, at that moment, made him wish, just for a split second, that he *was* the sort of man who'd at least threaten to lash out. He pushed the thought from his mind, disgusted with himself.

'When you came down to the pool this morning, Rob, what was the first thing you did?' Georgie spoke with precision. Clearly she'd been preparing the line all day.

'When I came down to the pool? Let's see . . . . Well – first I laid my towel out, and I must have put my book down. Then, if I recall correctly, I picked up the sun cream and began to smear myself with it. That what you're after?'

'Okay, play games. But the first thing you said this morning was: "I wish you'd find a better class of loser to entertain yourself with."'

Rob was momentarily silenced. That was not his recollection of things at all. He hesitated. 'I don't think that's what I said . . . .'

'Really? You don't remember? Your first words of the day to me?'

'No – I mean – I was joking, Georgie, if I said that! And I don't think I said it like that!' Rob had been happy that morning, unconcerned by anything, especially unconcerned by Michael, to whom he'd given barely a thought. So he'd been careless, then; that was it. It was easy for him to be careless when it came to Michael.

'So I'm making it up, am I? This is all coming from me?'

'I didn't say that, Georgie, but still, whatever was said, was said in jest – you know that as well as I do. We've joked about it enough, haven't we? So why now? Why today? You don't mean to tell me you've been festering all day because you wanted to defend *Michael*?'

'NO!' She shouted, startling him. 'No, you stupid idiot – it's *you*. You. You just blunder in, completely oblivious. You think you know everything, you've got it all down pat. Always a joke, always a line.'

'Did Michael hear me? Is that what you're worried about?'

'It's not about Michael.'

Her voice was so loud that Rob glanced around anxiously, worried suddenly himself that Michael could be in danger of hearing her through their windows.

'It's about *you*, Rob – about how pig-headed you are and how you miss what's right in front of you. You obey every passing whim, every little fancy, as if it's the dictate of God on high. If you're in the mood to be cruel or nasty, so be it – everyone's got to play along with you. You're upbeat and happy? How can it be possible that the world doesn't instantly follow suit?'

'So I interrupted an intimate moment, did I? Is that what you're saying? I blundered in and screwed up some confession, some little psychiatrists' session?' He couldn't keep the nervousness from his tone and cursed himself for it. Rob knew that Georgie was dangerous in this mood, that her sarcasm could be withering. She made him feel vulnerable, stripped bare. A casual mood of irritability had morphed in to a ruthless character assassination. Did she really judge him so harshly? Was he honestly as she saw him: a selfish, unworthy bastard?

His words hung between them, the timorousness of his tone at odds with the defiance of his question. Perhaps it was the tone that got to Georgie, for she sighed suddenly, her shoulders drooping, defeated. Rob wasn't being dense on purpose, if that was what her sigh implied, and he stepped forward to explain, to appeal to her reason, hoping she would soften her ruthless vision of him. As he approached, Georgie shook her head.

'I'm sorry,' she told him. 'I'm sorry. I didn't mean that – any of it. I don't know why I'm so angry.' He touched her lightly on the shoulder, relief beginning to bubble. She didn't shake him off, but nor did she look at him. 'It's not about Michael, the poor guy. It's nothing to do with him. Or you – not really.'

'But did I say something bad? Did I spoil something?'

'No, no, not at all. Even if you were a bit harsh about him this morning, I know you didn't mean it.' Rob bowed his head, taking the criticism, though it was spoken lightly.

'Anyway, it wasn't that. I can't even remember what we were talking about – me and Michael, I mean. Nothing at all probably. It's not what you think, down there. I'm not engaged in some sort of project.'

'I know you're not.'

'I'm just . . . sometimes I feel . . . I just feel really – disconnected from you. I don't know why. But today . . . .' Rob listened, careful not to interrupt her delicate admission. 'I sit there sometimes in the mornings, chatting away to Michael, and you're up here fast asleep. Oh . . . it's ridiculous.'

He squeezed her shoulder gently. 'Go on.'

'It's just . . . . Sometimes I think I could be anyone, you know? Anyone at all and it wouldn't matter. When it comes to you, I mean. I listen to myself sometimes, talking away, trying to be nice – talking about all sorts of things I know Michael doesn't have the faintest clue about, and it makes me think . . . . It makes me feel a bit pathetic. It's all rubbish. I felt it so strongly this morning. I was telling Michael something about us – nothing major – just something about the way we like to go to the same restaurant all the time, and I suddenly stopped. Not because of him or because of that, but something made me wonder . . . .' She began biting her lower lip, reluctant to continue.

'What did you wonder, sweetheart?'

She looked up at him. 'Why me? I don't know why you're

with me. Why I seem to make you so happy. I wonder if some-one else might do a better job. I sometimes think you could replace me with someone else in the morning and they'd do just as well. Better even.'

'Oh, Georgie.'

At last, the tears had begun to flow, and Rob had felt a surge of relief that it wasn't anything too serious, anything he had to truly worry about. And selfishly, it reassured him to discover that his pangs of feeling replaceable were mirrored by her own. He wanted to tell her, wanted to explain that he had had exactly the same thoughts once or twice, standing on the balcony, watching her with Michael, but she was too upset to hear him. Later – he would tell her later, when she was calmer.

'You're trying so hard, Rob. All week you've been trying. You've been amazing. You want to make everything perfect – we've only got this snatched time together. And I'm messing it all up. I'm sorry. I'm so sorry. You're right – I'm a child, a spoiled child.'

Rob comforted her, reassured her. Georgie's unwarranted insecurities regarding their relationship had surfaced once or twice before, though her anxieties were usually trained on her work. She had had a somewhat chequered past before meeting Rob: two failed relationships with men who had ended up hurt-ing her quite badly. When they had met, Georgie had been reluctant to embark upon anything new, but Rob had talked her round. He had never mistreated her, not like the others had done; had never given her cause to mistrust him, sexually or emotionally. Indeed, it had been a badge of pride for him, the seriousness with which he had taken their relationship, even in the earliest days. Some of his friends had mocked him for it at the start, for Rob had a history of serial monogamy, always swearing at the end of a break-up that he would stay single for a while, have some fun, but then invariably he would meet some-one 'serious' within three months or so. He had known it was different with Georgie from the very beginning, but his friends had taken some convincing. And now, apparently, she needed to be convinced as well.

Rob took her in his arms, holding her close, and, though she didn't want his embrace, didn't feel she deserved it, she didn't resist it either. He told her that he loved her, that her happiness was the most important thing in the world to him. That he couldn't imagine ever being without her. That he wanted to spend the rest of his life with her. She looked up at him, baffled. He had never said those things before, not so clearly, or with such strength. A sudden impulse overtook him.

'C'mon – let's get out of here. Let's go somewhere different for the night.'

'What? Where? It's nearly suppertime.'

'Tomorrow, then – let's go somewhere tomorrow. We'll get out and do something, just us. Have an adventure.'

She shook her head, half-laughing, her tears still very close. 'We are together – just us – that's why we came on holiday!'

Rob got up quickly and took the guidebook she kept by her side of the bed. 'Come on. Let's make a plan. Or we can take the book to dinner with us if you like. If you're starving.'

She shook her head. 'No, I'm okay for the moment. Go on then. Let's have a look.'

He sat back down beside her, still in his towel, and scanned the book's contents. As he was reading, she gently pulled the sheets down and covered his shoulders with them. He glanced at her, touched by the gesture.

'Thanks.'

She nodded, still abashed. Rob smiled. If only she could know how all encompassing his love for her really was. How he thought of no one else – nothing else.

'Okay, my darling,' he said, 'where shall we go?'

~

The crowds had been worse than usual. It was the weekend and scores of Greek youngsters had descended from the surrounding villages, flooding the town, hoping for some easy pickings amongst the annihilated tourists. Certain nightclubs had been so packed that the doormen were turning people away, causing more than one drunken fight to break out on the pavements outside. The police had been out in force patrolling the streets, permanent expressions of disgust on their faces as they surveyed the mayhem.

Michael had not had an enjoyable night. It had started harmlessly enough, with a couple of pints in the British Bulldog pub, which was frequented mainly by guys around his age. He had chatted for a while with a group of Liverpudlian lads, younger than him, nineteen or twenty or thereabouts. One of them, a trainee plumber named Alan, had even bought him a drink. Alan was the shy one of the group, and had been sent up to the bar most often to get in the rounds for his mates. Michael had been perched at the corner, and when Alan was waiting for drinks for the third time in a row, they had started to talk.

Michael was surprised how easy he found it now, making small talk with strangers. He supposed that was how things happened in life: necessity forced you on to your own resources, and the more you practised doing unusual things, the easier it became. He'd bantered with Alan, and had had no problem explaining his situation, how it was he'd come to be on holiday on his own. Alan, who could not imagine life without his mates (no matter how they might treat him), was deeply sympathetic.

'C'mere, man – come and join us.'

'Oi, Alan! What's taking so long?'

Michael felt a pull of compassion for this evident underdog, and helped Alan take the eight pints to the table.

'This is Michael,' Alan explained. 'You'll never believe what's happened to him.'

It had been nice for a while, the camaraderie of the group, and Michael could see the attraction of it, though he found a couple of the guys a bit too loud and dominating, reluctant to let anyone else get a word in. But they were a nice bunch: high-spirited, relatively good-natured, as long as things were going their way. Yet when the conversation progressed beyond general chitchat, Michael couldn't help but feel the odd man out, by virtue of his age. It was a mere gap of three or four years, yet the lads seemed to be from a different generation. He couldn't follow half their talk. They were going on about something called 'meow, meow' for a long time. Michael didn't know if it was a silly catch phrase or what, until Alan turned to him quite innocently and asked him if he'd ever tried it. 'Way better than E, man, and legal too. God, you gotta try it, and you gotta get off with someone on it. I swear to God, she can be the biggest minger and you'll still feel like your balls are going to explode!'

Michael had instinctively recoiled at the vulgarity, but he knew that Alan meant well. When the conversation moved on to their various sexual escapades (apparently one of them, Barry, was notorious for getting blow jobs from fat girls in the back of nightclubs), Michael excused himself to go to the bathroom, and slipped away. They wouldn't notice. They were already too far gone.

The clubs were a disappointment that night. Too many people were crowded in – there was barely room to move, and the noise level was so high, there was no point trying to talk. Even from Michael's favourite spots upstairs on the balconies that overlooked the dance floors, he wasn't able to enjoy himself. There were too many bodies down below to pick out the one or two he might want to watch. Pissed off and claustrophobic, he had almost been involved in a fight with two girls. Michael hadn't intended any confrontation, but they'd barged past him, one of them elbowing him hard in the abdomen. *Slags*, he'd muttered under his breath, but not quietly enough, for the second one heard him and turned on him, eyes flashing. She'd been a sharp-looking sort, all bones and angles, long nose, thin lips. Too much make-up and too few clothes, like all of them.

'What did you say?' she demanded, reaching out to grab her friend, a plump girl, the one who'd pushed into him. They always seemed to operate like that, girls: one fat, one thin. Even when they travelled in groups, it was an even enough ratio, as if some form of natural selection had declared that there should be a wide array of choice on offer. 'Carol, hang on – this wanker here has something to say to us.'

They were spoiling for a fight. The girls were as bad as the boys for that; worse, actually, for they could let loose their aggression and claim the protection of their gender if anything came of it. It had been the same at school. Taunting and teasing had moved on to outright threats and violence, more often than not. Packs of girls picked out the weak ones, weak boys their favourite targets, the humiliation factor being so much sweeter. The worst was that there was nothing you could do. It was no good trying to treat girls like that with any consideration or politeness, any appeal to their better selves. The only way was to give as good as one got, or to give in quickly and suck it up. Michael could feel the familiar knot of nerves clench in his stomach as the two girls squared up to him, and he bitterly resented it.

The fat one, Carol, came up very close; so close that Michael could smell the booze, cigarettes and burger on her breath. 'You got something to say, fuckface?'

Michael held her gaze, prepared to stare her out, but her friend, the skinny one, had quickly rallied support from a group of lads nearby, who approached with all the righteous anger of the chivalrous.

'Oi! What the fuck? You giving these ladies a hard time?'

One of them shoved him. Michael couldn't go far, since he was pushed back against the balcony rail, but he could feel the strength behind the action. He was outnumbered; defeat was certain. With a contemptuous glance at the two women, he elbowed his way through the little group, making for the exit. He could hear the catcalls and cries behind him of 'tosser!' and 'twat!' but he didn't turn back. His heart was beating fast and his thoughts were red-hot. *Fucking little bitches. I hope those lads take 'em outside and fuck them up the arse. One by one. Like the fucking slags they are.*

He didn't bother with another bar or club but headed straight to the beach, consumed by his rage, feeling it power his muscles, drive him forward. Though it was still relatively early, the beach was full of the usual mass of bodies, and Michael stepped over and around them quickly, resisting the impulse to lash out and kick them. He headed away from the busiest bits, farther down the coast where he could have a bit of peace. Rather than calming him, the walk only increased his anger, pumping him up, and when he was alone, he took it out on a pile of sun loungers stacked up outside a posh hotel, kicking them hard, over and over, until he hurt his foot. Only then, breathless and in pain, did he stop, hurling himself onto the sand, curling up tight into a ball, as if to squeeze out his feelings. He didn't know how long he stayed there, only that he heard distant voices approaching: probably the police or a security patrol, who made a show of coming out on the weekends to protect the rich hotels' bits of beach.

Michael didn't want to go back to his hotel. It was still dark, and the thought of sitting alone in his room or on his balcony with nothing to look at bothered him. Besides, he was cautious now about his routine. Any break in it and something might happen – he ran the risk of falling asleep and missing his morning session with Georgie.

Georgie. Just the thought of her brought a smile to his face. The anger seemed to melt away almost immediately, the shock of his confrontation with the two women already a memory, hazy, as if a dream. He had done the right thing, he decided, bowing out of any fight. By doing so, he'd gained the upper hand, kept his dignity, refused to play up to what they wanted. He could see it all so much more clearly now, how obvious the game was with people like that: how much they invested in their little victories, how it took the humiliation and pain of someone else to make them feel good about themselves. Michael determined that never again would he give them the satisfaction, any of them. Oh, he might once have given off the air of someone to be messed with, to be taken advantage of, but that was all changing. He was learning not to be frightened any more. For there was nothing to be frightened of.

Take Georgie: beautiful, gentle Georgie, who deserved so much. She had got herself stuck with Rob, smarmy, full of himself, no better than a worm. He treated her like crap. She'd confessed as much – not in so many words, but then she was like that, too polite. And, of course, she was scared. All the things she wanted for herself but couldn't get, thanks to that bastard! Like spending her money on things *she* wanted. Making a different sort of life for herself: travelling, having fun, letting her hair down a bit. Freedom.

Only that morning, Georgie had let slip that Rob used to laugh at her when she'd suggested she'd like to get away from it all permanently, that she had fantasies of running away to an island like this one, to live on. Michael had barely been able to contain his excitement. How he longed to tell her of his plans for the little island in the middle of the bay. But he'd controlled himself, recognising that he had to tread carefully, follow Georgie's lead and not startle her into anything too soon. She had a lot on her plate. He knew he couldn't rush her. She needed gentle encouragement. So, instead, he had contented himself with casually remarking how he loved being able to sit outside in the mornings, how he enjoyed not having to wear such heavy clothes all the time like back home. That had been enough to set her off. She told him that a part of her wished she could really opt out, have the courage to follow her heart and live in a beautiful place, eat good food – have all the simple pleasures, the sun, the sea, and pursue her work at the same time.

'I know it's ridiculously naive and a total artist's fantasy, but it's not entirely impractical, not for me, anyway. I don't really have to be in a particular city – I can work anywhere, and I can always get on a plane and travel if I have to have a meeting or something. And it's cheap out here; we could live so much more cheaply. Even Rob – okay, it's a little more complicated for him because, at the moment, he has to physically be at the plant, but he's talked about doing freelance consultancy for ages. If he did that, he could be based anywhere, and just travel when he had to. There's no reason why he shouldn't have more freedom, work for himself. He doesn't have to be tied down if he doesn't want to be.'

Georgie had paused, her eyes doing that distant thing that told Michael she was drifting away. His heart had been beating fast, rendering him dry-mouthed and hesitant. But before he could speak, before he could tell her of his plans, she had started again, quietly – so quietly that he had had to strain to hear her.

'I sometimes wonder if I'm not the biggest coward going, d'you know that? Not in any obvious sense – not even in an important sense, but just . . . within myself. If I were *truly* brave, I'd go off and live the life I wanted, instead of whining about it from time to time and letting myself forget, instead of letting bills and jobs and friends, and just doing the normal bloody thing, get in the way. Not letting Rob talk me out of it, or not take me seriously. I'm a hopeless romantic, according to him. But I'm not so sure. I think I'm more of a coward, if anything. I'm a fucking coward.'

Michael had never heard her swear like that before, and he'd been shocked. The word sounded different coming from Georgie: it had a power and an explosiveness of feeling that he had never registered, not the way other people bandied it about. And though he didn't like hearing the word on her lips, didn't like the way her mouth twisted to pronounce it, he felt more sorry for her than ever. That Rob should laugh at her! Michael could see it in his mind's eye, could see the man all primped and preened, buff from the gym, building muscles that were all for vanity. Oh, Rob would have taken the piss all right, would have laughed in her face, told her she was an idiot – her, an idiot!

And though it made Michael's blood boil just thinking of it, something else struck him. For all Rob's posh talk, his easy, off-hand manner, his strutting about the place as if he owned it, when it came down to it, he was just like any of the scumbags Michael met on the streets of the town. It was all about power, feeling like top dog, bending everyone else around you to your will. And though Rob didn't need a posse of mates to back him up, and had somehow managed to be king of his little world without resorting to violence (as far as Michael knew), he recognised that the impulses were just the same. Rob was a bully. And if Michael wouldn't give in to a bunch of slags or lads who threatened him, then why on earth would he give in to Rob?

'When I was a kid, I was scared of my own shadow,' Michael had told her, wanting to lead by example. He had learned to be brave. He was still learning. So could she.

Georgie had smiled at him, that warm, kind smile that made her eyes crinkle at the edges. 'You are a treasure, Michael. Really, I should pay you, making you listen to me, on and on – all crap, the lot of it.'

'Fifty quid then!'

She'd grinned, punching him playfully, and he had amused her by feigning injury. Though it had still been on the tip of his tongue to tell her about the island, he'd held back, sensing that there was still a little way for her to go before he could reveal his plans. And Michael wasn't at all sure how best to broach the Rob issue. That sinking feeling had come again, that *he* had so far to go before his plans could become reality; so much to do, so many things to worry about. There was no way things would be ready for Georgie soon; it would probably take at least a year. Would she be happy, waiting about in an apartment on the mainland for a year? No matter. Time enough still to talk about it. They had so much to talk about.

Thinking of Georgie as he lay on the beach, curled tight, thinking of how he'd see her again in a few hours, Michael became peaceful. Cheered by the thought of their imminent meeting, he went and bought himself a coffee and a sandwich and returned to the beach, oblivious now to the crowds around him. In the darkness, their little island was invisible, but soon the sun would rise and present him with his vision of the future. He could wait. Michael was good at waiting.

~

Unusually, it had been Rob who'd had to drag Georgie out of bed, jolly her along and supervise her preparations. He had barely slept all night, but felt great when the alarm went off at seven. Georgie, on the other hand, was sound asleep and it took him a while to wake her, help her find her bearings. Rob was impatient to get them moving, excited about the day and night ahead.

'Don't bother with a shower – you can have a swim when we get there.'

The boat left at eight from the little harbour. They didn't need to take much, just one overnight bag, but Georgie was at sixes and sevens, clumsy in her movements. When she dropped her hairbrush for the third time in a row, Rob burst out laughing, and gently steered her to the edge of the bed.

'You tell me what you need. I'll do it!'

It was amazing how busy the town was at that early hour, full of people who hadn't yet finished their night's entertainment, wandering around, dazed, in the sunshine, the heat and the excess of alcohol making them slow and dopey.

'I can't imagine the hangovers,' Rob whispered to her as they passed a particularly dejected-looking group of men. 'They'll have been drinking all night.'

According to the guidebook, Strogili Island was less than two miles long, with no permanent inhabitants, but a luxury guesthouse which operated during the summer season. Facing straight out to sea, hidden from the mainland on the far side of the island, the guesthouse was a 'private idyll of relaxation', specialising in spa treatments and beauty therapies, with a top-class restaurant. Visitors could expect the highest quality of care, and would also have the opportunity to roam the little island that was full of rare plant species. Rob had called the guesthouse the night before, delighted to discover that a room was available, though he didn't dare tell Georgie how much it cost. It didn't matter. This was a treat, a necessary indulgence, and he booked it happily, taking down the details, noting how out of date the guidebook was, which had all the boat departure times wrong.

Once outside, Georgie perked up and bought them both coffees to take with them as they strolled through the town and down to the harbour. Her outburst of the previous evening seemed very far away, though she was still ashamed that she should have turned on Rob so violently. She couldn't really work out why she had snapped, but knew that something had been building for a long time.

'I'm glad we had it out,' Rob told her, squeezing her free hand. 'It's all over now anyway.' And it had cleared the air, even if she felt a little foolish for it.

'You know I didn't mean it, don't you? Any of the . . . horrible things I said.'

'Yes, I know, sweetheart. I know.'

Georgie had never seen Rob so simple, so sincere – so truly himself, at ease. When he had told her of his feelings for her the night before, she had believed him; more than that, she knew them, finally, to be true. And though what he had said to her was important – vital – more significant still was that she had privately confirmed her own feelings. Being with Rob the night earlier, showing herself at her worst, at her most vulnerable and childish, and seeing the result: knowing then that he loved her for all she was, Georgie had discovered, with a certainty that elated her, that she truly loved him too.

They were the only passengers on the boat, and it made them laugh with happiness, standing at the bow, the wind in their hair, the spray on their faces. Nothing could shake them now, not stress or strain or their own inner doubts or petty immaturities. No rules. They felt free and invincible as the boat chugged towards the little island, hazy in the middle of the bay. It was going to be a wonderful day and a wonderful night.

~

Michael had hardly noticed the time passing, even though he'd sat on the beach for far longer than usual. The only thing that made him realise how long he'd been there was bad stiffness in his legs and lower back when he finally stood up, ready for the walk to the hotel. He wobbled on his feet, slipping in the sand. Someone called out 'steady, mate!' A few of the bodies on the beach were fast asleep. Staff from the beachfront hotels would be along soon to clear them off, barking instructions in rapid Greek as they struggled to lay out their sun loungers and umbrellas.

As usual, the town was busy enough, with the late-night stragglers making their weary way home, or stopping for a desperate breakfast in a vain attempt to soak up some of the alcohol that was poisoning their systems. Michael got himself a pastry, warm from the oven, for the stroll back to the hotel. What had been a dreadful night had turned into a lovely morning. Staring out into the darkness on the beach, he had settled into an almost dreamlike state, untroubled by the noise around him, peaceful in his thoughts. And as the sun came up, revealing the distant beauty of his island, he had returned to his planning, contemplating the different colours he would paint each hut, working out the equipment he would need to furnish them, especially the little studio and the guest cottage. A long-forgotten memory had floated up, unbidden. Michael as a very little lad, holding someone's hand – he couldn't remember whose – watching as big men mixed cement, laid bricks one on top of the other. He himself was lifting a brick in both hands – it was heavy – and carefully laying it on the wet cement. Someone laughing, helping him press it down firmly. 'Perfectly level! He's got your eye, Jack!' A pat on the shoulder, more laughter. Michael had forgotten the experience and couldn't place it in his past. But he must have been with his father. Strange. He could count on one hand the number of times he'd seen his dad work.

Strolling through town, Michael stopped briefly to watch a group of workmen on a small building site, wedged between a nightclub and a bar. The men were stripped to their waists, and the structure they were working on was half-completed. No doubt it would be another bar or club, or possibly another off-licence. Large slabs of grey concrete formed the outline of the building, solid and imposing, creating an invitingly cool space within. The workmen moved quickly, efficiently, trying to get as much done as possible before the heat became insufferable. Michael watched, half-hoping they might trigger other memories from his childhood, though nothing came. But it pleased him to watch them work. It made him realise how, with a bit of practise, he would be able to do similar work himself; that, and a bit of engineering. He'd be more than capable. And how nice to be able to work outdoors rather than being stuck in a warehouse all day, stacking and packing and breaking his back for no real reward. At least on his island he'd have something to show for all his labour. Something of his own.

As he came to the top of the town, just before turning up the little road that would take him back to the hotel, Michael had a very strange sensation. A large crowd of lads, still high from the night before, was hanging around on the corner, clutching bottles of beer and shouting back and forth to a large group of girls in a similar state, who were gathered on the pavement opposite. This impromptu meat market, combined with passing traffic and other pedestrians, caused Michael a bit of difficulty in getting by, and it was while he was in the midst of the group of men, threading his way through as politely as he could (he had no desire for any sort of confrontation, not again), that he had the extraordinary sensation of hearing Georgie's laugh. He stopped for a moment, so vivid was the sound. He strained to see past the guys crowding round him, but at that very moment some of the girls chose to come and shout a little closer, and the net of men around him tightened in anticipation.

When he was eventually able to extricate himself, Michael knew it had only been an illusion. There was no chance that Georgie would be down in the town at that hour. But the incident didn't unsettle him; on the contrary, it made him smile. It was just another sign of the closeness of their connection and, besides, his mood had been dreamy. Yet how lovely that he should have heard her laugh, out of the blue like that! Halfway up the dirt track that wound through the little olive grove before the hotel, Michael stopped with a sudden pang. He wanted to bring her something – something special. It seemed fitting somehow, this morning, with all his plans bubbling and the way she'd talked yesterday about similar things, about wanting to get away. It would be the right thing to do, to make a gesture, make her an offering. Apart from their daily coffees, Michael had presented her with nothing since the guidebook.

He agonised for a brief moment, checking his watch. He didn't want to sacrifice one moment of their hour together, but if he were quick and didn't have a shower back in his room, he would have enough time. He strode back into the town, sidestepping the group of girls and lads, who were now congregated in the middle of the street. He nipped in to a little tourist shop a couple of feet along (they were all tourist shops down there) but he'd noticed this one on a couple of occasions. It had a better selection of jewellery than any of the others, and women flocked to it like a magnet.

Surprisingly, Michael didn't have to spend too long making a choice. The necklace leaped out at him at first glance, and he knew it would be perfect for Georgie. A little polished shell that reflected the light, it wasn't garish or ostentatious, and the chain itself was only a piece of leather, simple, pretty. Just a token, a little something. Nothing to make her feel uncomfortable (or, perhaps more importantly, to make Rob suspicious). Michael could tell her that he'd won it, maybe, or that he was buying gifts for people back home and had got one extra by mistake, if he were forced to justify himself. And they were all excuses she could use to Rob, should he happen to notice the new adornment, which Michael doubted. The guy barely gave Georgie a second glance when he came down each morning. Though it was wildly overpriced, Michael didn't bat an eyelid when he handed over his money. Hearing her voice so close to him on the street like that – it had been a sign. Couldn't you hear voices when you held your ear to a seashell? You were supposed to hear something. Perhaps Georgie would hear his voice, if she ever chose to listen.

It was still early when he arrived back at the hotel: his detour hadn't taken long. Georgie wasn't yet down, so Michael went upstairs to his room and showered, changing his clothes, putting the necklace carefully in his pocket, ready to be presented at the right moment. If it proved to be more awkward than he anticipated, if the mood wasn't quite right for such a gesture, or if his shyness kicked in again, he could always pat his pockets and pretend to find it quite by chance, pretend he'd forgotten all about it and offer it to her that way. But with any luck she would be receptive, after they'd talked for a while, after she'd told him more about her unhappiness. It would be a welcome salve, a reminder to her that things didn't have to be that way, that anything was possible. And that she was known, really known, and cherished for who she was.

Michael was excited. He sat on his balcony, waiting for Georgie to arrive. The elderly couple were settled in their usual spot in the shade; the woman had noticed Michael as he stepped out, and had waved politely. Michael was happy to wave back. There was no threat, nobody looked askance at him any more.

He watched as Les pottered about, radio on, preparing himself in his little hut for the day ahead. Funny – that first evening, Michael had thought that Les might be someone he could attach himself to, might be someone to hang out with, even spend a crazy night with out on the town. How naive he'd been! How limited his sense of possibility. It had taken Georgie to point out how inappropriate a man like Les was for Michael. And though it had been a bit of a shock at first, discovering how blind he was to people's real quality, how easily he could be taken in, Michael knew that it wouldn't happen again. Not with Georgie by his side. She had a proper sense of things, and she was teaching him. He would learn to see the world through her eyes.

His thoughts were running away with him. He wasn't alone on the beach now: he had to steady himself, calm himself down before she arrived. Things were delicate for her. He had to proceed with caution; nothing could be rushed. She was frightened, he could see that: frightened of Rob, who bullied her. Michael needed to imbue her with all his strength and courage, to reassure her, promise her that she would be all right – more than all right. She'd be free at last; free to be who she was, to follow her heart. Free to love the person she should love.

Bored with sitting on the balcony, Michael made his way downstairs. So what if he was there before her? It wasn't how they usually did it, but it wouldn't matter. They no longer had to be quite so formal. It's not like she would stop or hesitate if she saw him sitting there. It was nearly half-past nine, half an hour later than her usual arrival time. Perhaps she'd had difficulty sleeping – maybe she'd had indigestion. Michael knew she was prone to eating too much late at night, a habit she wanted to shake, particularly because she was trying out her new fitness regime in the pool. He smiled. There was nothing more charming than the day-in, day-out knowledge of all the little details of someone else's life – well, of Georgie's life. On the island, she'd be able to swim. It would have to be in the sea of course, but that was even better than a pool, wasn't it? She loved the sea – she'd told him that, lamenting the fact that the beach in the town was so packed with other tourists, and so dirty. She and Rob had taken a wander down there one afternoon early on in their stay, but had been put off by the loutishness. It was more relaxing staying by the pool.

Michael bought two coffees from Les. Georgie wouldn't be much longer, he was sure of it. He was offhand with Les, and Les was offhand with him, piqued by his lack of interest. Michael thought he heard him mutter something disparaging under his breath, but he couldn't be sure. Only when he was turning to leave, coffees in hand, did Les offer casually, 'You waiting for the lady?'

Michael hesitated, his pride rearing up, ready to bite if even vaguely ruffled. Before he could reply, Les continued. 'She gone, my friend. First thing this morning.'

Michael stared at him. Les's expression was innocently neutral, but Michael knew enough about men like him not to trust it. 'What are you talking about?' he asked, as evenly as he could.

'She and her husband, they leave first thing. I saw them walking down the path.'

It was on the tip of Michael's tongue to snap that Rob wasn't her husband, but he held back, determined not to bother rising to Les's pointed barb. So that was it then: an early morning stroll, a breakfast in town. It must have been Rob who hadn't slept, since he'd not be up at this hour otherwise. Poor Georgie, having to give up her morning to traipse about with him. But at least Michael was reassured, so much so that he almost laughed. When Les had said she'd gone, he had felt a blind panic rise in his throat, clouding his vision, taking him over. Maybe he'd got his dates wrong – maybe they were here only for a week and were heading home! Or maybe something had happened, something to send them away. How irrational, stupid. There was a perfectly simple explanation for it, he was sure. Georgie would be back soon, would make her apologies and tell him what had happened; take him aside perhaps, all casual, where Rob couldn't hear. She was probably agonising right that minute, wondering if she should have left word, left a note. Michael forgave her, of course – forgave her instantly.

Les was watching him, grinning broadly. Les had information. He'd seen them, had probably spoken to them that morning. He knew where they had gone and was clearly angling to tell, angling to have Michael wrest the information from him, make himself look desperate. Michael sipped his coffee, trying to look unconcerned.

'They've probably gone to the beach. She likes the beach. I was just down there myself. Makes a nice change.'

Les shook his head, enjoying his position of power. 'Nah, I don't think so.'

Michael shrugged, aware of Les's eyes on him, conscious of

the amusement in his tone.

'You're quite buddies with the lady, huh?' Les seemed to feel he'd gained ground; he was confident, cocky.

Michael sipped his drink, keeping his focus sharp. How right Georgie had been about him! He was nothing but a scumbag.

'You and she, always talking in the morning.'

'We have coffee together.'

'Yeah, yeah, I see that. But you like her, right? I see you like her. It's pretty clear, my man. It's no good, waiting around for a lady – especially married lady. Trust me – I know.'

'She's not married.' He sounded sharper than he'd intended, and he cursed himself inwardly for giving in so fast. Les's eyebrows shot up in amusement. Michael could feel the heat of a blush rising on his cheeks. 'She's nice, that's all. I like talking to her.'

'And looking at her. It's okay, man – she's hot stuff! I like to look at her too, though not as much as you.'

Before Michael could think of anything to say, Les turned away with a final smirk. He'd probably been waiting all week to have a go, get his revenge on Michael for having scorned him. And he hadn't even told him where they'd gone! If he even knew in the first place . . . .

Michael's hands tightened around the plastic cups. He must look like an idiot, holding two coffees, when no one was there to share them. Les started to whistle along with the radio, an insolent whistle, too loud, tuneless. Clearly Michael's foolishness had made his day. But Michael wouldn't allow it. He wasn't going to let this upstart, this pathetic, dirty-minded *shit* of a man, make him feel small. Georgie would never allow it. With what he hoped was an air of confidence, Michael turned on his heel, and settled down in his usual spot by the empty sun lounger where Georgie should have been. He wasn't going to be defeated so easily. If nothing else, his nights out had taught him that to give in was the worst thing you could do.

Michael knocked the rest of his coffee back quickly. He took it black with lots of sugar, loving the buzz that came so rapidly afterwards. Everything tingled, the caffeine masking his exhaustion, making him alert. Georgie's cup sat untouched by his feet, and he picked it up gently, almost reverently. She took her coffee with lots of milk and not much sugar. She loved sweet things, she'd confided, ruefully. If she could, she'd have sugar with everything. But it was terribly bad for her, she knew, and she had to be careful, had to watch herself, so she was strict with the sweetness of her coffees and her teas. Michael longed to tell her that, as far as he was concerned, she didn't have to worry about a thing. If she wanted to see fat – really fat – she should come downtown with him at night! Georgie was a slip of a girl really. She could double in size and she'd still look beautiful. Mind you, Michael supposed it was better in the long run that she wanted to take care of herself. Though he couldn't imagine it, if he encouraged her to let herself go, there might come a point in the distant future when she would be really old and out of shape, and that wouldn't be good. So it was better that she was a bit on-edge about her appearance now, just in case. Michael would dread ever having to have a conversation with her about anything like that.

He sipped her coffee cautiously. It was lukewarm and not sweet enough for him. He didn't like the way the milk diluted and changed the flavour of the coffee, but he was grateful for the opportunity to taste what Georgie tasted every morning. It made him feel closer to her somehow, and renewed his confidence. He shook his head, smiling. He'd been so silly to allow Les to get to him, even for a moment! He had so many things to practise, to get better at. It was strange. Never in his life had he felt such an urge for self-improvement. He had been resistant to anyone who'd tried to change him before – even small aspects of him, like what he read or didn't read, what he thought or didn't think – though he hadn't had much to complain about really, since neither his teachers nor his parents had cared enough to try more than once or twice. As long as he'd stayed quiet and out of sight, his parents hadn't bothered him. They hadn't bothered about much, really, both of them sunk in misery and defeat, spiralling out their dismal days in a haze of alcohol and medication. Michael had felt nothing when they died, one after the other like a pair of mice in a cage. He'd been seventeen then, and already out in the world on his own for a year. Apart from their neighbour, he was the only person at both their funerals. When the priest had asked Michael what he'd like him to say, he hadn't had the faintest idea. They'd done nothing with their lives. They'd offered nothing to their son. They were better off dead.

The pool was getting busier, the young families splashing about. The two English children, the brother and sister, had become progressively less well-mannered over the course of their holiday. They were slower to respond to their parents' instructions, more prone to bickering, louder than they'd dared be at the start. Michael would never have had the balls to be so forward at that age, answering back, sulking so obviously. But, then, he'd not had a sibling, never had anyone close in age to spur him on, give him courage. He had always thought he need-ed that support and encouragement; had told himself he'd been hard done by, and that was why things were as they were. Hence Patrick had been such a godsend, an eye-opener, showing him the ropes, giving him that little nudge. But look at him now: here he was, doing well for himself, and all alone. He didn't need Patrick at all out here. In fact, Michael dreaded to think how things might have gone had Patrick been with him. He would certainly not have met Georgie, not properly. So the whole thing must have happened for a reason. And though he was fleetingly sorry for Patrick's loss, he knew that it had had to happen; that somehow, this had all been planned.

Whatever Rob and Georgie were doing, they were taking their time about it. Probably Rob had insisted on something that suited him, and she had been forced to agree, no matter what she might feel about it. But it was getting close to eleven, and Michael was feeling the heat. If he didn't get out of the sun, he'd burn again. He was pleased, though. He had sat out for a good hour without feeling anyone's eyes on him, without feeling self-conscious or foolish. Even Les, who had come by once or twice on the pretext of clearing up rubbish, hadn't been able to ruffle him. That was Georgie's doing. She had made him that strong. Michael would thank her for it later.

Back in his room, he settled into bed. He figured that even if they did come back in the next hour or so, she wouldn't be alone anyway, so he might as well get some sleep, refresh himself a little. He set his alarm for mid-afternoon. And if Rob were down there with her later, he would go and say hello, regardless. He had already proved himself twice over that morning, acquitting himself admirably. Not even Rob could hold him back now. And though Michael was sorry to have lost his morning with Georgie, he was content with the promise of the afternoon ahead. A hushed and rapid explanation, her sorrowful apology, his reassurance. Giving her his gift. It would be lovely.

Almost immediately he fell into a dreamless sleep.

~

The guesthouse was far more impressive than Rob had expected. Calling it a guesthouse was deceptive. It was a luxury spa, catering to the wealthy housewives of the mainland, and the bronzed and buffed tourists who came from Italy and France. He had been entirely unprepared for its grandeur. Approaching the island, all that had been visible were some dilapidated old storage huts, a bit of an eyesore up close – concrete, ugly.

'Oh God – I hope we've not been conned,' Georgie joked, scanning the headland.

But the boat had veered around the side, hugging the shoreline, and to Rob's surprise, the island extended farther back than he'd imagined. Front on, it appeared to be a thin sliver of land, but as they circled the side, he saw that it was a trick of perspective. The front of the island was actually a small cliff, hiding a long flat plane behind, which sloped back a good few miles. The island must have been twice as wide as it was long, but you wouldn't know it until you got there. It pleased Rob, this discovery of the hidden section, almost as if he had created it himself. Georgie caught him grinning, and teased him. 'You look like the cat who got the cream.'

'I feel like it!' he told her, pulling her close against him.

A young woman, a member of staff, stood waiting to greet them on the little pier. A couple of small speedboats were tethered there, with the guesthouse's name written on the sides. 'We would have come and collected you,' the woman told them rather sternly. 'You should have left instructions when you made your booking.'

Georgie glanced at Rob, a little surprised. He shrugged it off. 'I didn't know. No one mentioned it.'

That wasn't true, and Rob felt momentarily awkward. He hadn't wanted to say anything, but the hotel's pick-up and drop-off service would have added another hundred to the bill, which was already going to be very steep, what with lunch and dinner and the spa treatments he wanted Georgie to take advantage of. Not that the money was in and of itself a big deal. Rob could have covered it with ease. He never worried about his finances, and rarely stinted on things he wanted. He had a good salary, and had an eye for opportunity, making canny choices with his employers, choosing to remain on a temporary contract rather than going permanent, meaning his salary was almost doubled.

So it was odd that now, with money in his pocket, and on holiday, Rob should have a sudden pang of mindfulness about expenditure, especially on something so trivial as a boat service. But it wasn't about the boat, or indeed, the money. It was to do with his new vision of himself – himself and Georgie – his vision for the future. Rob wanted to be responsible, wanted to think ahead, wisely.

For since he had decided that he was serious about spending his life with Georgie, a new sense of things had taken root in him: a practical sense, a sign of his commitment to the long term. Alongside his desire to make her happy, make her proud and fulfilled, he wanted to be able to provide for her. Not that he'd ever tell her; he knew how much she valued her financial capabilities and contributions. And it wasn't that he wanted some old-fashioned set-up, far from it. But he wanted, privately, to make sure she would always be comfortable, that she could always rely on him. He wanted to ease the burden of the vagaries of her employment, and free her up to take the work she wanted without fear. So while Rob had already spent hundreds on this little night away, he had decided that hiring a speedboat was a wasteful luxury, even as he knew it was a silly gesture. Georgie would laugh at him if she knew, and unpick his shaky logic in seconds. Not that it mattered. His had set his plans in motion, shifting his priorities without fuss. He would show her through his actions that he had a more mature approach. That was the way to build trust, create confidence. If he talked it all up now, if he over-presented things, she would find it difficult to believe him.

They checked in to their room, which turned out to be a proper suite. 'If there's anything you need, don't hesitate to ask.' Nothing was done by halves at this resort. They had a bathtub that doubled as a jacuzzi, and a gorgeous balcony looking out on the vast sea beyond. There was a personalised welcome package waiting for them on the bed, listing all the treatments available. It seemed the entire place was designed to cater to every desire. They could order whatever they liked from the kitchen at any hour of the day or night. If they wanted massages in the privacy of their room, that could be arranged – anything at all.

'It's a bit crazy, isn't it?' Georgie had said, delighted with it. 'It's like something out of the movies.'

Their day of pampering began with a leisurely breakfast served to them on the terrace downstairs. Other guests lounged around in white cotton bathrobes, taking small breaks between treatments to refuel. Rob and Georgie were the youngest guests there by at least a decade. The other clients all had that slightly leathery, well-kept Mediterranean look to them. Their skin glowed like burnished mahogany, and they had the ease and equanimity of the exceptionally well tended to.

'They all look like playboys, don't they? Or extras in a Fellini film,' Georgie whispered, almost alarmed, watching a group of plump middle-aged men chatting genially over their fresh fruit. 'And the women. God. They take care of themselves all right, don't they? Not a wrinkle among them. Botox or something – has to be, doesn't it?'

Rob knew Georgie felt a little uncomfortable, even as she relished the luxury. She wasn't one for standing on too much ceremony, yet she couldn't bear to feel out of place. He reached over the table and took her hand. 'This is for us, sweetheart. We're here to enjoy ourselves, and that's that. Bugger the lot of them!'

She smiled, grateful for his understanding, and cheered up immensely when the waitress placed a steaming plate of pancakes in front of her. 'I can't resist,' she'd said, when she had scanned the menu, and Rob had encouraged her. To see her excited by something so small was a delight. 'I'll swim it off later,' she assured him. 'I'm doing very well with that.'

'You don't even have to think about it, you know,' he'd told her, sincerely. 'I wish you wouldn't torment yourself with all that stuff.'

'So you'd like me old and fat then?'

'I'd like you however you looked. So just stop worrying, okay? At least for today. You're beautiful – always have been, always will be. So please relax. Relax and enjoy, my love. That's all I ask.'

They spent the day separately. Georgie threw herself into the spirit of the place, as Rob wanted, and booked herself in for no less than five different treatments: massage, facial, body scrub and wrap, manicure and pedicure. Rob booked in for two: a full body massage, which turned out to be as good as advertised, and a special Indian head treatment later in the afternoon, designed to 'soothe the mind and invigorate the senses', a somewhat contradictory approach that amused him enough on paper for him to give it a go. In between, Rob did as the others, and hung out on the terrace in his robe. He had his book with him, but didn't get much reading done. He was happy to just sit, gazing at the azure ocean, utterly content with his lot.

They met in their bedroom at the end of the afternoon. Georgie was glowing from all the attention, and showed off her beautifully polished hands and feet, made him feel the softness of her skin post-scrub, girlish with enthusiasm. He happily obeyed, pulling her onto the vast bed, the smell of scented oil on her skin invigorating him far more than any head massage. They bathed together afterwards in their jacuzzi, cracking open the bottle of complimentary champagne that Rob had discovered in their minibar, giggling, tipsy, pressing up against the jet streams.

At dinner, they amused themselves to the point of hysteria, gawping at the other guests who were decked out in all their finery. Most of the women wore garish prints and heavy, ugly jewellery – so ugly that it had to be hugely expensive. There was a barely disguised air of decadence amongst their fellow guests, who exchanged meaningful glances and flirted outrageously with people who weren't their partners. Rob reckoned that they were probably staying in the dirtiest hotel in Europe, suggesting that most of the couples would wife-swap later that evening. He proposed that he offer up Georgie for the night, in return for a wad of cash or, failing that, the loan of a yacht.

'That's all I'm worth, is it? Not even a full yacht – just the loan of one!'

'I'd ask for a dinghy, darling, but I don't think they'd know what that was.'

There was a path leading down from the terrace to the beach below, tastefully lit with fairy lights and torches. Recklessly, they had ordered a second bottle of wine, and, with the waiter's beaming permission (nothing was off-limits here), took it with them to have on the shore. No one else was there. Taking off their shoes, they waded into the warm sea, holding hands, feeling the light breeze on their faces. They were quieter now, their earlier energy spent a little, but both profoundly happy. So when Rob turned to Georgie, standing in the ocean, his trousers rolled, the hem of her dress splashed with water; when he turned, still holding her hand, and asked her if she would marry him, it seemed almost inevitable that she should accept. And she did, with a sudden, inadvertent cry of pleasure, of surprise.

'Oh, Rob. Yes! Yes – I want to – I really want to.'

He scanned her face. There was nothing there to throw him or make him falter even for a moment. Without warning, his eyes filled with tears. She threw her arms around him, causing them to stumble, and in an instant they toppled over into the sea. Laughing, gasping for breath, they grabbed for one another, pulling each other to the shore, collapsing in a sodden heap on the beach.

'There – you see? Even God and nature agree. We've just been baptised into our new life.'

Rob couldn't argue with her logic. He pressed his mouth to hers in a salty kiss, and praised whatever or whomever it was that had blessed him. He would be forever grateful.

~

When Michael awoke at half-past three in the afternoon, it was to a churning feeling in his gut, but he sensed that it was no physical sickness. With a flash of realisation, he knew that Georgie wouldn't be back at all that day. She was gone, off with that man, apparently without a second thought. And she hadn't said a word. Even though Michael was suddenly certain that she had known long in advance that she'd be away all day.

He deliberately took his time getting up, going to the bathroom, delaying the moment when he would step out onto the balcony and prove himself correct. He wanted to preserve even the smallest shred of hope for as long as possible. It was like a little game – Michael against the world – and it was a game that he would win, whatever happened. Let it be a welcome, joyous surprise should he be proven wrong, should Georgie be down there. And should if he was proven right, he'd have won, anyway.

But when he ran out of things to delay him, he had to step outside, in to the bright sunlight, blinking, hoping it would take a while for his eyes to adjust. It took seconds. Georgie was not down below, as he had known she wouldn't be. Michael had won, but it brought him no satisfaction. Grimly, he stood on his balcony in full view – no hiding for him now – and stared down at the pool. The usual suspects were there, plus a couple of glaringly pale new arrivals – couples, mainly – who held no interest for him. Across the way, Georgie's balcony door was closed, the curtains drawn. The shutters on the bedroom window were closed as well. Though it was possible that she had retreated for one of her afternoon naps, Michael was certain that she wasn't there and hadn't been there all day.

He was exhausted, but he would not contemplate sleep again. With a bitter laugh he recalled how only a few short hours ago he'd settled down happily, convinced of Georgie's imminent return. It didn't seem possible that he should have been so naive! He'd become too cocky, too sure of himself. Things had been going too well. He had forgotten to doubt, going too far the other way, taking things for granted. Without warning, his mother's voice rang in his ears. *You're a fool, Michael, if you think people do what they say they're going to do. You're a bigger fool than I thought.* She was right. And now he had to face it: face the results of his pathetic hopefulness, his childish faith. His over-confidence. No one could be relied on: not his parents, not Patrick, not Georgie . . . .

Michael swallowed back a sob. He had done everything wrong, he saw that clearly. He had tried to play the game without having the first idea what the rules were. Pathetic! Who was he trying to kid? Too nice, that was his problem. He was always too nice, too easy to take advantage of. People saw through him immediately, saw him for the soft touch he really was. A wave of self-pity engulfed him and he turned back from the balcony into the coolness of the kitchen. And as he wept, he knew that he deserved it, knew that he was being punished correctly for his idiocy. His crime was unforgivable: he'd let himself believe. Had he not learned his lesson? Would he ever learn his lesson?

When the rawness of his grief began to ease, and he became aware of his surroundings again, Michael noticed with surprise that his phone had beeped through a message. He fumbled with it, clumsy. Though he'd had the mobile for some years, he very rarely used it. Nobody ever called him – only work, to rearrange the odd shift, and Patrick sometimes, when he was bored and wanted some attention. Michael felt a small surge of hope rise in his breast as he pressed the button to reveal the identity of the sender. It might be Georgie – had he given her his number? He didn't think so, but perhaps he had. Yet almost instantly, as he felt hope rise, he quashed it. Something steely took control of him: a stern, strong voice from within that he didn't recognise at first. What had he just been crying about, like the big baby he was? *Don't be a fool. See the world clearly. You understand the situation. Stop playing games. Stop kidding yourself.* It took Michael a moment or two to register that the voice, the authoritative voice, was not his mother's. It was his own.

And within seconds, he was grateful for the sternness and clarity: his cold and unsentimental sense of things. For, sure enough, the message was not from Georgie but from Patrick. It was the first Michael had heard from him since he'd left him at the airport. *Funeral yesterday,* the message read. *Lots of family around. Total nightmare. Loads of shit to sort. How's the holiday? What you been doing? Want to hear everything. You'd better be having some fun for me. I could do with it.*

Though the thoughts were barely formulating, were semi-incoherent, Michael suddenly knew what he had to do. His grief had rattled him, stopped him thinking clearly. Of course

Georgie wouldn't text him. Rob would never allow it. Michael had no right to blame her for her silence, for her disappearance. It had nothing to do with her; she had no say over things. She hadn't betrayed him, not of her own volition. He had to get a grip – had to separate the truth from his own messy feelings. Otherwise, he'd be in trouble.

There had been so many times in Michael's life when moments like this had arrived: moments in which he had to make a choice, take decisive action. Either he had been unable to recognise them before, or had been too scared to do anything. Not any more. Not this time. Because there was more at stake this time than just his own personal happiness. There was Georgie to think of, and clearly she was in more trouble than Michael had realised. She was like a hunted animal – vulnerable, easily got at. Michael saw her cowering in front of Rob, forced against her will, her fragile strength destroyed. How easy it might have been to overlook how much she needed him. How she was relying on him to do what needed to be done. He would not let her down. He *must* not let her down.

Taking an ice-cold bottle of beer from the fridge, Michael went into the bedroom, picking up the small pad of hotel notepaper and a pencil from the top of the bedside locker. Returning to the sitting room, he settled himself on the sofa, placing the beer, pad and pencil carefully on the coffee table before him. He took a moment to gauge his state, to breathe deeply, relax. But he was already steady and calm. When he was ready, he picked up the phone and, instead of replying to the text, he dialled Patrick's number. In a voice that he barely recognised as his own, he spoke.

'Patrick. Hi. All right? Been meaning to give you a ring . . . .
Yeah. See how you're getting on. Yeah . . . ? Shit. Well, it's funny,
actually, there *was* something I wanted to ask you . . . . You know
this island pretty well, right?'

~

It was very late by the time they returned to the Hotel
Bougainvillea (Georgie never failing to sing the name, rather
than say it), which had come, after their night away, to feel like
home. They had spent a second full day on the island, being
pampered, though, that day, they managed to contrive being
together as much as possible: getting massages side-by-side,
Georgie eventually convincing Rob to take a mud bath with her.
Rob had offered to get them a second overnight, but she had
declined. It had been wonderful, two full days and a night, but
there was a limit to the amount of spa treatments she would
enjoy, and besides, they had a perfectly good hotel back on the
mainland. Anyway, didn't Rob want to seal the deal as it were,
and start looking for a ring? Plenty of jewellery stores on the
proper island – some high-end ones, too, so he mustn't think
he'd get away with any old tat! They should plan a shopping
expedition.

They had taken the boat back at around six, Rob having
been forced to use the guesthouse speedboat, unable to feign
ignorance of it a second time. Hungry, they stayed in town for

dinner, rather than going back to the hotel first, and it had turned in to an unexpectedly social evening. Dining at their little taverna were another young couple, and the man, Keith, vaguely knew Rob through mutual friends – they'd met once or twice before. Rob and Georgie joined them for the meal, which went on into the night, with drinks afterwards, all of them getting on like a house on fire, toasting Rob and Georgie's engagement.

It was a sudden and unexpected pleasure to reconnect with the world from home. It reminded them that their ordinary lives were now extraordinary, made significant by their decision. Happiness and planning and parties and celebrations awaited them upon their return, evenings with friends and family, eager to share in their joy. So it was well after three in the morning when they finally stumbled back to their room, clutching their overnight bags, desperately trying to be quiet but giggling like kids, tipsy and light-headed. They tore at one another's clothes, their passion heightened by the intensity of the evening – the wine, the pleasure they'd taken in the company of others, and their now public and publicly celebrated status as fiancés.

Rob woke to an empty bed, and it took him a moment or two to reaccustom himself to his surroundings. Georgie had clearly slipped effortlessly back into her old routine and was probably down at the pool, waiting for him. Rob didn't know how she did it, for no matter how little sleep she'd had the night before, she always got up and out. He had slept far later than usual, even for him. It was nearly lunchtime, and his stomach growled with hunger.

Virginia Gilbert

Rummaging around in their little kitchen, he saw that they were low on supplies and would need to do a supermarket run, probably the last one they'd make before returning home. They had three days left. Stepping out on to the balcony, Rob stretched and yawned, feeling the heat of the sun penetrate him, letting it prolong his sleepiness, keep him slow and relaxed. Apart from his grumbling stomach, which begged for breakfast, he had never felt so good in his life: strong, healthy, well rested, clear-headed. And loved. The warmth and security of that knowledge flooded him with happiness. He smiled broadly at the world below; ready to be of service – to love back in return – and do whatever Georgie wanted for the rest of the week.

Her towel and book were on the sun lounger, but Georgie herself was not. Rob scanned the poolside. It was busy; new arrivals, instantly recognisable thanks to the whiteness of their skin, were laid out next to the old hands, who were now almost as dark as locals. The English family was there, as always, the kids wrestling with large inflatable lilos in the pool. The family with toddlers was also there, sitting in the shade of their umbrella. The elderly couple sat in state. She was reading, her husband dozing. Les was in his hut, busy with lunchtime orders. Rob watched from his sly vantage-point, amused to see Les drop a freshly made sandwich on the floor behind the bar and surreptitiously put it back on the plate.

Georgie must have gone to do the shopping, he thought. Typical Georgie: mindful, taking care of them both. Rob would do more of that from now on. He would be the one to notice when they were running low; be the one to think ahead. She wouldn't have to shoulder any burden alone, no matter how minor, how domestic. Never again would he be blind to the small actions that made all the difference – or indeed, the bigger ones that really counted. After showering quickly, Rob dressed and grabbed his wallet and key. He'd walk down and meet her on the way back from the supermarket, give her a hand up the hill, surprise her, show her that he recognised her thoughtfulness and wanted to match it. Show her that this was the way it would be from now on.

Strolling around the pool, nodding a hello to the familiar faces of the staff and guests as he passed, Rob reckoned that he and Georgie should make plans for shopping for a ring. He'd look in the guidebook after lunch for good boutique suggestions. If necessary, they could hire a car for a day and head to the capital. Though it wasn't vital that they buy it abroad, Rob felt it would be lovely if the ring Georgie was to wear for the next God knew how many years came attached with memories of Greece, memories of this turning point in their lives. He wanted the ring to be extra special.

The supermarket was busy with shoppers, locals on their lunch-break, buying supplies before the place shut for siesta. Though inconvenient for the tourists, the strict adherence to siesta time was touchingly impressive to him. He loved the rhythm of life in hot countries. The early starts (though he himself wasn't able to manage them) to take advantage of the relative cool, the sleepy afternoons, the long nights. It was a civilised rhythm, he felt, geared to what the human body needed, to what nature dictated, not thoughtlessly given over to the demands of the industrial machine, though Rob knew that if he lived in a climate where siestas were taken, he'd get half as much work done. Of course, in theory, the working day was split: one was supposed to work through into the night, stopping at around eight or nine, so that if you totalled up the hours worked in the morning and the hours worked in the evening, it made up a full day. But Rob knew he'd give in far too easily to temptation – would more than likely wake after an afternoon sleep and not be able to get back to things. It might suit him, working only half-days, taking a more relaxed attitude to his career; sacrificing extreme ambition for simple, happy days. But then, Rob reasoned, perhaps that was why so many of the hotter countries were so poor and underachieving, with shaky infrastructures and industries. It was all to do with siesta culture. He'd make a bet that the ancient Greeks or Romans hadn't shut down their empires every afternoon because it was a bit too hot.

Rob took his time wandering the aisles, certain that he'd spot Georgie at any moment. With a belated pang of guilt, he realised that he hadn't actually made it to the supermarket before, and now that he had, he found himself intrigued at the range of different products available. Georgie had told him it was very well stocked (one excuse for why it always took her so long), and Rob was amazed at the variety on offer. Georgie was the self-designated 'foodie' in their relationship – hence she was more than likely lingering somewhere, poring over a delicacy. She loved foreign supermarkets, an obsession that Rob had never quite understood. But as he was becoming more in tune with his wife-to-be, more interested in her habits, her tastes, he found himself picking up a couple of bits and pieces – olives and stuffed vine leaves and a tin of what he hoped was aubergine in oil – excited suddenly by the prospect of something new to try. Georgie had ended up buying a spare bag when they'd been in Sardinia, to stock up on food to take back home. They should do the same here.

Rob couldn't see her at the checkout. Annoyingly, he had left his mobile back in the room. It was possible that she had gone all the way into town – there was a fresh fruit stand on the main strip that she'd been to once or twice for watermelon – or perhaps he'd just not spotted her in the shop soon enough and she was already halfway back to the hotel. Either way, Rob didn't want her to arrive in their room and find him away without a word, so he paid for his few purchases quickly and walked briskly back.

But Georgie wasn't by the pool and she wasn't in the room – nor were there signs that she'd been and gone out again. She must be downtown then, to get her watermelon. Rob retrieved his phone and texted her, asking her to let him know where she was, so he could join and give her hand with the shopping. Perhaps she had been distracted by some of the jewellery stores. Rob added humorously that she was not to make a purchase without consulting him.

His hunger was really gnawing at him. If Rob didn't eat with mechanical regularity every couple of hours or so, he crashed, becoming cranky and disorientated, liable to make poor decisions or procrastinate over simple things. Nothing he had bought in the supermarket was suitable for breakfast. Slightly reluctant, remembering the dubious attention to hygiene Les had shown with some hapless guest's sandwich, Rob strolled down to the poolside hut and ordered one of his own, keeping a close eye as it was prepared.

The elderly woman who sat reading with her husband all day in the shade came up to the bar as Rob was waiting. Her husband was fast asleep, his book still open on his lap. Rob nodded to her politely. Though they had seen one another every day for nearly ten days, they had yet to exchange a word. In a strong, strident voice, utterly at odds with her fragile, decorous appearance, the woman ordered a sandwich and a coffee, and stood next to Rob, waiting for Les to bring the food. It amused Rob to see how different she suddenly was in person to what he had imagined. He'd observed the couple a little over the days, for they had reminded him of his grandparents – quiet, mild. But from the sound of the woman, he'd been entirely wrong.

'Are you having a nice time?' Rob asked her pleasantly. She had been looking at him, clearly hoping for a chat. To his surprise, she merely shrugged, half-rolling her eyes, as if he'd asked her something foolish.

'It's not very *clean*, is it? It's supposed to be four star!' Her tone was petulant, whiny. So she's a moaner, Rob thought, and almost laughed. To think she'd looked so placid, so sweet, sitting there day after day in the shade with her husband. 'Our room. The tour operator told us they would clean the rooms every second day but I don't think they've been in more than twice since we've been here! Lazy. That's what they are. Lazy and dirty.'

Thankfully, Les was ready with the woman's food, serving

her before Rob, even though he'd placed his order first. The men exchanged brief glances, both aware that she was a difficult sort. She inspected the plate closely, suspicious.

'No mayonnaise this time? You swamped it yesterday – it was inedible.'

'No, Madam, no mayonnaise. Just as you asked.' Les spoke politely, quietly, unwilling to be drawn in. Without a thank you, the woman turned away, pausing only to repeat to Rob her issues with the hotel cleanliness. 'You should speak to them. We all should. It's disgusting!'

Rob nodded vaguely, not in the least in agreement with her, and turned his back. He watched as Les turned to make his sandwich, and suddenly felt a pang of sympathy for the man. Having to deal all day with rude, obstinate people, being treated like shit most of the time, especially by those who looked so decent. Rob tipped him generously and stayed at the bar to eat, certain that Georgie would be back at any moment and probably reproach him for buying his lunch there. She didn't like Les – thought he was slimy. Poor guy, Rob thought. Hitting on the ladies was probably the only fleeting bit of enjoyment he got out of his day.

'Is okay?' Les gestured to the sandwich Rob was already halfway through.

He nodded, his mouth full. 'Delicious. Thanks.'

Les took the compliment, grateful. 'You want a beer? On the house for you. Because you had to wait,' he added, apologetically.

Rob knew the real reason. Les wanted a chat, wanted to relieve the boredom and reassert his status, after his display of

Virginia Gilbert

servility in front of the old woman. But Rob had drunk too much the night before, and knew if he indulged again the day would be lost.

'No, thanks. No beer. Coffee would be great, though.'

Les shrugged. These foreign guys, they made so much of their capacity to handle booze, but they were pussies really. Still, he made them both a coffee and came out front to join Rob, leaning next to him against the bar, surveying the poolside.

'How much longer you here?' Les asked.

'We go back Thursday.'

'You've had a good time?'

'Oh yes. Wonderful. We'll be sorry to leave.'

One of the English kids hurled himself into the pool with a loud shriek. 'Thomas, don't *do* that!' His father's voice was plaintive, weary. Thomas ignored him, splashing about happily.

Les tutted. 'Too many kids this year.'

Rob smiled. 'They're not so bad. Pretty harmless. I was much worse at their age.'

Les glanced at him, curious. Rob didn't seem the sort to indulge children. 'You got kids?' he asked.

'No, not yet. But we'd like to. In a couple of years, maybe. If Georgie – if my wife's up for it!'

Rob felt a sudden surge of pride in the use of the word. He was going to have a wife! He laughed at his incredulity and sense of good fortune. Georgie was going to be his wife. He loved the proprietary nature of the word, loved hearing it roll off his lips. He never thought he'd feel such happiness at the thought of being married.

Les smiled. 'She's sleeping late today, your lady. Did you keep her up last night?' He winked. If Rob hadn't been holding his coffee, he was certain Les would have nudged him. He sensed the man's desire for locker-talk, realising suddenly why Georgie disliked him so. It *was* a bit sleazy, even a bit creepy, the way everything had to have a double meaning, laden with innuendo.

Rob stood up straight, preparing to leave. 'She's out. Up early, as usual.' He wanted to defend Georgie's honour, make sure Les knew she was not someone he could joke about, even lightly.

'Oh. Yeah, that's right. She was down here early like usual. But I thought she must have gone back to bed.'

Les went around behind the bar, recognising that the conversation was a non-starter. Rob was puzzled.

'What do you mean? She didn't stay here?'

'No, man, only for a bit, I think. Half-an-hour maybe. You know, she sits out usually all morning – has a coffee with that guy, you know – the big guy. She's very friendly, your wife.' It was a pointed dig, but Rob chose to ignore it. He was baffled. How long had Georgie been gone?

'So what – she didn't have coffee this morning? She didn't stay by the pool?'

Now it was Les's turn to look surprised. 'No. Like I say – she was here. She talked with the guy a little. They have their coffee like usual. But I had to go inside for stupid staff meeting, pain in the ass. When I come back, she not here.'

'What about him – Michael? Was he here?'

'I dunno, man. I'm working. I make the coffees, make the sandwiches! I dunno.'

There was a defensiveness to Les's tone that sent a sudden prickle of fear down Rob's spine. The man was talking as though something had happened, as though something untoward had occurred – something that he didn't want to get involved with. Rob took out his phone. Georgie hadn't replied to his text message; indeed, he'd forgotten all about it until this moment. He rang her. It went straight through to voice mail. His heart started to beat faster. Georgie never turned off her phone. She was almost superstitious about it, even keeping it on during flights, 'just in case'. It was a long-standing joke between them, because more often than not her mother would ring, at the most inappropriate moments.

Rob's stomach clenched. He tried to calm his thoughts: thoughts that were racing ahead of him in panic. Her battery was dead, that was probably it. She'd gone into town to do some shopping, had lost track of time . . . . No. That was entirely unlike her. Georgie wouldn't do that, not without telling him.

Les was studiously ignoring him, refusing to be drawn in. Rob suddenly twigged the reason for his discomfort. He must think there's some affair going on or something. He thinks Georgie's off with Michael – thinks they're running around behind my back. A sudden blaze of anger shot through Rob, directed at Les. As though Georgie would go *near* a man like that. That he could even *think* she'd lower herself. He turned to Les.

'So let me get this straight. Georgie – my wife—,' Rob

stressed the word, defiant, '—was here this morning, early, but you haven't seen her since, what? Ten? Ten-thirty?'

'Yeah, I guess. Ten. Yeah – ten. I was back here after the meeting.'

It was nearly two o'clock. Four hours. Where the hell had she been for four hours?

~

It had been so easy when it came down to it. All that Michael did now surprised him: not so much the actions themselves, but the ease with which he accomplished them. Everything was changing, and in so swift a time. And every step was simple. What had he been so worried about all this time? Spending all his adult life wondering how other people did it, how they managed, how impossible it all appeared. Up until now, Michael's greatest personal achievements had been passing his driving test and owning a car, renting a room and paying the bills, and holding down his job. They had been the huge hurdles, the major tests of character for him. To think he had once taken such pathetic pride in these small badges of his maturity! That they had been the sum total of his participation in the adult world. Before, Michael had marvelled at other people – how they did it, how they made it seem so effortless, all the things that normal people did. Buying a house, having a family, doing things with friends – even booking a holiday. He'd let Patrick take care of all that. But now Michael knew how it felt to be in charge, confident, not cowed by authority – any authority, from a shop-keeper to a bank teller to a tax inspector. What had he been so scared of all this time? It had all been so easy. Nobody questioned him, nobody told him off. He had only had to assert himself in the smallest way. People respected him, didn't look twice. That was all it had taken. It was a revelation.

The first thing had been the hiring of a car. There were three car rental places on the main drag, and Michael chose the one farthest away from the hotel, towards the far end of town, away from the beach. He had steeled himself for trouble, but miracu-lously he had brought everything he needed on his first go: driv-ing licence, cash. No trouble, no bother. He only needed it for a couple of days, just to do a bit of sightseeing, he told the bored receptionist, who had clearly wanted to be elsewhere. Michael had been amazed at his inventiveness – the little story he'd spun so casually, just dropped in to the conversation.

'It's my girlfriend really. She loves history, always got her nose in a guidebook. Wants to see everything. Can't sit still for a moment.'

The receptionist had barely nodded. Her mobile kept beep-ing text messages. Perhaps she was having a row with a boyfriend, for each time the phone sounded, she reached instinctively for it, a worried expression on her face. But then she would remember that she was dealing with a customer, and she'd move her hovering hand back to her keyboard. Michael was grateful for her distraction. She didn't ask him any ques-tions.

The car he was given was pretty banged up, but he didn't

care. All the better really. The receptionist had been unapologetic.

'Height of season. Most cars are taken. You should have booked earlier.'

But not even a hint of reproach could sway his mood. The woman carefully checked the vehicle with him. It took Michael a moment to figure out what she was doing (he hadn't wanted to ask), but apparently they had to go around the car and note down each bit of damage, each dent and scrape, so that when he returned it, she could tell if he'd done damage of his own. The whole process rather amused him, and he became quite involved once he understood what was going on, pointing out minute details, really tiny little scratches that she dutifully wrote down, grunting with impatience.

It took him a little while to get used to driving on the wrong side with everything in the car the opposite way around. Leaving the car rental place, getting on the main road, Michael realised for the first time how appalling the Greek drivers were. Partly it was because the roads were very bad, full of potholes and dips which drivers swerved around at the last minute. Even still, the Greeks were unnecessarily aggressive, ignoring common courtesies, casually breaking speed limits. Yet far from being frightening or annoying, it suited Michael. He had always been a bit over-cautious when it came to driving, and the other drivers' recklessness filled him with a sense of freedom. No point being the only fool to obey the rules when everyone else broke them with such abandon.

The rental place had given him a map with the car and,

though he stumbled over the place-names, he traced his route easily enough. It was a long drive, nearly two hours, though he lost his way once or twice. Closer to an hour and forty without all the wrong turns; an hour and a half if there was no traffic. Easy. Michael drove back without a hitch, getting more and more used to following the unfamiliar road signs and markings, taking in his surroundings as much as possible so as to be able to drive the route smoothly when he had to do it again.

He left the car at the supermarket. It wasn't like the car parks back home which closed when the shop did, or which kept a strict eye on people, making sure they were 'customers only'. Here, vehicles could apparently stay for as long as they liked. There were no security guards or cameras. Michael knew the car would be safe overnight. No one would look twice at it. The only thing he did before leaving was to remove the sticker on the front windshield with the car rental company's name on it. With that gone, it looked like any local person's car.

The rest of the evening was spent in careful preparation. No distractions. He heard Rob and Georgie come in very late, giggling and hushing one another theatrically. Though he felt a little flutter upon hearing her, Michael hadn't bothered to go on to the balcony to look. He didn't want to see anything. Didn't need to. Things were different now. He was in charge. He wasn't going to rely on a flimsy routine, wasn't going to put his faith in that any more. It would be foolish, after everything that had happened. And in light of everything that *would* happen. For there was an unstoppable momentum now, a momentum that Michael was creating.

~

By four o'clock, Rob was frantic. He had just spent the worst two hours of his life. After speaking with Les, he had left the poolside bar quickly, going back up to their room, suddenly fixed on the idea that Georgie might be there; that she might have snuck up, unnoticed by him while he was talking; or worse, that she might have been there all the time – stuck, hurt, ill. It made no sense and, of course, the room had been empty. Without thinking, Rob had rummaged through her belongings, searching for – for what? A clue? What was he looking for? Could she be having an affair? Was that really it? Catching himself midway through emptying her drawer, he recognised the ludicrousness of his actions. He was out of control, and it had happened so suddenly. He had to calm down, not panic; think things through.

Michael. He had been with her that morning down by the pool, as usual. Rob pounded on the door to Michael's room. If he wasn't there, Rob knew he'd have all the answers he needed. His thoughts ran wild, uncensored. He knew there was something – he'd always known, right from the start. This shambling, lumpen guy, so sweet, so innocent. Too good to be true. His instincts had told him so. Why in God's name had he not listened to them properly, not forced Georgie to sense them too? Forbidden her to have any contact with him, told her to stay away – even that first night when she was so determined to be nice, show Rob how good she was to adopt the lonely creature. Oh, he'd pay for it – Rob would make him fucking pay . . . .

'Rob. Hey!'

Michael stood in his doorway, in a T-shirt and boxer shorts, rubbing his head, dishevelled, clearly only just awake. His state of undress and baffled disorientation threw Rob and, at the same time, made his stomach churn with a ripple of disgust. There was something so unprepossessing about the man, the size of him, the slightly sweaty, clammy skin.

'Is everything okay?'

Michael's concern sounded genuine.

'Georgie's gone,' Rob told him curtly. 'She's been missing since this morning. No one's seen her since.'

Michael shook his head, not understanding. 'Sorry, Rob – what do you mean?'

'Can I come in?' Rob didn't wait for a response but pushed past him, recoiling inwardly at the brief physical contact as he stepped into the kitchen-cum-living-room, the mirror reverse of his and Georgie's. It was dark inside, curtains shut.

'Rob, what's going on? What's the trouble?' Michael spoke gently. Rob could well imagine that that was the tone he used each morning with Georgie: solicitude, kindliness, winning her over so effortlessly. The fucking bastard.

'Do you know where she is? Have you seen her?'

Michael shook his head, apparently still unsure as to what was happening. He play-acts beautifully, thought Rob. Much more skilled than I'd have given him credit for. A little warning voice told him not to be too hasty, not to judge too fast, but he ignored it.

'Not since this morning. We had a natter, as usual, when she was down by the pool.'

'But you left early, right? Normally you stay with her till I come down.' It sounded strange to Rob's ears, giving voice to a daily routine that all had participated in but none had spoken about, except in jest. Perhaps if they had made it more concrete, examined it more closely . . . .

'I was knackered. The only reason I'm down there in the mornings is 'cos I haven't gone to bed yet. I go out at night, y'know? I'm young, I'm single – that's what I do.'

Rob noted the careful defensiveness in Michael's tone. He was sculpting his persona, right there, in front of Rob, practising it for later, for when he'd have to explain himself to the police. Because by God he was going to talk to the police if Georgie didn't show up.

'By the time I get back at around nine, everyone's already up, starting their day. So I have a cup of coffee, chat with Georgie, if she's there, then I come up to bed. I'm only just up!'

'But today was different. You didn't stay long. Normally you stay longer.'

If Michael was surprised that Rob had this information about his movements, he didn't show it.

'I told you, Rob, I was exhausted; I couldn't keep my eyes open. It was quite a big night last night.' He smiled, open, inviolable. 'Georgie was laughing at me this morning – said I was wearing myself out with all the shenanigans downtown. She told me to go to bed. I must have been terrible company.'

She could be here. She could be here right now, right at this moment – hidden somewhere, tied-up, drugged – worse maybe.

'She didn't tell you what her plans were for today? Didn't say she'd be going out?'

'No, nothing like that—'

'So what the fuck did you talk about then?' Rob cursed himself as he spoke the words. He was showing his hand far too early, letting his suspicions be seen. Such transparency weakened him, made things worse. He shook his head, refusing to let Michael answer. 'Sorry. I'm a bit stressed.'

'You say she's been gone all day?' Michael spoke gently, carefully.

'Since ten. People saw her leaving at ten. She hasn't come back.'

'That's not like her, is it?'

Rob knew he had only asked the question as a courtesy to him. Michael probably felt that ten days' passing acquaintance with her was plenty to validate his authority as to her little ways.

'Have you spoken to the police?'

'Not yet, but I will. Since you were the last person to speak to her, I wanted to check with you.'

Michael's face betrayed nothing but concern. 'Yeah, course. Jesus, you must be in bits.' He took a step towards him. Rob held his ground. 'Let me throw on some clothes and I'll go out looking for her – if you like. If that would be helpful.'

Rob nodded, not really thinking about his offer; more anxious to have a couple of moments alone in the place, so he could look around. His mind was already ten steps ahead of him.

'I'll just be a minute,' Michael told him, and slunk off into the bedroom.

There was nothing on the table of interest, nor on the kitchen counter. A half-eaten sandwich, empty beer bottles. The man was a slob. In the rubbish bin only food and old wrappings. Without asking, Rob went into the bathroom. Nothing there either, nothing suspicious. Only the sad evidence of a young, single man, who clearly wasn't much focused on personal grooming: a lone toothbrush, a razor and a can of cheap deodorant. The bedroom then, there had to be something there.

Michael hadn't closed the door fully and Rob could see glimpses of him as he bent to pull on his jeans. He couldn't think of anything rational to say, any relevant question to ask to give him a pretext to push the door wide open and step inside so as to hear him better.

'Are you ready?' he asked, entering the room as he spoke. Michael glanced up at him, surprised, but he didn't protest.

'Just about.' Michael turned his back on Rob to button up his shirt.

Rob glanced around. One of the two twin beds was rumpled, clearly slept in. The other was still made. On the bedside table, a bottle of water, sun cream and a lamp. The wardrobe doors were open. A couple of shirts were hanging up. An open suitcase on the floor. Nothing more. Nothing suspicious. Rob didn't really know what he was looking for anyway. Suddenly feeling foolish, he was about to step out of the bedroom when he saw it.

'What's this?'

He stooped to pick it up from the floor, half-hidden under the bed. For the first time, Michael appeared discombobulated, flushing a deep red. Rob held the necklace up for inspection – a cheap bit of tourist tat. He hadn't seen Georgie wearing it, not that he could remember; but then, he didn't have an eye for all her bits and pieces, and she had a lot of jewellery. It could be hers.

'Oh, that's —'

'Where did you get this?'

Rob knew he was out of line but didn't care. He had no right to interrogate the man – Michael could quite reasonably become offended, but instead he shook his head, embarrassed.

'It's some girl I was with the other night . . . . She took it off when we were, you know. She asked me to keep it safe for her. I forgot to give it back.'

A trophy – didn't some people keep trophies? Not from sexual conquests, but from murders, violent acts. Serial killers. Rob gazed at Michael shrewdly.

'So you fucked a girl and stole her necklace?' He wanted to shock him, kick him to the truth.

Michael grimaced. 'Well, I wouldn't put it like that, but . . . yeah, basically. Yeah.'

Rob didn't believe a word of it. He pocketed the necklace, his eyes fixed on Michael. To his surprise, the man held his gaze and suddenly, without warning, moved swiftly towards him, coming close.

'Look, Rob. I know you and me – we haven't really spoken

much. But Georgie, she's a lovely lady. She's been very kind to me. You must be worried sick. I'll do anything you like – whatever I can do to help, okay?'

They walked together in silence down to the town, splitting up once they hit the main drag, Michael promising to call should he find anything. Rob watched closely as he ducked in to a bar, reappearing quickly afterwards. He went in to a second, then a third. Rob turned his back, striding quickly down the street.

His thoughts were racing. Had he been completely stupid, cornering Michael as he had? Should he have gone to the police first? Alerted the hotel management? Called the hospitals – perhaps Georgie had been in an accident, so badly hurt that she couldn't speak, couldn't give them Rob's details? Had she bumped in to someone she knew – the couple they'd been with last night perhaps – and got carried away, figuring Rob would call her when he woke up, not realising her phone was off? No, none of it made sense. The only thing that *did* make sense was Michael. Rob knew – he *knew* – that Michael had done something.

At the police station, to Rob's surprise, he was taken seriously from the start and was ushered into a little room where he was questioned by a young policeman who spoke fluent, Americanised English.

'So your fiancée's been gone since ten this morning?'

'As far as I understand it. I was asleep until lunchtime.'

'We shall call the hospitals for you. Wait here.'

It hadn't taken long. There were only four hospitals on the

island. Nothing. Rob didn't know whether to be grateful or not. Georgie's absence was still unexplained. And something in the policeman's manner had changed when he came to tell Rob there was no record of her having been admitted anywhere. There was a weariness to him, an over-familiarity. He was too used to dealing with tourists and their bad behaviour; the unexpected consequences of too much booze – rapes, fights, theft. He had put Rob into that category, the category of useless, loutish tourists who got what was coming to them.

'This man at your hotel. Michael. He has been bothering her?'

'No . . . . Not like that. I mean, he hasn't ever . . . . But it's weird, you know, he goes up to chat to her every day. And she's too polite to say no.'

'But he's out at the moment, looking for her?'

'Yes, but . . . of course he would! It would look too suspicious, otherwise, wouldn't it?'

The policeman sighed, shaking his head. Rob fought a sudden urge to hit him.

'And this couple you hooked up with last night. She is friends with them?'

'No. I know the guy only vaguely. Georgie met them both for the first time yesterday.'

'Do you have a number for this couple?'

Rob shook his head. They had pledged to exchange numbers at one point during the evening but had forgotten.

'You say you just got engaged, right?'

'Yes, yes – I told you all this—'

'Sorry, just one moment. You got engaged two nights ago, is that right?'

'Yes, but if you'll let me—'

'Do you think it might be possible, and please don't take offence, but do you think it might be possible that your fiancée is a little bit . . . . How do you say? Overwhelmed? Uncertain? Perhaps she wanted some time to think?'

The notion was so preposterous that Rob barked out a laugh. The policeman's expression did not change.

'Think! What would she have to think about? She was delighted – we both were – *are*. There's no problem there.'

'So you have been very happy, both of you? There's been no fights, no problems?'

Rob felt that things were getting out of hand. He struggled to keep his tone neutral, struggled to hide the defensiveness he suddenly felt. 'No, nothing. Things have been great.'

'So there would be no reason, as far as you know, that she would want to go off on her own for a while?'

It sounded so plausible – the policeman's tone was so plausible – that it gave Rob pause. Reasons, the man was asking for reasons as to why Georgie might want to be alone for a little while. An unwanted wave of rationality swept over Rob, silencing his instincts that something was profoundly wrong, preventing him from feeling the intensity of his convictions, from communicating their intensity to the policeman. There were some good reasons why she might want a little time to reflect. Soul-searching. Doubts. Fears. Perhaps Georgie felt she had been swept along too fast; perhaps now everything was crashing down on her. Perhaps she felt she'd made a mistake.

Rob stood abruptly. The policeman also rose, more sympathetic now. 'Please, don't be alarmed. We cannot do anything until she has been gone for twelve hours anyway. But more than likely, she will return to your hotel very soon. If not, you can come back and I will personally handle things. Okay?'

Outside, back in the late afternoon heaviness of the heat, watching as tourists and locals went about their daily business, Rob felt as though he'd made a mockery of everything. It was outrageous, the policeman's suggestion, beyond outrageous, and he'd fallen for it. He was about to turn on his heel and march back inside, demand that they start searching for Georgie, demand that they take the whole thing seriously but at that very moment the policeman who'd so casually dismissed him came outside with a colleague, busy, preoccupied. Noticing Rob, he shot him a glance, a warning glance, telling him not to bother approaching; he'd have no joy here. They got into a squad car and drove off, the policeman's eyes firmly on the road ahead as they passed.

It was close to six. They wouldn't act until she'd been gone twelve hours. *Twelve!* Anything could happen in that time – it was an eternity. A whole life could hinge on the decision of a minute, let alone hours and hours. He couldn't just stand there; he couldn't be inactive. He toyed with the idea of phoning Georgie's mother, on the off-chance Georgie might have called her, wanting to talk about the events of the holiday, discuss her acceptance of Rob's proposal, express any possible misgivings. Georgie was close to her mother – if she were going to talk to anyone, it would be her. Rob stopped himself short. He could feel his panic rendering him childlike, afraid. He had to think clearly. He must not allow the policeman's wry suggestion to unnerve him, alter his focus. Alarming Georgie's mother now would do more harm than good.

He took out his phone and dialled.

'Michael, where are you?'

~

Though he hadn't gone downtown at all, Michael had been up the previous night regardless. His body clock was wired to his new nocturnal rhythm, and it suited him. He had always hated getting up early for work, had always struggled with the 7 AM starts. This was a much better routine for him and he thought that when he got back home, he might start looking for something that would enable him to work at night. Then he'd laughed at the silliness of it. Thinking about work, about home! As if he'd be going back, perfectly normal like, at the end of the week.

When the sun had risen, Michael had left the hotel complex and wandered down to the supermarket, closed for another half-hour or so. There had been no one around in the car park – no security, no early shoppers. He had moved the car to a dirt track farther down the road, not too far, but well out of sight of prying eyes. Strolling in to town, he bought himself a coffee and a bite to eat, mingling with the drunken revellers, making sure he chatted with the guy who served him, just in case he might need to be placed doing his normal thing at that hour of the morning.

At seven, he returned to the supermarket and, though it was early, the place had been busy. Michael had bought what he needed, and taken the bags to the car. It was unlikely that anyone had noticed him here, he thought, though if they had, it was a risk he had to run. The cashiers had been tired and grumpy and most of the customers, all locals, were on their way to work, preoccupied and hurried. Leaving the car where it was, Michael had taken a shortcut through the olive grove, back up to the hotel. The only notice he'd attracted was from a dog, tethered to a tree in the middle of the grove. It barked furiously as Michael passed. But no one had come or called out, so he hadn't worried.

He had followed his morning routine to the letter, arriving back at the hotel, calling a greeting to Les, retreating to his room for an hour or so, sitting on his balcony, then coming back down at nine, when Georgie had appeared. It was delightful, watching how smoothly everything unfolded, without a hitch, almost like magic. Though he had been prepared for anything, had been ready to change things as events occurred, it seemed as though nothing was going to get in his way. It was as if God himself were smiling on his plans, willing the world to make things as easy for him as possible.

He had approached Georgie, friendly as always, buying the coffees, settling himself down. With as much nonchalance as he'd been able to muster, he asked where she had been the previous few days. Had she and Rob taken an excursion? Gone sightseeing? He had been ready for tears, for a confession, but Georgie was full of excitement – a welling, bubbling spring of urgency that she could barely conceal. Oh, they'd been to the most marvellous place – did Michael know about the little island off the coast? Only twenty minutes by boat. You'd never think to look at it, but there's the most magnificent hotel and they had a wonderful time.

It had shocked him profoundly. To hear that his island was not his at all and never would be, that it was already taken, already inhabited – that he would have to get rid of his dream just like that – it sickened him. And Georgie went on and on about it, wouldn't shut up. Hearing her describe it brought a lump to Michael's throat and he had struggled to keep his cool. But just as he thought he might be dangerously close to losing it, that strong, hard voice came from within, saving him at the last minute. *Get over it. No more dreaming. You're past that now and you know it. In fact, it just proves you're doing the right thing. No more dreams. Time to get real. Time to do it properly.* It gave him confidence, hearing that voice – his voice – feeling that strength. He didn't have to give in to sorrow or self-pity. He was being tested, that was all. It was a test of his strength.

But Georgie hadn't finished. There was more to come, much more. Something significant had taken place there, on his little island: something magical and wondrous and just '*so right, Michael! It feels so right!*' It had been like a punch to the stomach, and Michael had had to take a moment to recover, turning away. Not that she'd noticed anything, the way she'd been blathering on. Oh, she'd had no idea why Rob was taking her, had thought it was just a little treat to make the holiday really memorable. Had felt guilty about it, because she'd been a bit off-sorts with him. It was such a surprise, when he'd asked her. And yet, in a strange sort of way, not surprising at all. She had known instantly that she wanted to. She didn't even have to think about it.

It was the only time Michael came close to faltering. The magnitude of it caught him short, and all thoughts of what was to come went clean out of his head. For in spite of all that he knew about Georgie's situation, about how things were with Rob, he felt at that moment that she had seriously betrayed him. And, for the first time, he felt a stab of anger towards her – anger that had been reserved for Rob up until now. A cold chill went down his spine, frightening him. Had he been mistaken? Had he seriously screwed up somehow, got it all wrong?

Georgie had gabbled on for some time, unfazed by his silence, his withdrawal. Michael wasn't really listening to her. He hadn't been listening properly since hearing of her acceptance. She had said yes! To Rob, to marrying him. After everything she'd said to him, to Michael! After all their talks, all their conversations – after all the honesty and facing of facts, she'd done the unthinkable! All right, Rob was a bully, could turn nasty if not handled carefully, but she hadn't had to say yes outright. She could have stalled, bought herself time – anything. And to do it on his, on Michael's, island . . . . If she'd wanted to hurt him, she couldn't have planned it better.

He had been silent for so long that Georgie had nudged him

gently. 'Michael, are you okay? You haven't been listening to a word I've said, have you?'

He covered well enough; at least, he thought he had, telling her how pleased he was, how surprised, what a nice story. He tried to speak fluently, tried to find the right words, but they wouldn't come out straight. This was the one thing, the *only* thing, he hadn't foreseen. He should have, of course, and he cursed himself for not having thought of it. It seemed so obvious that something like that would happen. The bastard – the conniving, controlling, manipulative bastard! Taking her away all alone, bullying her in to it. A marriage proposal! And yet – *Oh God, please let me be wrong* – she didn't seem at all concerned; quite the opposite, in fact. She wasn't asking for advice, she wasn't making another of her confessions. She was gleeful, positively elated. It had thrown Michael into a panic – a panic Georgie sensed but didn't understand. And, for a fleeting moment, he didn't understand *her*.

'Michael?' She'd spoken gently, sensitively. He could see it in her eyes: she felt sorry for him, pity. She thought she knew how he felt, and wanted to comfort him, reassure. It was all he could do at that moment not to reach out and strike her.

'I'm sorry, Michael. I should've . . . . I mean . . . . You and I, we've become mates, haven't we? I didn't think, I mean – I don't want to upset you. I don't want . . . . Oh, God . . . .'

She hadn't been able to articulate it properly, but then, it wasn't in her nature to be so brazen, Michael knew. She hadn't had the nerve to say it straight, lay her cards on the table: *You love me, Michael. I know you do, and I feel the same way. Only*

I'm weak. And Rob . . . Rob is . . . I have to do it. I can't say no.
It gave him some small comfort, thinking of it this way; reminding himself that she had been caught by Rob, was not a free woman and could not speak freely. She had had to protect herself; she'd had to say yes. To have refused, stuck alone with Rob on the island, might have brought her into danger.

Michael nodded, conveying as best he could this unspoken understanding, though a part of him was still furious. But it was mostly fury with Rob. His anger at Georgie's weakness, well . . . that was something they could talk about. Later. That could wait.

'I've got to nip down to the supermarket. Don't s'pose you fancy a stroll?' His heart had been in his mouth when he'd asked her. He had other options prepared, but he hoped against hope that he wouldn't have to use them.

'Oh great, yes. We're low on everything. I should grab something for Rob's breakfast. Well, lunch, more likely, by the time he gets up.'

'I'll just go and get some cash. Meet you out front?'

'Perfect. Oh, and – Michael?'

She was standing, her arms held slightly open as though she were welcoming him. 'I just want you to know, I . . . I really value our friendship. I'm glad I was able to tell you this morning. You're the first, you know. You're the first person I've told. I've not even rung my mother yet.'

Michael didn't know if this were true or not but at that moment he didn't care. Because as he looked at her, standing there before him, her arms outstretched, her eyes wide, he was suddenly struck by the force of her message. It pulled him sharply out of his own head, and he saw with total clarity that she was reaching out to him, more overtly than she had ever done before. Oh, he knew well that she was speaking in code – she'd done that from the beginning: her hidden, desperate pleas for assistance and action, barely disguised by her words, but this was almost too obvious. Michael looked into Georgie's hopeful, expectant face and was suddenly filled with a rush of love for her. He could forgive her weakness, could forgive her cowardice. After all, it was hardly her fault that she had been reduced to this. He would help her; show her that she could relax, be herself, without fear. It might take some time – she'd been too long with Rob – but Michael was a patient man. *It's coming, Georgie,* he silently told her. *It's all coming. Just hold on.* He'd smiled at her and she'd returned the smile, broad and warm. She knew then. She had probably known all along (or hoped), but had probably never dared think it might actually become a reality. Michael could almost feel her gratitude, it was that strong.

Upstairs, he took his time gathering the things he needed, securing them safely about his person. Not that he needed much, but he couldn't afford to screw up now at this last, vital moment. He checked and double-checked everything and, finally satisfied, left the room, leaving the balcony door and curtains open. Rather than going back down via the pool, he took the long way, all the way around the back of the hotel where, thankfully, he ran in to no one (even though he'd prepared for it if necessary, ready to explain that he thought he'd dropped something stumbling home drunk a day or so before).

Georgie was waiting out front.

'Rob's still out like a light. Lazy sod!'

They had strolled down to the supermarket. And from there, it had all gone amazingly well. It was an accomplishment Michael knew he would look back on with pride in years to come; and a certain amount of baffled amazement that he'd managed to pull it off. Of course, by then it would be a shared experience, between him and her and whomever else they'd chosen to have in their lives. A tall tale to make the grand-children incredulous.

Michael had lingered just before they arrived at the super-market, claiming he had to send a text message to Patrick and explaining to Georgie that he had been in touch finally, want-ing to talk. She had been very understanding and had gone in to do her shopping, leaving him alone. Michael went down the road as quickly as possible, down to the little dirt track where he had parked the car. It was still there, untouched. What a great country! Back home, someone would have done something to it, or have tried to make off with the bloody thing.

He kept an eye on the front of the supermarket, hovering on the corner of the track and the road. He saw Georgie when she came out, laden with bags, bemused, wondering where on earth he was, why he hadn't been in to do his shopping. Michael had called to her, waving her over. He knew she couldn't hear him properly, couldn't make out what it was he was shouting (which was nothing in particular, not at first). He watched as she sighed theatrically, her shoulders drooping, and started walking towards him.

'Michael, what is it? These are heavy! What're you doing there?'

'Come here. I've something to show you.'

She had half-laughed, but Michael could tell she was a bit annoyed, readjusting the weight of her bags between her hands. She craned her neck to see around the corner as she approached the track.

'What? What is it?'

Michael shook his head, smiling at her, backing away so that Georgie really had to turn the corner, out of sight of the supermarket, and step on to the dirt track. He was ready for her. She glanced at the car, then glanced at Michael, not connecting the two, her mouth slightly open to ask again why he'd brought her there. Perspiration beaded on her brow and there was a damp patch on the front of her T-shirt. The sun was very hot, and it seemed to Michael that it was almost audible, beating down on them in slow, rhythmic pulses. The cicadas hummed loudly in the olive grove, adding to his sense that the whole world seemed to be urging him on, pushing him to continue.

Georgie had been about to speak and turn back, pissed off, impatient, when he got her, square on the side of the head. Out cold at the first blow. It hadn't been a pleasure hitting her. If there had been any other way, he would have, but it had had to be done. Luckily, he got her on the first go, so she probably wouldn't have felt anything. Michael had practised a bit the night before. It had been some years since he'd had to do that sort of thing to someone and he'd been slightly worried that he might not remember properly, might get it wrong. But it had been as smooth as anything. It seemed his reflexes had a memory of their own.

Michael had estimated that he would have only a few minutes before Georgie began to come round, so, as quickly as he could, he'd lifted her into the car. She was heavier than expected. Maybe she did need to swim her laps, after all. Her shopping had scattered when she'd fallen, and a carton of milk had burst, spilling its contents into the dust, attracting almost instantly a large group of flies. Michael had tied her up firmly, efficiently: knees bent, hands underneath them, so that she made a compact little bundle. She would be uncomfortable, but it wouldn't be for too long. He'd checked the gag, made sure she could breathe properly, then put on the blindfold. Not that it was strictly necessary, since she'd be down on the floor of the car, in the back, but still, it seemed appropriate.

He gathered up the rest of her shopping and kicked the burst milk carton into the bushes. The puddle on the ground was already close to dry. In another couple of minutes nothing would remain. Watching it for a moment, Michael was reminded of their first real encounter, his and Georgie's, over his spilt milk in the supermarket. How long ago that seemed now. How much had happened since then. He'd never understood it before, when people talked about time being relative – hours feeling like days, or weeks flying by like minutes. But to think that, in real time, he and Georgie had known one another for only twelve days – not even. It sounded ludicrous, spelled out like that. Impossible. Yet now, they had a lifetime ahead of them. Michael hoped those years would stretch out slowly, hoped that he could enjoy every moment.

His reverie hadn't lasted long. A muffled groan came from the car. Georgie was coming round faster than anticipated. Perhaps he'd been a little bit too gentle, too cautious. Quick as a shot, Michael got in the car, turning to check that she was securely wedged on the floor behind the passenger seat, and had set off. It had taken less than five minutes. The worst was over. All that remained was to settle her down, then take a little bit of time to cover his tracks. Beyond that, everything was sorted.

Michael drove in a haze of pleasure. Every ounce of intelligence, every inner resource had been called upon those past few days and he'd risen to the challenge. They could say what they liked, but no one could deny that he'd performed magnificently. No one could say he was stupid now.

~

It was hopeless. Far too many people. All the young tourist families were out for their early dinners and quite a few over-keen youngsters were already in the bars, warming up for the night ahead. Greek families still lingered on the beach while others made their weary, sun-baked way up the main drag, laden down with towels and beach toys, inflatable chairs and all the paraphernalia needed for an afternoon on the sand. The crowds would only get worse as the evening wore on, Rob knew. It was like looking for a needle in a haystack and he cursed himself for having wasted a precious few hours trying.

Something had happened to Georgie and that bastard was involved somehow, Rob knew it in his bones, even though Michael had rung him not an hour before to check in, arranging to meet at nine o'clock in the taverna.

'If we haven't found her by then, we can go to the police together, Rob.'

Fuck the police and their twelve-hour rule! Abandoning his search, with Michael's words still ringing in his ears, Rob went back to the station, demanding to see the young policeman who had spoken to him earlier that day.

Of course, it had all been bullshit. All the reassurance, the 'I will personally handle things', just an easy fob-off to another pathetic tourist. Cold fear sunk deep into Rob's bones. He ought to have seen it, ought to have known it earlier. He had spent the whole afternoon in a haze of half-belief, hanging on to the words of authority when all the time he'd known that something dreadful had taken place.

Never in his life had he made such a scene before, but then, his contact with the police had been minimal. They were the good guys, the omnipotent ones – Rob had always thought of them that way, when he'd thought of them at all. The blind faith of a nice middle-class boy. It was only as he stood there, raging at the semi-competent youngster behind the front desk, that Rob realised, with a sudden flash of horror, that the police were just like him or anyone else: lazy, tired, getting things wrong – badly wrong. The thought petrified him.

He knew he wasn't making sense, wasn't telling his story coherently but his panic and fear were too overwhelming. What made matters worse was that he was raising his voice, flailing about, unable to remember the name of the officer who'd dealt with him that afternoon, if, indeed, the guy had given him his name. His thoughts were out of control. Perhaps it was some vast conspiracy and everyone was in on the disappearance of his fiancée! Was there anyone who could be trusted, anyone who would take him seriously? As the young man at the desk went off in search of someone to help, Rob stood mute, silenced by the overwhelming sensation of utter loneliness. With Georgie gone, he had nothing he could call safe. Nothing he could call home.

'Come this way, please.' The young policeman's voice was high and boyish, his English clipped and correct, though far from fluent. They must put their new kids through a training programme that gives them stock phrases to deal with crazy English tourists, Rob thought. The strange, sinking sensation in the pit of his stomach; the reckless, childish wildness of his thoughts, told him he was close to hysteria. If he was met with dismissiveness or lack of interest now, it would tip him over the edge.

Rob was brought to a small office at the back of the station. Had he been designing a set for a film, he couldn't have done it better. Cramped, run-down, flaking plaster. A whirring ceiling fan set the papers, overflowing from every cabinet and stacked on every available space, rustling gently. Any increase in breeze and sheets of vital information might be lost. And then there was the policeman himself, a detective. The youngster proudly introduced him as Detective Alexis Antoniou.

Antoniou's physical presence was strangely familiar to Rob. A stooped but still powerful frame, greying stubble. Hooded eyes that had retained their warmth, in spite of the horrors they must have seen, the knowledge of human wickedness and weakness they'd encountered. Antoniou was the embodiment of every ageing detective Rob had ever seen on film and television and, though he recognised the banality of the comparison, he could have wept with relief.

'Please. Please sit down. My colleague tells me you were here earlier today? I've seen his notes. So. Your fiancée?'

Perfect English, though heavily accented. Rob suddenly felt that with this man all would be simple. With a small but grateful smile, he carefully explained the day's events. And equally carefully, but with an insistence that he had lacked when speaking with the other police officer that afternoon, Rob told the detective how certain he was that something bad had happened, something involving the guy from the hotel who had been hanging around Georgie all holiday. The guy who was, at that very moment, supposedly out looking for her, due to meet him, Rob, in half-an-hour to assess the situation.

At the first mention of Michael, Detective Antoniou straightened up. 'This man, he has been spending much time with your girlfriend?'

'Not that much – just a coffee in the mornings. But it's been every morning, regular as clockwork. He got stuck here on his own – he was travelling with a friend, another guy, who went straight back home as they arrived. He said his friend's mother had died, or something, I don't know. Georgie felt sorry for him. She . . . . She only wanted to be kind.'

Rob broke off, close to tears. Antoniou eyed him closely. Glancing up, it occurred to Rob that perhaps he himself was under suspicion. Or if not, at the very least the man was trying to get the measure of him, to gauge the veracity of his story, of his emotions. A sudden self-consciousness overtook him and he coughed, trying to shake it off. The situation was too important for him to fuck it up by doing something wrong, something misleading.

Antoniou seemed to sense his nerves, however, for he didn't question Rob's obvious accusation of Michael. Instead, he pressed him on it. Had this man said or done anything that bothered Georgie, unsettled her? Had Rob noticed anything strange in his behaviour? Had anything untoward happened, however minor or seemingly unimportant? Rob had to answer honestly. Georgie had never mentioned anything. But with a sudden clarity of memory that surprised him, he did recall something; something so tiny, he was amazed it had stayed with him, amazed that it had even registered. The first day – the first morning – he'd seen Michael watching them from his balcony. When Rob had locked eyes with him, Michael had instantly turned away.

The detective made a note. Rob was still baffled that he should have remembered such a thing.

'It sounds ridiculous, doesn't it?'

'Your instincts were speaking to you. It may be something, it may be nothing. But this man, Michael – you went to see him today? You went to ask him about Georgie?'

Rob liked the way the detective spoke her name, softly pronouncing all the vowels, the 'e', the 'o', elongating the word slightly. It seemed to draw out the very essence of her somehow, made her feel alive in a way that Rob had never experienced: alive in someone else's thoughts and mind. Georgie was someone that the detective – this stranger – was now holding close to him, making her a part of himself. She was the bond between them, her absence made yet more powerful by their shared concern for her.

'Michael had been the last to see her, as I understood it. He'd gone down to talk to her this morning, as he does every morning.'

'And he offered to help look for her?'

'Almost immediately.'

'You thought that strange?'

'Not so much that . . . .' Rob frowned, trying to articulate exactly what it was in the encounter that had so rattled him, his preconceptions of the man aside. 'He seemed worried about her, concerned, as I imagined he would be. It was . . . . There was something . . . . It was like he wanted to show me how simple it all was, how . . . I don't know. There was something in his manner. . . . He hid it well, but . . . it was a bit like he was showing off, in a way. Quietly. He didn't stop me when I walked in on him getting dressed he didn't say anything. I would have, if some guy who clearly didn't like me barged in. It was as if he was trying to prove something to me.'

Antoniou didn't react, just kept his eyes fixed on Rob, taking it all in. 'There was something strange – this necklace,' Rob fished in his pockets for it. 'It was on the floor by one of the beds.'

'Beds?'

'It's a twin room. Because of his friend, I guess.'

Antoniou nodded and made a note. Rob pressed on, an increased urgency to his tone.

'I don't know if it's Georgie's. She has so much jewellery. He claimed it was from some girl he'd slept with. Said she'd asked him to keep it safe for her, and he'd forgotten to give it back.'

'But you didn't believe him?'

'I don't know what to believe. I was rude to him. He didn't react – not in the way I would have, anyway.'

'But he offered to help?'

'*Insisted* on it. He told me that he knew we didn't get on but that he wanted to help Georgie. Said she was a lovely lady, that she'd always been kind to him. I . . . . It seemed so unreal, so strange. He'd never been like that before, so . . . trying to be intimate. He's this big, heavy, shy sort of guy – the kind of man you don't look twice at. The kind of person you just think is happiest down the pub with the boys, knocking back pints or something. He's not the sort of person who . . . who talks about kindness or being lovely. '

Rob trailed off. Antoniou got up suddenly, making him start.

'I think we should go and meet Michael. You are due to meet him—' he checked his watch '—in fifteen minutes?'

'Yes, at the taverna Georgie and I go to every night. We took him there for dinner the night we all arrived.'

'Well then. Shall we?'

They went in a squad car, taking the backstreets so as to avoid any possibility of Michael spotting them along the main drag. Antoniou had ordered two other cars to meet them there in case of difficulty, should Michael prove in any way unwilling, though privately, he had his doubts that Michael would arrive at all. Rob glanced at him as he drove, his eyes fixed on the road ahead, concentrated, focused.

'What do you think, Detective? What do you think's going on?'

Antoniou glanced at him for a moment, and, though his expression reverted to neutral almost instantly, Rob swore he glimpsed a flash of apprehension in the man's eyes.

'I do not know, not yet. But I think it is important that we speak to this man, this Michael. I have sent men also to your hotel, in case he has returned there for some reason.'

'So you don't think I'm crazy? I've felt like I've been going crazy all day.'

Antoniou smiled, shaking his head slightly. If anything, he was far more concerned than Rob would ever guess. The mayhem that ensued during tourist season required him to be open to any possibility, however strange or outrageous. There was little he hadn't seen in the past twenty or so years, as the holiday industry boomed in his country. The rapid expansion of the towns, the cheap hotels and tacky bars that seemed to appear almost overnight. The corrupt building deals and land grabs.

The behaviour of the youngsters, planeloads of them all summer long, who came to drink themselves into oblivion for two weeks. Rape was the most common of the incidents Antoniou had to deal with – rape made hazy by too much booze, and frequently by drugs. Most of the women who reported could barely remember their attacker's first name, let alone what he looked like. These women were easy targets, prey ripe for the taking, and no amount of warnings either from government campaigns back home or locally (each hotel had a notice pinned up in reception) seemed to make any difference. Theft and assault came next on the list, but again, most complainants had too vague a memory of the actual incidents, and the chances of them ever receiving satisfaction were slim to none. It seemed to Antoniou that his job during the summer months was less that of genuine problem-solving than it was pure psychological management. Reassure the public that you take them seriously. Make them feel that there is some order amidst the chaos, some hope, some natural law of justice. That in spite of all the hedonism, the wanton abandon, when sense returns, there will be some reward for it.

But this case was different. Antoniou had sensed that immediately, the moment he first saw Rob. This was no lager lout, coming to complain about a feckless girlfriend, who more than likely had hotfooted it off with a pal of his. Antoniou had seen that scenario played out countless times.

He cursed his colleague Zaglanikis, who had interviewed Rob earlier – arrogant and spoiled, he had misread all the obvious signals. Zaglanikis was related to one of the local politicians and lived out the cliché of the useless brat, ruined by nepotism, believing himself to be invulnerable. *I'll make sure he knows just how badly he's screwed up this time*, Antoniou thought grimly to himself. *And if there's a body – if this (God forbid) turns out to be as bad as I have a feeling it might – that bastard's off the job.* If Antoniou had been there that afternoon, he would have known instantly how seriously to take the situation. Though he was resorting to type in his assessments, his instincts told him he could not fault them. A well-behaved, middle-class woman gone missing unexpectedly – this was no accident, no minor slip of behaviour. Whatever the bubbling depths beneath the mannered, polished exterior that Rob presented (and, Antoniou imagined Georgie would present equally well, if he ever had the opportunity of meeting her), they would not be enough to drive her to cause such panic. Something had happened to her, and it might already be too late. The hours that had been wasted by Zaglanikis's incompetence could never be recovered.

Rob went first into the taverna, without stopping to consult Antoniou, who took his time, approaching carefully, casually, taking in everything. Rob looked around wildly and sought out Antoniou with his eyes, desperate. Michael was not there.

'Sit down,' Antoniou told him. 'Just wait. I'll be over there.'

Rob did as he was told, a haunted look in his eyes. It still felt impossible to him that everything should be so far out of his control, so beyond his powers of rationalisation. Antoniou had a word with the owner, who seemed genuinely distressed to hear of Georgie's disappearance. Yes, she and Rob had come every night for nearly two weeks – well, almost every night. They had been away for an evening and told him all about it when they returned, celebrating their engagement. He had offered them a bottle of wine on the house. Of course he'd do whatever he possibly could, whatever Antoniou wanted.

The other man? A frown of confusion, clutching at memories, straining to recall. Yes, vaguely, only vaguely, over a week ago he had been there. Georgie and Rob had eaten alone every night, except the night before when they'd met with friends. Perhaps the first night, he could half-remember something, another man, but . . . . He struck his forehead with frustration. So many people, in and out all the time! Whoever it was, he couldn't be sure, didn't know if he'd be able to recognise him. Antoniou calmed him. It wasn't important. The man was due to show up here at any moment, anyway. And if not . . . well, that would tell him all he needed to know.

Rob and Antoniou checked their watches at exactly the same time. Ten minutes late. Rob glanced over at him, nervous, agitated.

'Should I call him?'

Before he could reply, Antoniou's mobile rang. It was his colleague, Sergeant Petrous, up at the hotel.

'No sign of him, boss. All his stuff's still in his room.'

'Passport?'

'No, that's not there. Nor his phone or wallet. No personal documents at all actually, except for a welcome package from the tour operator, about the hotel. That's under a different name, though – Patrick Connor. But he's left some clothes here.'

'Have the boys ask around. Knock on every door, summon all the staff. And find a contact for this Patrick Connor – get on to the tour operator. Get both their details. And the couple's room. Every inch, okay? If there's anything, anything at all.' It had to be done. Though Antoniou didn't really doubt Rob's sincerity, one could never be entirely trusting of one's instincts.

Rob had called Michael, unable to wait for instructions.

'Straight to voice mail. What's happening? What did they say?'

Antoniou stood. 'I think we should go. There's no point waiting here. He's not going to come.'

The colour drained from Rob's face. 'Who was that on the phone? Have they found something?'

Antoniou felt a strong pang of sympathy for the man. He could see how hard Rob was trying to keep his cool; how he was struggling not to give in to panic. With a certain type of person, this control could sustain indefinitely, but nevertheless, it did its damage. Something was fracturing inside Rob, Antoniou's practiced eye could tell. And even if the result was good – even if he awoke from this nightmare to blessed comfort and relief, to the return of his beloved – the experience would leave its mark. Caution and restraint would become an instinctive part of Rob's armour from now on. Impulse and spontaneity would be quickly suppressed, or carefully weighed in the balance, measured, before being acted upon. It saddened Antoniou, even as he knew it was inevitable, and knew also that it was certainly not the worst thing that could happen to a human being. Not remotely the worst thing.

He patted Rob's arm gently, almost tenderly, wanting only to reassure. 'This man is not at the hotel. And it doesn't look as though he's coming here, but I'll leave one of my men, just in case. But we should go back to the station. I think we ought to talk further.'

~

It had not been a frequent occurrence in Michael's life to give thanks for the kindness of other people. But he had spent most of the past twenty-four hours or so pouring down blessings on Patrick's head. Though Michael needed only temporary shelter, only a brief period of sanctuary, it was a definite need and he wouldn't have been able to put things in motion so smoothly without Patrick's help, even though Patrick was unaware of just how much he was helping, which somehow only added to Michael's sense of gratitude. Thinking of all that had happened, it seemed suddenly credible to Michael, in a way that he had never thought about before, that there was some grand design operating in the universe, some unseen hand guiding every-thing. Why else would Patrick's mother have died so suddenly? For what had once seemed like a crisis – being stuck alone in a foreign country – had become the defining experience of his life. Without some level of preordination, nothing made any sense. It had all come together so perfectly.

He didn't need long, but he required a bit of time, and he counted on the forces of the universe to come to his aid again. He had estimated about twenty-four hours. If he could just have that, then all would be well. Georgie would take a little while to recover; a little longer perhaps to understand what Michael had in mind, and then some time would be necessary for her to confront her fears, admit her weakness and finally face the truth. Michael prayed that there would still be time for them both to savour the joy before the inevitable disruption, the confrontations that would have to be dealt with, but if the worst came to the worst, that didn't matter so much. There was a lifetime ahead of them. As long as he was able to get her to the point where her courage was strong, her resolve unshakeable, nothing else mattered.

The provisions were basic but perfectly adequate. Camping gear – had she ever gone camping? He would ask her one day, but not now. Either way, it didn't matter. It wasn't going to be for long. When they had arrived at the cottage, Michael had laid Georgie out gently in the back room, and covered her up with a sleeping bag. It wasn't cold, but he reckoned she was probably in a mild state of shock and should be properly looked after.

Georgie had been wide awake, and her eyes had held Michael's own unremittingly, whenever he glanced at her. He'd checked the gag: it wasn't too tight but tight enough to prevent her from speaking. She had made no sound though, no grunt or groan. He had left her arms and legs bound, although as soon as he'd got her inside, he had straightened her out a bit, getting her out of the uncomfortable position he had had to put her in for the car ride. Without wanting to overstep the mark, but sure that she'd be stiff and sore, he had gently rubbed her arms and legs, trying to soothe the muscles. Only then had she moaned. She wriggled slightly, trying to evade his touch. He stopped at once. The last thing he wanted was for her to think him improper.

There were no keys to the cottage, so locking her in had been impossible, but Michael had planned for that. She was securely tied, and the small room he'd put her in was window-less, so even were she somehow able to haul herself upright, there was very little she could do to attract attention. And even if the gag came loose and she shouted or screamed, there was nothing – no one – around for miles. Having explained to her that he would be back very soon (a bit of a lie – he knew he'd be gone for most of the day), Michael had offered to fetch her a bite to eat before he left, but she'd made no indication that she want-ed anything, and he didn't want to press the point. In a way, he was relieved. Being alone for some hours would give her time to think about the situation. She was sharp, Georgie, clever. More than likely, by the time he returned she would have faced up to things, and be ready to talk with him, listen to him; hungry for his certainty, his sense.

Still, Michael wasn't taking any chances. Closing the door on her, he shifted the heavy wardrobe that he'd been delighted to discover in one of the bedrooms the day before, in front of it, effectively sealing her in. She would have enough air since the door didn't quite touch the floor at the bottom (badly made, he noted), but he left the tiniest of tiny gaps between the wardrobe and the wall, to make sure. It would be hot and claustrophobic no doubt, but certainly not dangerous. The wardrobe covered the entire doorframe so completely that you would never know there was an entrance to a room beyond. Georgie wouldn't be able to move it. It had taken Michael close to an hour just getting it down the hallway. But such a stroke of luck that it had been there in the house! Another bit of the puzzle had slotted into place without him even having to think about it. God was smiling on him for sure.

Patrick had been more than a little taken aback when Michael had asked him about the cottage when he'd phoned. Michael had tried to come at it as lightly as possible, but he supposed it must have seemed a bit odd. It was the first time they had properly spoken since the crisis at the airport and all Patrick had wanted was tales of drunken debauchery – a bit of vicarious living to liven up what had been a terrible ten days for him. Michael had had to stretch his imagination to concoct a story, but it had worked, because when Michael pressed Patrick for the information he needed, he'd come through. It had taken some quick thinking, and a good deal of encouragement, but Michael had managed to get Patrick to remember not only the name of the area but even a brief description of the place. Patrick had actually been amazingly accurate, considering it had been a good many years since he'd been there. For example, he remembered the strange little water tower, long abandoned, rusting in the heat, which marked the turning-point for the track that led to the cottage. Michael planned to congratulate him on his powers of memory. He would be eternally grateful.

'So who's this bird, then? The one from round there?'

Michael had grinned to himself, so pleased was he with his story. It was one he knew that Patrick would buy, even though he had sounded dubious at first. In a different mood, Michael might have taken offence. Patrick had made it pretty clear that he found it hard to believe that Michael was capable of attracting a woman on his own, let alone a local who happened to be from the area Patrick had spent time in as a kid. But Michael had convinced him, telling him all about her, without hesitation, as if it were the most natural thing in the world.

'She's lovely, Patrick, really nice. Works here at the hotel. Cleaner. We've just been chatting a bit. When she said where she was from, the name rang a bell. I couldn't place it at first, but then I remembered you and your mum's boyfriend. Am I right? That's the place, isn't it? That's where he lived? I thought so! God – funny how it stuck in my head like that, all random. But it's nice to have something else in common with her. They're a bit shy, these Greek girls, a bit nervy. I'm going to take her out, take her for dinner or something.'

Patrick had been happy to give Michael the details that would (he hoped) help him score. 'Long as you don't do anything stupid like fall in love with the bird and try and bring her home. Or, worse, stay out there. Can't work, mate, trust me. Culture clash. I've seen it all before.'

Michael had reassured him it was just a bit of fun, and so easily did Patrick fall for the story, he'd had to bite his lip to prevent himself from laughing with delight. Funny, he talked so long about his imaginary paramour – Rosa, he'd called her –

that, by the end, Michael had almost convinced himself of her reality! He could see her in his mind's eye: small, dark – very dark – with long curly black hair and shy, downcast black eyes, whose lashes fluttered slightly as they rose to meet his own. And though it pained him, he admitted to Patrick, when pressed, that she was indeed well-endowed. All that a guy could wish for. He'd had to say it. Patrick loved that sort of detail.

But how cool it was that Michael would be able to tell her that he knew her neighbourhood, knew where she was from, thanks to his mate, who knew it very well. 'Cos wasn't there a water tower close by? And a few abandoned cottages where the quarry was supposed to have been? Yeah, tough going for Rosa's little part of the island all right – just a series of disappointments, one after the other. Patrick told him there was supposed to have been some regeneration scheme years back, but it had all fallen through. Loads of the locals had had to move to the resorts to find work, much as Rosa had clearly done herself. That's why his mum's ex-boyfriend had left, in the end. There was bugger all there.

'It's a total kip. Don't tell her that, I mean – not like that, but Christ, it was like a ghost town.'

It sounded perfect to Michael and, indeed, it turned out to be.

Michael had basked in his triumph for some time after his conversation with Patrick. He was turning in to some storyteller and he hadn't even had to think about it too much. But he hadn't sat long on his laurels. Though he had a reasonably accurate description, he still had to find the place. And there was no guarantee that the cottage – Patrick's mother's ex-boyfriend's cottage – would still be standing; or even if it were, that it would be unoccupied. It was a hell of a long shot, but Michael had had to do something. His island was out of the question. There was no way he could get her over there, it was far too open and public. Besides, it was already inhabited and ruined by what she and Rob had done there. That dream would have to be replaced. The cottage, however, even if it were far-fetched, was at least something to go and look at. And, as it had turned out, it was perfect. Couldn't have been better. God bless Patrick. And his mother (rest her soul) and that good old ex-boyfriend of hers, wherever he might be.

Michael had made his preparations in a delicious bubble of anticipation, amazing himself at how capable he was becoming. If ever he needed a boost in confidence, if ever he had to prove himself again, he would remember this experience. How with focused effort and the proper application of his will, he had achieved so much and in so short a time. He'd got the car, mapped the route, approved the isolation and remoteness of the cottage, bought the supplies, stocked everything they would need there. And now – now, a mere twelve or so hours later – Georgie was actually there, waiting for him!

All that remained for him to do was buy them a bit of time, and all would be well. To Michael's surprise, when he had returned to the hotel after leaving her, ready to kill the afternoon hours before he could slip away again and get back to her, he had fallen almost instantly asleep. Thank God that Rob had come calling for him, or he might very well have slept the day through, which would have been disastrous. Once again, every-thing was working in his favour.

Michael had known from the beginning that Rob would turn on him as a likely suspect if Georgie went missing. Rob would love nothing more than to accuse him, haul him down to the cops; finally vent his jealousy and anger. So he wasn't at all sur-prised when Rob turned up – in fact, he wondered what had taken him so long. He didn't feel affronted, not even when Rob just barged in without being asked. Not even when he walked in to Michael's room while he was dressing. It was all over for Rob now. How a part of Michael had longed to tell Rob it was all over! That he must let go of his pipe dream, that Georgie no longer belonged to him; that in truth she never really had, because he was an arrogant bully and not fit to scrape the shit off her shoes. That she had understood her error, seen what a fool she'd been, had had enough of his nasty, arrogant ways and was through with him. If he had any sense, Rob would pack his bags and leave. It would have given Michael such satisfaction!

It was on the tip of his tongue, and he had really had to con-centrate, remember to play his part, remember why he was doing what he was doing – buying time, steering Rob off course. He reminded himself how much more satisfying it was going to be to hear those words spoken not by him, but by Georgie her-self, to Rob's face, holding Michael's hand for comfort and strength. It was all coming. He just had to be patient.

Of course, the moment they'd split up in the town, Michael knew he had to move. He could see Rob's bristling impatience, could sense the anger of the man against him. Rob didn't trust

Michael, and Michael sure as hell wasn't going to trust Rob. As soon as Rob was out of eyeshot, Michael had gone back to his car and sped away, each mile bringing him closer to Georgie, closer to the confrontation that he knew would have to come, but closer also to the joy. They didn't have long, so he hoped she had spent the day thinking, hoped she was ready.

It was cool in the cottage when he returned. The cement walls, stripped bare of any protective coat of plaster or paper, radiated no heat. Michael hadn't really thought about that – keeping warm. Still, it was only for one night at most. A bit of discomfort wouldn't kill either of them. And she had a sleeping bag. At least he'd thought about light: two good camping lanterns and a torch, just in case. Before going in to her, he prepared a couple of plates of food; nothing fancy, just a bit of meat, cheese and olives that he'd bought at the supermarket the day before, leaving them out on the kitchen table. Georgie had eaten plenty of olives on that first night at dinner, so he was sure she liked them.

With some difficulty, Michael shifted the large wardrobe and opened the door. It was pitch black inside the room and a waft of stale air struck his face. A sickly, acidic smell greeted him and he recoiled. Lifting the lantern high above his head, he saw Georgie staring at him, still bound and gagged. It was only for a fraction of a second, but Michael could swear that what he saw in her eyes was hatred. It unnerved him, but before he had time to look more closely, she turned her face to the wall, away from him. It became clear what the smell was. As he gazed at her body, stretched out on the mattress, he saw that her little summer dress was soaked through below the waist. She'd pissed herself.

He felt sick. No wonder she'd turned away. It was disgusting. He fought the urge to run out of the room, to shut her back in. He tried to rally himself – no – no – it wasn't her fault, it was his. He hadn't thought – it hadn't occurred to him. There was no running water in the house, so they couldn't use the lavatory, tucked away behind the kitchen. They'd have to go outside if nature called. He'd have to go with her – God, how awful! He hadn't anticipated it.

'You're all wet.'

He said it without thinking, just to have something to say. And it couldn't be ignored, after all. It had probably got on to the sleeping bag and mattress. The lot would be ruined. She would be cold that night, after all.

'I don't have a change of clothes for you.'

Georgie still had her face to the wall and wouldn't move, wouldn't look at him. Michael couldn't bear to stay in there, not with the smell. He put the lamp on the floor beside the door. Gingerly, he approached her, a faint wave of nausea rising in his throat. He couldn't stand the smell, the wet. He had always hated it, even as a kid when he wet the bed, waking every morning to chafed, sore legs and a sickening sense of failure. But no matter his reluctance and dismay, he had to move her. It had to be done.

Georgie's whole body went rigid at his touch, as if electrified. He explained to her as calmly as he could what he was doing: that he was going to take her into the kitchen for supper, make her comfortable, but she still wouldn't co-operate, wouldn't soften her limbs to make it easy for him.

With some difficulty and not a little revulsion, he scooped her up, the wet dress pressing down on his forearms, and manoeuvred her through the doorway, out in to the corridor and down to the kitchen, where the food was waiting, lit prettily by the other lantern. Breathing heavily, he managed to deposit her on a chair, and leaned back against the counter, catching his breath. He took one of the bottles of water he'd bought, and drained it, wishing it was beer. That was another thing he'd forgotten – wine, beer – something to loosen them up. A sharp stab of panic bit at him for the first time, though the cause was minor. A small detail like beer wasn't going to change anything, but, still, Michael couldn't help but wonder what else he might have overlooked.

Georgie was staring at him fixedly. She looked awkward and uncomfortable. Her legs were stretched out straight in front of her, tied at the ankles, her arms bound at the wrists behind her. She seemed precariously perched and looked as if she might slide off the chair at any moment. He asked if she was all right and it took him a moment to realise that she couldn't answer him even if she'd wanted to, because of the gag. He stepped towards her.

'I'm going to take off this gag now, Georgie, but I'm warning you – any noise and there'll be trouble. Not that there's anyone around to hear it, but still, no fuss.'

Michael kept his tone light. There was no need to threaten her, not Georgie. But he wanted to make sure she understood who was in charge; for the moment, anyway. He came behind her and untied the gag. She opened and closed her mouth a few times, stretching her jaw. He saw that it had left nasty red marks across her cheeks. He hadn't realised it had been on so tight.

'Sorry,' he blurted, and then felt foolish. Georgie was staring at him, watching his every move, as though at any moment she expected him to pounce, or do something to hurt her.

'Are you okay?' he asked her, still feeling sheepish about the gag.

She opened her mouth and closed it again, as if she had been about to reply, but had thought better of it. Michael stared at her, unnerved. This heavy silence wasn't at all like Georgie. He knew her quiet moments, knew when she was sad or thoughtful. None of her silences had been like this. He was about to repeat the question, in case she hadn't heard properly, when she suddenly spoke.

'My head hurts. My arms and legs are numb. My wrists . . . my ankles.'

She sounded more or less normal, a little quieter than usual perhaps, more controlled. But Michael could have laughed with relief. At least she was talking! They could almost have been back by the pool, were it not for her fixed gaze on him; a gaze that he had not seen from her before. She didn't say any more, and Michael realised it was up to him to make a decision.

'If I untie you, you promise not to do anything stupid?'

It was a vague request, but he hoped she understood. She nodded, still looking at him. She'd been tied up for hours. He reckoned that she would probably behave herself, and, anyway, there was no reason for her not to. He only wanted to talk, that was all. Yes – he'd untie her and then they could settle down to a bit of supper.

He crouched down and tried to unpick the knot at her feet. It was too tight; he would have to cut through the rope. Luckily, he had plenty of rope, just in case. In two swift movements, he freed her arms and legs, stepping away from her quickly, putting the knife out of reach; watching to see what she would do. She made no sudden movements. She brought her arms around in front of her, wincing with pain. She tried to flex them and her face grimaced. It was a little better with her legs: she bent them at the knee, one after the other, and rolled her feet around. Then she tried her arms again, gently, slowly, lifting her shoulders up and letting them drop, rubbing her hands.

'All right?' Michael watched her movements, fascinated by her concentration. Finally, her eyes weren't on him.

'You've really hurt me.'

She didn't look up at him, nor was her tone particularly accusatory. Just a neutral statement of fact.

'I'm sorry, Georgie. I didn't mean to.' It was true – he hadn't anticipated her being in pain. 'I'm sure it'll wear off.'

'I'm freezing,' she said, still not looking at him. Michael hesitated. If he nipped back to the room to get the sleeping bag, she could very well bolt. She seemed to guess his thoughts because she glanced up at him contemptuously.

'You needn't worry. I'm not going anywhere. I couldn't even if I wanted to. I don't think I can stand yet.'

He knew she was probably right, but it wasn't worth the risk.

He glanced around. There was nothing there he could use, no bit of old fabric or curtain. The windows were all shuttered from the outside, firmly closed. Seeing no other solution, he pulled off his T-shirt, which was damp with sweat. Somewhat shame-facedly, disliking being half-naked in front of her, he held it out. She stared at him, open-mouthed, then turned away with dis-dain.

'You don't want it?'

She didn't reply. With a small shrug, Michael pulled it back on. He'd done what he could. If she didn't like it, it wasn't his fault. Things weren't going as well as he'd hoped. She bent over, massaging her legs again. At least her hands and arms seemed to be working better.

'D'you want something to eat? Something to drink?'

When he spoke, his voice sounded higher than normal to him. He felt like a fool, hovering by the counter, not knowing what to do. He thought she would have been more vocal, chat-tier, ready to talk to him after the solitude of her day. He moved closer to the table, pushing a plate of food towards her.

'It's nothing much, but there's olives and cheese. Some meat – cold cuts. I've got fruit, if you want. And biscuits.' Even though he knew she was on a bit of a health kick, trying to watch her weight, he had bought the biscuits anyway. He thought she would appreciate the comfort of sugar. 'Go on, you should have something. You haven't eaten all day. I don't want you getting faint or anything.'

To his surprise, Georgie suddenly burst out laughing. But it wasn't a joyful laugh; not that bubbling of mirth Michael knew from their mornings together, when he'd say something silly to amuse her. The laugh was sharp and harsh – angry, mocking. It reminded him of the girl on the beach, laughing at him, taunting him, spoiling for a fight. He swallowed hard, trying to quell his nerves.

'You're concerned about my health, are you? My general well-being? Oh, Michael, you really are something!'

He was confused. Georgie's words implied jest, but her expression did not. He half-smiled but got no response. It didn't make any sense. Was she teasing? Of course he was worried about her, after a long day alone without food. And, after all, this whole thing was because he was worried about her, wanting only the best for her! Hadn't she realised that? Michael's thoughts went slowly, lumbering along, one after the other, the tumbling swiftness of his logic, which had buoyed him for so long, suddenly abandoning him. He felt clumsy and deeply unsure of himself. And it had all happened so fast! This wasn't the Georgie he knew – she wasn't the sort to make him feel foolish and slow. She had never done it before, so why was she doing it now? He scanned her face desperately, searching for any sign that she was joking, playing with him. He had been able to read her so well up until now. Why, then, could he not get the measure of her?

Georgie broke his gaze, turning her eyes slowly away from him, as if he were nothing more than a speck of dirt. Had she not understood then? Was that it? Had she not allowed herself to understand? It was possible, although Michael had never imagined she would refuse to face up to things. What, then, should he say to her? How should he begin to explain? She was usually so quick, so on the ball.

And then it struck him. She was testing him. She had tested him before, with all her hidden signs and veiled pleas. He'd seen those – he'd understood. It was her way – to dance around things, hint at them, never come out straight with anything. She was doing that now, even though there was no need for it. Michael was missing some vital cue. He'd not been alert enough. He would have to work harder.

'So then, Michael – out with it. What's this all about? Are you planning to rape me? Kill me? Is that it?'

She sounded almost cheerful, but she was looking at him again, her eyes cold and hard, boring into him, not letting him away with anything.

'What are you talking about?' He was genuinely dumbstruck. She was joking, she had to be joking. Testing. He wished she would stop.

'You lure me from the shop, knock me out, tie me up, dump me here. I must say, Michael, this has all the trappings of a proper kidnap. Is that the idea? Is it money you're after? A ransom?'

He couldn't speak. It was so ludicrous. Money! What made her think it was about that? She had misunderstood so badly, and he was thrown. 'Georgie,' he pleaded, desperate to explain, to make her see, 'you've got it all wrong. I don't want to do anything bad!'

At this, she started. Her face registered a mixture of shock and a vague sort of triumph, as if she sensed she had the advantage somehow, but didn't yet know why, or what to do with it.

'You don't want to do anything bad,' she repeated slowly, letting the words hang between them, imbuing them with a meaning that was above and beyond anything Michael had intended. The way she spoke, the repetition of his words, made him feel foolish. It was getting too much. He had never treated her that way, not even jokingly! He bristled. It was perfectly simple. Why was she being so *blind* about it all?

'So what is it you *do* want, Michael?'

She folded her arms, looking for all the world like a stern schoolmistress waiting for a naughty child's excuse. A chill ran through him and he shivered, trying to cover it with a shrug. His back was still damp with sweat, his T-shirt sticking to him uncomfortably. He felt himself to be at a disadvantage, standing over her as he was. It was all wrong, all skewed. He needed things to be more familiar, more recognisable, so he took a seat at the table opposite her. The two plates of food sat between them reproachfully, the cheese curling a little at the edges. Michael longed for things to be more normal. Surely she wanted the same thing?

'Would you like a drink of anything? I've no wine, I'm afraid—'

She slammed her hand on the table, hard, causing him to start. 'Spit it out, Michael! What the fuck have you brought me here for?'

He gazed at her, hurt, puzzled. She had never spoken so rudely to him before, had never sworn at him. And her tone. It was the same tone she'd used with Les, and it stung. Michael struggled to keep calm, to bite down his rising panic, his uncertainty. He couldn't make her out, couldn't take his cue from her, and it was frightening.

'You and I both know why we're here . . .' he began.

'Do we?' Her voice dripping with sarcasm. He decided not to rise to it, suddenly realising that it was all a part of her test, though it was more cruel and unnerving than any she'd served him with before. Nevertheless, he could understand it in a way. Georgie needed him to prove himself at this crucial moment; needed his strength, his resolve. It was but an extreme version of everything he knew about her. Very well. One final proof to give her confidence. He could do that.

'Yes, Georgie, we do.' He spoke gently, the tone he knew worked best with her. 'You can pretend all you like, but it won't wash with me.' He paused, anticipating a response, but she simply gazed at him, her expression hard and cold, waiting. He continued, his confidence quietly increasing. 'You said it yourself – we all need help sometimes. We can't do it on our own. And you're right.'

'What the fuck are you talking about? When the fuck did I say that?'

She sounded so outraged that Michael was tempted to laugh, blow the whole thing, seize the moment and let them both collapse into the joy of the occasion. But he sensed that it was too soon. He had to play on a little longer, indulge her a bit more.

'Oh, Georgie, come on,' he chided gently, letting her know he was humouring her. No harm in that. 'Days and days we've spent! Hours and hours. You think I wasn't listening? You know I was – and you were too. Everything we've said, everything we've done . . . Georgie. You mustn't feel worried or anything. I *wanted* to help you, right from the very beginning, the way you helped me. We've helped each other from the start, haven't we? Right from the very start. It was a miracle, us meeting the way we did. It's like everything's happened the way it was supposed to. If Patrick's mum hadn't died, then I wouldn't have met you at all probably. And if you hadn't been stuck on your own all the time too, because of *him,* well . . . . But it's like you said. How you have to be brave, have to think about what you want for the future. I know what you mean, I really do. And it's like us being friends and all. Your other friends – they aren't brave enough. They won't change. But us, together – that's what we want. We want the same things! You've been on your own too long. You've tried to help everyone else, but no one's helped you. That's all over. You don't have to be frightened any more. I'm not. There's so much I'm going to do, Georgie. I won't leave you alone. I won't tell you what's what or anything, or boss you about or run away to work. You don't have to be frightened. We'll do every-thing together from now on. 'Cos that's what friends do, isn't it? Help each other. So you don't have to worry. You're not on your own any more. I'm here. I'm here to help you.'

He sat back, shaking. Adrenalin pumped through him. He had never spoken at such length, without interruption, in his life, and it was an extraordinary feeling. He hadn't taken his eyes off her, not the entire time he was talking, and it was as if some invisible force had drawn them closer together, closer than they had been before, if that were possible, binding them in a way that made him want to shout with joy.

Georgie shook her head slightly, as if to free her hair, and looked down at her hands resting on the table. The red marks from the rope were still visible on her wrists, and she slowly traced a finger over them. Eventually she spoke.

'You're mad. You're completely mad.'

Michael had half-opened his mouth to speak even before she'd started, so ready was he to burst forth with mutual expressions of gratitude and disbelief at their good fortune. But as Georgie's words sank in, with her eyes still averted, his confidence began to falter. Had he botched things up? Gone too fast? Not explained properly, or not in the way she wanted? Had he once more fucked things up because he was too slow and stupid? Had he failed yet again? His stomach lurched painfully. He wanted to beg her to stop – stop the test, stop the game. It was too much. Yet still she would not look at him, would not give in, give up.

'Georgie?' he asked, pleading for some respite, some response – anything. 'I'm not mad. You know I'm not. Let's not joke, now. I just – Georgie, please. Just . . . talk to me.'

She looked up at him suddenly, her face somehow smaller, less robust than he remembered it. He attempted a smile, hoping against hope that she would respond. It came out as more of a grimace, so odd and unsettling was her gaze. When she spoke, she sounded calm, almost weary, but at least the anger and coldness had gone away.

'Michael, you've made a mistake. A terrible mistake.'

He frowned, and pushed his chair away from the table, suddenly uncomfortable, sitting there like a lump across from her. She half-rose: 'Michael!'

The movement surprised him, making him start towards her. She sat back down again hastily, holding up her hands in surrender.

'Don't worry, I'm not doing anything!' She seemed frightened. He'd moved quickly. Her voice shook a little as she spoke.

'Listen – listen to me, Michael. I think I understand, okay? I really do. You're right. You're not mad, not like that. I think I'm to blame for this, in a way. I think I've . . . I think you've really misunderstood. We've misunderstood each other. I mean . . . oh, God, Michael, this is all . . . . This is crazy! I know *you're* not crazy – I didn't mean what I said. I just mean . . . I think we need to talk about this rationally, calmly. I think I know why you . . . why you've done what you've done, but, Michael, this isn't what I want! This is a big mistake.'

It was too much to take in. She was speaking so urgently that he could hardly follow her. All he heard was 'mistake' and 'crazy'. He stood very still, trying to remain calm. His legs were shaking and he knew that if he moved, he might lose his footing. Georgie was watching him. Slowly, carefully, she rose from her chair and took a step forward.

'It's okay, Michael. It's all going to be okay. But you have to listen to me. You've made a mistake bringing me here. I don't want to be here. Things I've said or haven't said – you've got it all wrong. I understand why you – I mean, I think I do, but . . . . It doesn't matter. I'm happy, Michael, really I am. I'm happy. So you don't have to worry about me, or do what you're doing. It's okay, you know? It's all going to be okay. All we have to do is turn around and walk out of here, go back to the hotel and we can forget about it.'

She smiled at him, a sweet, shy smile, and it was almost enough to soften the blow of her words. She saw his hesitation and pressed on, leaning into the table, beseeching him with her eyes, her hands, her words.

'I know you care about me, Michael. Believe me, I know. And I care about you, too. You're right – we're friends – good friends! You don't want to hurt me, I know that. I know you wouldn't want to do anything to make me unhappy. So you don't have to worry. You don't have to worry about anything. We'll just . . . get out of here and go back to the hotel, okay? That's all. It's simple. Easy. No one's suffered, nothing bad has happened. It's just a misunderstanding. No one's going to get in trouble. But we should go, Michael – we really should go back. It's late already. People will be worried.'

Michael knew she was waiting for him to respond, to tell her that she was right and he was wrong, that yes, they should just go back. Georgie was so passionate, so genuine, that had he not known her better, he would have believed her. She believed herself, so strong was her cowardice, so fearful was she of every-thing she needed to do. She had even less resolve than he had thought. She needed him more than ever.

'I don't think you do understand, Georgie,' he told her. 'I don't think you do. You've got some pretty serious things to face up to this evening, and we're running out of time.'

~

Waiting in the police station as the night went on had a similar quality to Rob's childhood trips to the hospital, when he'd been dragged along as a toddler by his frantic parents, worried about his sick infant brother. James had had a series of illnesses, one after the other, blighting the first eighteen months of his life. Rob, not quite three when James had been born, remembered only the feeling of tension, of barely suppressed panic that his parents hadn't been able to shield him from. He remembered knowing that something was seriously wrong, but not what it was or what was being done about it. Things were hazy in his memory, in atmosphere and in specifics: just flashes of feelings and vague moments. Kindly nurses who brought him chocolate or a glass of milk; the smell of the orange plastic chairs he waited in and fell asleep on, their slightly bumpy texture, fun to run your fingers over, a bit frayed at the edges of the seat, enough sometimes to pierce the skin. Long corridors with shiny floors, the lino squeaking underfoot, making his shoes stick a little as he walked. The early morning light outside, cold and grey. The relief in his parents' voices when they came to wake him, came to take him home. The way his dad scooped him up, held him close, burying his head in Rob's neck, breathing him in. The kindness that was inherent in disaster. The closer one was to tragedy, the gentler people were. It was the same sitting patiently in the police station – the same watchful and sympathetic glances, the same attention to his comfort and well-being, the same kid-glove treatment that was so well meant and yet so alienating.

He had dialled his parents three times already, hanging up before the first ring. He didn't know what was preventing him from following through, from calling them, explaining, letting them know. Rob wasn't frightened of telling them – at least, he didn't think so, for, as yet, there was nothing solid he could say, other than that Georgie had disappeared. If he didn't ring them now – if things dragged on with no end in sight, he would have more to say, more to explain, and they would wonder why he hadn't called them earlier. And yet, the thought of hearing his parents' voices on the phone, their shock and concern, their immediate insistence that they fly out to be with him, that they contact Georgie's mother, bring her over: the mere thought of all that activity was too overwhelming. Rob felt that if he called them, something in him might break.

The police had left him alone for quite a while, in a little room just off the main reception. A television was on in the corner, and Rob had glanced at it, on and off. Some sort of game show was in progress, but he couldn't make head or tail of it. The studio audience was loud and boisterous and clearly involved in an integral way, because the camera kept swooping down amongst them, zooming in on individuals with whom the host, a middle-aged man in a very tight suit, would engage in banter. Showgirls strutted about the stage doing very little other than pouting and looking pretty. A panel of judges – or perhaps they were contestants? – stood on stage behind strange little platforms, but for all Rob could tell, they were barely involved in any of the chaos around them. Paper and ticker tape and balloons were dropped from the ceiling at apparently random intervals, signifying God knew what. All in all, it was a whirlwind of movement, distraction and noise, and when the programme broke for commercials, Rob turned it off. Watching it made him feel spectacularly lonely suddenly.

A sturdy policewoman looked in on him every so often. At first, Rob was vaguely touched that they should be so solicitous of him, but after an hour or so of waiting and three visits from the policewoman, he realised they were less concerned with his welfare than with his presence. Perhaps they thought he might flee. Perhaps he was their chief suspect and they were in the very process of investigating him! Antoniou had been quiet in the car on the way back to the station. In a moment of blind panic, his thoughts tumbling over one another, it had occurred to Rob that, thanks to Michael's no-show at the taverna, Antoniou might be in doubt as to Michael's very existence, and might therefore be suspecting him. Recalling this frightened Rob suddenly and he leapt up, about to call for the policewoman, to explain, before he remembered that policemen had already gone to the hotel, had confirmed Michael's existence, even though he was nowhere to be found.

He sat back down. In a way, it was only natural that Antoniou should suspect him. He had to do his job, be thorough. After all, wasn't it the people closest to a victim who fell most naturally under suspicion? The husband of a murdered wife, the father of a murdered daughter?

The phrasing had come unbidden. The words, the images.

Rob was having increasing difficulty censoring his thoughts, keeping a lid on their unremitting tendency to darkness – death, pain, horror. Phoning his parents, disturbing their cosy evening in the living room in front of the telly, seemed truly impossible now. Their world was unreal to him, their normality too far away. His mind couldn't make the leap. It amazed him, the progression of his thoughts. He realised with a shock that he had kept hope alive for only the briefest possible time. It was as if everything in him was straining to prepare him for the worst, and would not allow even a glimmer of uncertainty, much less optimism, to sustain him. It was most unlike him. Rob had always been far more resilient in previous crises. Not that he'd ever faced such a crisis as this, but, still, his instincts had always pushed him to be more casual, more nonchalant. He had retained a faith in the future: a faith that had been borne out more often than not. Yet now he was superstitious, and even his negativity seemed problematic, for Rob felt that if he indulged his dark thoughts, even in semi-realistic preparation for the absolute worst, then those thoughts – and thus, the worst – would somehow come to pass. It was the cruellest form of mental torture, this sense that he must keep control; that he, and only he, could, by sheer effort of will, force a happy outcome.

What was the detective doing? Where was he? What was the idea, keeping Rob under guard for hours at the police station, when he could be out on the streets, looking for Georgie? If they suspected him, why weren't they interrogating him further? Didn't they at least want his help? Information? Shouldn't he be

furnishing them with details about Georgie's appearance –
shouldn't he download photographs of her for them? The
policewoman stuck her head round the door.

'Can you tell me what's happening?' Rob pleaded. 'Is there a
reason why I'm being kept here?'

She was about to reply when something outside the room
caught her attention. She pushed the door fully open, and
Antoniou walked in.

'Forgive us – forgive me for keeping you. We had one or two
things to do.'

Rob stood before him, almost at attention. It never ceased to
amaze Antoniou how the effects of strain could be read in a certain type of person's face so easily. For in the space of a few short
hours, Rob appeared to have aged a decade. He had a pinched,
strained look, a hooding of the eyes, that no doubt was more to
do with fatigue than any permanent condition, but it made him
look much older than his years. Antoniou hesitated. It was not
ordinary protocol, what he was about to propose, but he had a
feeling there was more to be gained from taking Rob with them
than from leaving him behind.

'We think we know where your fiancée might be.'

'It's Michael, isn't it? He's taken her.'

'It looks that way. We've spoken to his friend back home, the
one he was coming on holiday with. He thinks he may have
some idea where Michael's gone.'

Of course, Antoniou wouldn't mention that they were still
pursuing other options, that he had men out, combing the
beach, investigating the more local spots where women were

known to have been taken, raped, dumped. The caves, the empty flats, the couple of disused nightclubs farther along the coastal road. There were so many possibilities, and there had been more cases than Antoniou cared to remember of vicious assaults on young women. He wasn't going to rule it out, though instinctively he was almost entirely certain that this elusive man, Michael, was responsible.

Antoniou had spoken to Patrick himself on the telephone, disturbing him from his dinner. The man had been silent for almost a minute after Antoniou explained the reasons for his call.

'He never told me anything. Not about this woman, I mean. Georgie, is it? He said he'd been seeing some bird from the hotel. Listen, are you sure you've got the right bloke? You know, Michael's . . . . He's not some . . . . He's really shy, you know? He's definitely not the sort to do something to someone – especially not a woman. I'll tell you, I was dead surprised he'd met some-one in the first place. It's not like him at all – he's rubbish with girls. Well, I s'pose he hasn't met a girl. At least, not like he said.'

There had been such disbelief in Patrick's tone. Working through everything he thought he'd known about Michael, rec-onciling the easy opinion he had held of his mate with the stark new evidence presented.

'Michael's . . . he's a bit of a loner, yeah, but he's *normal*, like – he's not some freak. He wouldn't do anything . . . *bad*.'

There had been a catch in Patrick's voice – shock. The sud-den flash of understanding that actually, it was entirely possible that Michael could have done something wrong. That he had no idea. That what lurked beneath Michael's surface was unknown.

'How many times have you spoken with him since the holiday began?'

'None, I mean, only the once – the other day. I've been so busy, what with my mother and everything.'

Patrick had sounded plaintive, as if fishing for sympathy. Antoniou had waited patiently for him to continue. A hint of pique became apparent in his tone.

'I texted him, to see how he was getting on. He called me just after. He sounded normal, you know? Nothing strange about him. Except this story about the girl – the Greek girl – Rosa, I think he said. I wasn't sure I really believed him. I mean, I thought there was definitely a girl, but I didn't think Michael was actually – you know – getting anywhere with her.'

Antoniou had the staff list. There was no Rosa employed at the hotel. Patrick had told Antoniou everything he needed to know: Michael's questioning of him, the details of the cottage. All in less than ten minutes. One thing stuck in Antoniou's mind, however. It had been so easy, had taken no effort at all, to discover Michael's plan. Was he really that naive? Didn't he think that the police, with only the most basic detective work, would be on to him like a shot? He must have done, since he had made no attempt to cover his tracks, get rid of any information about Patrick in his hotel room. Was it a trap of some sort? A trick? Was the man mentally unstable? Was he waiting to be discovered? He had kidnapped a woman, taken her to a cottage, an abandoned property. What the hell was it all about?

~

It stank. The whole thing stank from top to bottom. What was it he had heard so often, what was the phrase? *Dirty liar – he's a dirty, dirty liar!* Dirty. Stinking. Only he wasn't the liar this time. She was. Georgie was dirty. She was lying. She wouldn't stop lying.

Going near her had revolted Michael. He could smell the piss off her, surprisingly strong. She smelled like a tramp. Disgusting. Yet even in that state, she kept staring at him as if he was some kind of creature who was beneath her, someone lower, not to be bothered with. Couldn't she see herself? See what she looked like? Her hair stuck limply to the sides of her face, looking greasy. A spot was forming on one of her cheeks – a big one, bright red and swollen. Ugly. And the smell . . . . Nothing about her was appealing! Georgie, who primped and preened so much, took her time getting ready in the evenings, swam her laps every day, conscious of keeping her figure trim! She looked a sight, now, worse even than some of the dogs who went out to the clubs; fat, squeezed in to their tight little dresses, pale, sweaty, *ugly*.

And the lies. The endless, barefaced lies! It was amazing to behold, in a strange sort of way, watching as she struggled to keep up with herself, trying to remember what she had said, trying to cover her tracks. She didn't do it very well, she didn't lie with *conviction*, another phrase he kept recalling. Who had spoken to him about lying all those years ago?

'Michael, you must listen to me. Please – just hear me out.'

But he had had enough. Nothing she said was honest. And again, it was amazing, the sensation of calmness washing over him as the scales finally fell from his eyes. No pain, no fury, just peacefulness. He hadn't seen things clearly? Very well. He would atone for it without question.

Looking down as Georgie struggled under his grip, Michael felt the telescoping of vision that had happened when he'd gazed at his island. Everything else around him seemed a long way away. His focus, his entire world, was only on what mattered, right there in front of him. No, he hadn't anticipated what had come to pass, none of it, and yet he was remarkably at ease, trusting to his own inner sense of things; trusting that he knew what he was doing, and would know what to do as things occurred. He had come so far already, taking little leaps of faith. Why shouldn't he continue?

Every time he spoke to her now, she blinked, looking up at him wide-eyed, hanging on his every word. It was almost funny, how closely she was paying attention.

'You're not what I thought, Georgie. You're not who I thought you were at all. You played a good game, though. Fooled me proper, didn't you?'

'Michael, please!'

'Maybe you even fool yourself some of the time, you're that good. But it's over now, Georgie. No more messing.'

One hand could cover her entire face. She really was quite

small, he noted. She bucked wildly under his grip, her legs going rigid, and at the last moment, he released her and she gasped for breath, eyes streaming, face bright red and contorted.

'You look a right sight,' he told her. 'I'm sorry to say it, but it's true.'

Her sounds filled the air, loud, raking chokes as she struggled to normalize her breathing. 'Michael . . .' Her voice wobbled. She was crying!

'We're *friends*, Michael—'

'Friends don't lie to each other.' It was nice, him interrupting her for a change. It felt good.

'I haven't been lying, for God's sake.'

'Oh really? Only every day – every single day. It was funny to you, wasn't it?'

'Why are you doing this? Why? I've never done anything to hurt or upset you, never. I'd never want to.'

'You sat there, day after day, telling me all this . . . *stuff*. How unhappy you were, how you hated your life, your work – *him*.'

'You can't be serious. You can't seriously think I—'

'On and on and on you went. You're not sure if he really understands you, you're not sure where you want to go next. Every time you think of marriage and babies, you get a cold chill—'

'Because of my *age*, because of the responsibilities – nothing else.'

'You feel trapped sometimes. You look around and you don't know how you got here. You wonder if you should have done things differently, if you shouldn't just settle for what you've got.

You wonder if you're a coward, if you're just running away from something, not facing up to your bigger fears. You worry that you're frightened of being alone – so frightened you'll do anything to avoid it. You worry that you're not as talented as you'd hoped, that you'll never really amount to anything. You worry that basically, when it comes down to it, you're really not that *special* after all.'

He was breathless. Georgie stared at him, a strange mixture of horror and admiration on her face. It was a funny feeling, watching her looking at him like that. All her words coming back at her. Michael felt proud. More than proud – triumphant. She didn't think he'd listened, didn't think he'd paid attention. Thought she could just get away with it; get away with her endless lies, her manipulations, talking him into believing her, into caring about her. And when had she ever asked about him? As a matter of fact, now he came to think of it, she'd only ever talked about herself. Selfish cow. *As though the world revolved around her.* His mother's voice again, ringing in his ears, and he agreed with it. Now he had said it all out loud, it sounded so vain and petty. All her worries, everything she'd talked about, hours of it – such stupid, boring stuff. But he'd been taken in. Oh, yes, he had to admit it. He'd been played for a fool. And though it was not what he had hoped, not remotely what he'd hoped, Michael realised that things perhaps were better off this way. He had seen Georgie for what she was, in spite of everything, and it was far better that it had happened now, rather than later down the line. He wasn't sure he would have been able to cope if he'd continued being a dupe for another year or two. No, he would put this down to experience, a lesson learned. He was going to wise up. He wouldn't be conned so easily by the next one.

'All those things, all those things you said – the things you said I said, they were just . . . they weren't really *real*, Michael. Not that they were lies,' she added, hastily, 'but I thought you understood. We were just talking. Opening up, one person to another. I never dreamed . . . I never imagined . . . .'

She sounded weak, pathetic and she must have realised this, because she started sobbing. She would do anything to make him feel sorry for her, stop at nothing. Michael could see exactly how her mind worked now. She was no different from any of them. Just more airs and graces. Stupid bitch.

'Oh God . . . oh please . . . *please*, Michael – just let me go!'

Perhaps he should, he thought, watching her hunched over in her chair, her dress still wet and clinging to her thighs. She'd get a rash, all that soaked material chafing her skin. More blemishes. He almost wished Rob could see her now, see how she looked, how she *stank*. Would he be so keen to whisk her off for an afternoon 'nap' if he could?

He had to make a decision. The situation had changed completely. They would probably be here any moment, the police, and Rob, who would gaze upon his soiled love (Michael hoped) with disgust. That, at least, was satisfying. No self-respecting man could look at Georgie now and feel anything for her but contempt. She was worse than that fat girl who'd taken off her knickers behind the nightclub. He grimaced. To be thinking of that now, when he needed his mind clear. He had to focus.

They would be coming; there was no doubt about that. Michael knew he'd left things pretty transparent.

A sudden, unexpected pang of grief struck him, hurting him in his chest and stomach. How innocent he had been, a mere few hours ago, believing that she was someone better than she was. That they would be standing here, arm in arm, ready to face Rob, ready to tell him, show him how serious they were about one another, starting a new life. It had all felt so real, in his imagination. So exquisitely real. But she had fucked it up. She'd fucked it up with her little act. *He* hadn't been such a fool; it was *her*. Nevertheless, now things had to be dealt with.

Georgie was still crying and barely glanced up as he swept all the food off the table into a bag, paper plates and everything. Table cleared, Michael shot her a look, hesitating. She was moaning now, quietly but steadily. She sounded like a little girl in the playground looking for attention; tears spent, resorting to animal noises to attract some comfort. He smiled, relishing his newfound clarity. Is this what people meant when they joked about men being idiots when it came to women? Perhaps he wasn't so strange after all. All blokes were taken in at one stage or another by a particularly manipulative female. In which case, he didn't have to feel so bad about it.

Michael calculated he could risk it – a quick swoop into the back room to get her bag. He'd hold on to that so she couldn't phone for help too fast. But he would leave the lamp and the sleeping bag. He wouldn't be able to bring himself to touch it anyway, dirty as it was.

He was gone and back in less than thirty seconds. Georgie

was still hunched over, still moaning. Michael's mind was racing, working overtime. Thank Christ he'd been smart enough to bring his passport. Once again, some unseen hand had been guiding him, looking after him, helping him make all the right decisions. He'd debated at the time, thought it was entirely unnecessary, but a little voice inside had urged him just to take his passport, wallet, phone. But they had to hurry. He was running out of time. He had to get her to the middle of nowhere, as far away as possible from any town or village, then get himself to the port. He wasn't going to risk the airport with its busy charter flights, wasn't going to push his luck.

'Right,' he told her, 'I'm going to tie you up again. I won't do it so tight, but that's the way it is. I'm doing you the courtesy of telling you so that you can do the decent thing and not make a fuss.'

He sounded more pompous than he intended. She hadn't moved, hadn't looked up. He softened his tone a little. 'I'm not going to hurt you, Georgie. Okay? So just stay still.'

It was remarkable how quickly it happened. He approached her, ready to tie her hands first, in case she decided to lash out when he was doing the legs. She was so fast – so fast that he didn't realise what she'd done until it was too late. Hunched over as she was – what an idiot! What a fucking idiot! Why hadn't he guessed? In those thirty seconds, those precious thirty seconds when he'd been out of the room, she'd upped and squirrelled away the jar of olives he'd left, like a fool, on the counter. The olives he had offered her, back when he'd wanted her to be happy, when he'd believed her worthy and capable of happiness.

The blow was far stronger than he'd have thought for her size. All that swimming had strengthened her arms. The jar didn't break, didn't cut him, but the blow was hard enough to stun him, make him stumble and lose his senses for a second or two. It was enough. She was out the door before he'd understood what had happened. Out the door, sandals flapping, wet dress sticking to her – up and out and into the darkness.

~

Rob was strangely talkative during the car ride. Antoniou could tell it was bothering his colleague, Yannis, a taciturn, rather brooding young man who took his work immensely seriously. Yannis didn't recognise the panic driving Rob's endless stream of chatter. He hadn't yet seen enough trauma to know that there were as many variations on coping with mounting fear as there were reactions to tragedy.

'It's funny, last time I was here – in Greece, I mean, not on this particular island – I was staying at a resort with a couple of friends. Just lads, you know, on a week's break. There was a family in the hotel who had their rental car smashed in and all their belongings stolen. It was quite an event at the time – everyone in the hotel got to hear about it. They were very shaken. I think people were shocked because you don't really hear too many horror stories about bad things happening on holiday. Not on these types of holidays, anyway. Packages, you know – safe, boring, run-of-the-mill holidays. A bout of food poisoning's about the worst you ever get. That, or being ripped off somewhere or other. Of course, if you're backpacking or trekking somewhere more exotic – India or South America or somewhere – then you expect it to happen. But here, on a holiday like this. It just doesn't seem possible. It doesn't seem real!'

'Bad things happen everywhere,' Antoniou told Rob, soothingly, as if it would offer any comfort. There wasn't much point in engaging with him in his state. Rob was talking to keep the fear at bay. Yannis shifted uncomfortably in the driver's seat. Rob's nerves were getting under his skin. Antoniou glanced at his colleague, willing him to let it all wash over him, keep his mind on the job at hand.

'I know. I know they do. I just can't believe they've happened to *us*. Like this. We're getting married, you know.'

They did know. Rob had mentioned it at least three times already on the journey, yet each time he spoke the words, he sounded surprised, as though he'd only at that moment been informed of the news. He had little sense of anything or anyone outside his own wild thoughts. They tumbled over each other, one cutting off the other, half-formulated ideas or phrases instantly forgotten as another took their place. *Beat it back, beat it back*, like a drummer keeping rhythm: the underlying drive of the frantic confusion in Rob's head was to prevent him dwelling; force him to remain positive, open, in the moment. Nothing had happened – nothing was happening – nothing could be called definitive until he finally arrived to witness it. Until then, just keep going.

'It's quite far out, isn't it? I didn't realise he'd taken her so far . . . .'

'We're nearly there now.' Antoniou checked the GPS. 'I'd better call the others,' he told Yannis, who nodded, glancing in his wing mirror. There were two units behind them. Ten men altogether. And Rob. None of them had any idea what to expect.

'How are we going to do this?'

Antoniou didn't bother to correct Rob in his use of the collective. Rob wouldn't be doing anything. Rob would be staying well back should there be any difficulty, though Antoniou thought it better to explain that now.

'The men will surround the place, secure it. Sergeant Papadakis and I will enter the building.'

'He's there. I can feel it. He's there, and so is she. I can't believe it. I can't believe I didn't say anything – do anything. I knew. I knew from the beginning that there was something about him. I knew I shouldn't have let her . . . .'

Rob trailed off, weary of retreading this familiar ground. The more he spoke, the more he thought about it, the less he was really certain of what his instincts had initially told him about Michael. It all seemed a haze, already so far away. When he thought of their flight over, their first few days, he had the impression he was watching himself through the wrong end of a telescope. None of it felt real. Memories of earlier times – much earlier times in his and Georgie's relationship – kept flashing by, intruding, unbidden, apparently unconnected. The first time they made love in her shabby little flat. A meal they'd shared at an extremely fancy restaurant, to celebrate a big commission for her. She had eaten far too much and had complained late into the night of a sore stomach. Catching her one evening when he'd come home early; her staring into space when she should have been working, Rob watching her for a good long minute before she'd realised he was there. Georgie crying – over what? He couldn't remember, though he remembered the room they'd been in. His parents' house, his old bedroom. Maybe the first time they'd visited his folks? Christmas. The first Christmas he'd spent with her family; his first time breaking tradition with his own. Sardinia – lounging by the pool – holding hands between their sun loungers, her body bronzed and gorgeous.

'Good, okay. Five minutes.'

Antoniou hung up. Yannis glanced at him and he nodded. He slowed the car. They were approaching. Rob strained to see from the back seat. Ahead of them on the side of the road, a small cottage was becoming visible.

'Lights.'

Yannis obeyed, turning them off, and pulled over the car, cutting the engine. They were about a hundred yards away from the cottage. Antoniou turned around in his seat to look at Rob, who was staring, transfixed, at the place.

'I need you to stay here, Rob, do you understand? You must not, under any circumstances, leave the car.'

Rob appeared not to have heard him. Antoniou raised his voice. 'Rob, do you understand?'

'Yes, yes – I'll stay here.'

He sounded distant. Antoniou surveyed him shrewdly for a moment, then turned to Yannis, signalling they should move. Rob would more than likely disobey him, but with any luck he'd hang on long enough for them to find . . . whatever it was they were about to find. The two other cars were already parked behind, the men filing out silently, moving stealthily towards the cottage.

'Ready?'

Yannis nodded and removed his gun from his holster, opening the door. Rob started.

'You're armed,' he said, recognising the stupidity of the comment even as he made it.

'Don't worry,' Antoniou told him. 'We rarely, if ever, have to use them.'

'No, I'm glad,' Rob replied, his eyes for the first time in their exchange meeting the detective's.

Antoniou and Yannis approached the cottage cautiously. There were no lights visible from the outside. All the shutters were closed. But there was a car parked to one side, just out of view of the front of the house. By all accounts, Michael could be volatile. Push him into a corner and he might snap. What was it his friend Patrick had said of him? 'He's normal, Michael – totally normal. He's just a bloke. Granted, he's a bit shy at first, but he knows what's what. He's decent, really he is. Only has a temper on him when he feels something's wrong. Can't stand unfairness, Michael. Which is a good thing, isn't it?'

Patrick had been defensive, not only of his friend but of all men like him, like them; men who worked hard and were respectable, solid men, the sturdy underclass whom everyone wanted to exploit, who needed to stand up for themselves, since no one else would. Michael couldn't bear unfairness, injustice. So what perceived wrong was he attempting to correct in kidnapping a young woman?

The door was unlocked and the cottage deserted, but only recently so, they saw, as they flashed their torches round the rooms, their beams of light colliding with one another in their haste to reveal the scene. Plastic bags full of fresh food, rubbish cleared away. A sleeping bag, cold and damp with urine. They must have missed them by an hour at most, at absolute most. Unconstrained by silence now, the team sprang into action, issuing orders, strategizing, their excitement mounting. Michael had known they were coming – what was his next move? No car, unless he had a second one, which seemed unlikely. He had to be on foot, so it was going to be easy. It was open scrubland all around – with three cars, they could sweep the area in moments.

Antoniou frowned. He had that sinking sensation in the pit of his stomach that told him all was not well. Something had arisen, an unforeseen circumstance that had set dangerous wheels in motion. Though clumsy and transparently obvious in his preparations so far, there had been a certain logic, a certain meticulousness to Michael's plans: the hiring of the car; the organising of the cottage; the provisions for apparent comfort, for an extended stay. The man had even bought two varieties of biscuit. So why the sudden exit – why the overturned chair, the car still sitting outside, Georgie's handbag dropped carelessly on the floor? These items made Antoniou nervous. Predictability had given way to chaos, and now their window of time to prevent any real harm was narrowing rapidly. They couldn't be far. He turned to his men, ready to organise, when a faint cry from outside made him raise his hand for silence.

Quickly, Antoniou stepped out into the night. It was pitch black and eerily quiet. Even the drone of the cicadas – the insistent backdrop to island life – seemed softer than usual, as if they were aware of the fragility and tension of the situation.

'Over here! Here, quickly!'

It was Rob. The men ran out, torch beams flailing wildly. It was so dark, they had trouble picking him out in the vast expanse of scrubland. 'Here.' He was a good three hundred yards away, standing stock-still. Antoniou approached, panting. One of the men had reached Rob ahead of him and shone his torch directly onto the object Rob was holding.

'It's Georgie's. She's out here.'

A woman's sandal, dusty and still warm, sat in Rob's hand. Everyone fell silent, straining to listen, alert to any sound, any distant cry that would point them to her whereabouts. Antoniou thought fast. There had been a struggle. Georgie had made a desperate bid for escape. She was out here sure enough, as was her pursuer. The swiftest prayer he'd ever made flashed through his mind. *Let her still be safe. Let her be hidden somewhere, frightened – hurt, even – but alive.*

'You – you three – the cars. Bring them out.'

The men obeyed immediately. Without waiting to be organised, the remaining officers split off in different directions, striding quickly across the scrubland. Rob was at Antoniou's elbow as they headed on, Rob clutching Georgie's sandal tight. 'The strap's loose,' he muttered. 'She was going to buy a new pair before coming away but we didn't have time. Couldn't find anything she liked on the island.'

Antoniou swung his torch methodically to the left and to the right, the strong beam lighting the ground a good twenty feet or so ahead and around them. Something wasn't right, Antoniou knew. The silence, the stillness. He couldn't shake the feeling of being one step behind, one tiny pace that made all the difference.

'Perhaps we should call out?' Rob said, his voice unsteady.

Antoniou shook his head, every nerve strained, listening, focused. The silence was grim. No cries, no shouts from any of the others. Nothing.

'She's hiding – I'm sure she's hiding somewhere.' Rob couldn't bear the silence. He was close to the edge, Antoniou knew. About to break. The hysteria in his tone was unmistakable.

'She's a good runner when she wants to be – fast. She could get away. She's hiding – I can feel it. We should call for her.'

But there was nowhere to hide, bar the mountains some twenty miles off. Otherwise it was flat nothingness, deserted. Antoniou felt Rob tense beside him, felt the surge of angry impotence flooding through him, felt him struggle with the impulse to yell, to scream – something, anything! A noise stopped him short and he grabbed Rob hard with one hand.

'Listen!'

Had he imagined it? There was nothing now; only the low

hum of the cicadas, Rob's breathing, Antoniou's own heart thumping in his chest.

'What? What is it?' Rob was looking at the detective, eyes wide with fear, with expectation. He seemed so young suddenly, so alert, that Antoniou couldn't bear to look at him. It came again. A soft, muffled noise, almost like a cough – no, suppressed laughter: a child at play, giggling and trying to conceal it. Human – it was definitely a human sound.

'It's her!' Rob hissed, ready to move, straining against Antoniou's restraint. The detective shook his head, silent, listening. Slowly, keeping hold of Rob, warning him, willing him with his entire body not to act, not to give in to impulse, he moved towards the sound. It wasn't laughter, he realised – far from it. It was sobbing. Someone was sobbing.

Antoniou kept his torch held low over the ground, reluctant now to see too far ahead. The dread he had carried with him for the past few hours was reaching its zenith, clutching at his throat with an intensity that made it hard for him to even swallow. How bitterly he regretted bringing Rob along with them. He should have listened to his instincts, refused to think the best of things – he'd jinxed this! 'Oh, God,' he heard Rob moan, seemingly aware himself that each step farther was a step towards some unimaginable horror, a new, unbearable reality. But they had to keep going.

He was ten yards or so ahead of them when the torchlight finally, reluctantly, picked him out. Bent over on the ground, surrounded by nothing but bare earth, he knelt out there in the open, unprotected, vulnerable. Rob had been right: he was a big man, heavy, ungainly. Antoniou had seen so many of them fresh off the planes, ready to wreak havoc on the island, the quiet ones, the ones whose mates would make them the butt of all their jokes, could get away with it because these types so longed for any sort of inclusion. He'd been desperate for it too, hadn't he? Desperate for a little holiday with his friend; a chance to live it up for a week or two, hang off the coat-tails of his more confident and worldly pal. And there was Michael – on his knees in the earth, bent double over the scrap of a thing that not moments ago had been a living, breathing human being, whose heart had pumped, whose lungs had filled with air, who'd sped away as fast as she could on battered, bleeding feet.

Antoniou knew he had to look, had to make sure, even as he recognised it was hopeless. The blood from Georgie's head had turned the dust quite black in the darkness, and the rock that had caused such strange discoloration lay there placidly by her side. A strangled moan from Rob, matching Michael's sorrow, caused the man to look at them, his face contorted with the pain of loss.

Antoniou kept his grip on Rob, kept him close. Rob's moan came again, louder, disbelieving. The man, Michael, looked up at him, blinking back his tears, holding Rob's gaze with an intensity that baffled Antoniou. The way he looked at him, one would almost think they were family, well known to one another. It was a look that spoke of shared experience, connection. Rob started to shake violently and Antoniou moved closer to him, putting his whole arm out to steady him.

Michael knelt there, gazing at them both. When he spoke, it

was with such anguish that Antoniou felt a momentary pang of sympathy, until his eye fell again upon the limpness of the body on the ground.

'I'm sorry, Rob. I'm so sorry! I didn't mean to. You know I didn't mean to. I loved her. I *loved* her. She was my friend. She was my *friend*.'